JANET OPPEDISANO

The San Marco Heist

ISBN Digital: 978-1-7386998-4-1
ISBN Paperback: 978-1-7386998-5-8

Copyright © 2023
Cover Art Copyright © 2023
Cover Artist: The Book Brander

This is a work of fiction. Names, characters, places, and events are from the author's imagination or are used fictitiously. Any resemblance to actual persons, living or dead, business, companies, events, or places, is purely coincidental.

All rights reserved. No part of this publication may be used or reproduced in any form, whether by printing, photocopying, scanning, or otherwise without the written permission of the author, except for the use of brief quotations in a book review.

*To everyone who's learned that trust is
one of the greatest gifts we can give another*

FREE NOVELLA

To instantly receive the free romantic suspense novella *The Phoenix Heist*, the prequel to the Reynolds Recoveries series, claim your copy at

https://janetoppedisano.com/ThePhoenixHeist

CHAPTER 1
SCARLETT

My mark was late.

I ran a finger under the lip of the desk while cataloging every photograph, every book, every little statue in the private library. Pulled on the trunk of the ivory elephant. Nudged the wall sconces. Spun the inlaid globe to check if it wobbled. Started tugging on the drawers.

Nothing.

He must have seen you come in here. Either that or you're losing your touch, Scarlett.

"Library's off-limits to guests," came a low male voice.

Definitely not losing your touch.

I gasped as I turned to face him, my hand flying to my chest. "Oh!"

Greasy black hair caked with too much luxury pomade. Clean-shaven, tux with gray accents, shoes polished well enough to reflect the pot lights. No bulges or jingles to indicate wallet or keys from this angle.

He didn't even bother to look at my face. No, the dress was doing its job.

My hand lingered over my lungs, highlighting my plunging neckline. The shimmering golden gown with a thigh-high slit had garnered plenty of attention all on its own, but he deserved extra. I breathed deeply, swelling my chest, dragging the hand away slowly. Pulling his eyes with it. "You startled me."

"That wasn't my goal." He pushed back strands of hair which fell to his forehead and approached, shoulders squared, gaze finally lifting almost to my mouth. "But you still shouldn't be here."

"I just..." I leaned against the desk, gripping its edge. Girl next door? Femme fatale? Damsel in distress? Our research said bimbo. My least favorite cover story. Regardless, I pursed my lips and ran one crystal-studded Louboutin across the floor in front of me. "Someone at the party downstairs said there was a really cool book in here."

"We have a lot of those." He gestured absently around the room. Thirty feet by twenty, mahogany shelving, books enclosed by glass doors. Behind me, two arch-topped spring-line windows with a view of the gardens and pool.

One locked.

One not.

"Cool books turn me on." I blinked slowly, but the movement was lost on him.

His eyes followed my foot, like a predator waiting to pounce. I dragged it up to my other ankle.

"I wish someone could show it to me." I chuckled, low in my throat, and pushed myself off the desk, heading toward the door. As I passed him, I whispered, "But I don't belong here, so..."

He grabbed my wrist to stop me. "How turned on?"

Gotcha.

"Depends on how cool it is." I eased my mouth open and ran my tongue along my upper lip. *Come on, just show me already. We both know you're going to.* "Does it have pretty pictures?"

He closed the small distance between us, his chest flush against my arm. As repulsive as he was, as much as his vocal fry grated on my nerves, his scent was heavenly. Bergamot. Pineapple. Clive Christian, maybe? X? "They're called illuminations."

"Ooh!" I shivered, turning my body toward him. "Like lightbulbs?"

"Not quite." He smiled, a *You're not very smart* smile, and gestured to the other side of the room. When I moved, he walked behind me, to take in the exaggerated sway of my hips. "Medieval manuscripts have pictures in them, which are called illuminations."

"I like that." I stopped at the end of the room. As with the other walls, it was covered in dark wood shelves and crammed with books. But this section included flat file drawers without locks.

He pulled one drawer, which only came out half a foot. Far enough to reveal a keypad I hadn't found yet.

"Turn around," he said, fingers hovering over the numbers. "This is private."

Oh, no, you don't. I took his free hand in both of mine and positioned it over my eyes. Another giggle. He hesitated, but when I bounced slightly in excitement, he punched in the code.

Eight digits. Ridiculously easy.

"All done." His hand drifted from my eyes, along my chest

—but no touching—and circled to the small of my back, pulling me closer. This was a man used to taking what he wanted. Fortunately for me, what he wanted most was my reaction, and I'd gladly exchange it for what he was giving me.

Intel.

When the drawer opened fully, I sucked in a deep breath. The manuscript was exquisite. Fifteenth century vellum, the Latin lettering executed in immaculate black ink, framed in vines and leaves. Five oversized capitals of filigree and gold leaf. The top left contained an illumination of three men, two hills, and an angel.

The Codex of San Marco. Worth just shy of three-point-four million dollars.

Encased in an argon-filled titanium frame with double-walled glass. Not quite as secure as the Charters of Freedom, but that case certainly inspired this one.

"It's so pretty," I breathed, leaning against him to get a better look.

"You like?"

"Mm-hmm." I bit my bottom lip, fluttering my eyelashes, which he actually saw this time.

"Legend has it this manuscript points to an immense treasure."

"Ooh, that makes it even cooler."

He shoved the drawer closed, but it slowed on its mechanized track. A nearly inaudible click sounded before he spun me against the bookcase, one hand leaning against a shelf by my head, the other dropping to my hip.

My left hip. Dammit.

A quick check of the clock on the far wall. Eight forty. "What other treasures do you have?"

His hand eased down my side, inching slowly, and I slapped mine over it, halting his progress.

"I don't even know your name," I purred.

"Does it matter?" He dipped his head, lips brushing my neck, body pressing against me.

His name was Thomas Gregory Maguire. Thirty-three years old. Eldest son of Phillip Maguire. Shame of his father, yet heir to a property development empire. Oxford dropout. Broke up with his model girlfriend two months ago. Still lived in this immense mansion with his parents.

I slid his hand on my hip to my ass—eight forty-one—and hooked a foot around his calf. He was approaching my cut-off point. At least he smelled divine.

His lips found their way to my earlobe, and I groaned, pulling him closer. Eight forty-two.

"Eloise!" came a sharp male voice from the doorway, and I pushed Thomas away. Emmett charged toward us, chest puffed, face red. His black tux and shirt, paired with the slick dark-brown hair and close-cropped beard, made him look more intimidating than usual. "What the hell do you think you're doing?"

"Nothing!" I rushed to intercept him, leaving Slobbery-Mouth Maguire behind me. "Nothing happened, I swear!"

Emmett shouldered past me, finger raised. "If you ever touch my wife again, I will end you."

Thomas looked more put out than worried or upset. "She came on to me."

Instead of standing up for my honor, Emmett stalked back to me, grabbed my upper arm, and hauled me out of the room. "Typical."

He stormed down the hall to the front of the house,

muttering the whole way. 'Gold digger. Irresponsible. Unfaithful.'

I hazarded a glance over my shoulder to find Thomas leaving the library. He closed the doors behind him, fiddled with the handles, and slipped something into his pocket. I winked at him before turning back to Emmett.

"You're a brute," I growled as we arrived at the gallery overlooking the foyer. Dozens of well-dressed people milled about below us, spilling into rooms that radiated out like the legs of a spider. The study, the drawing room, the snooker room. Laughter and chatter echoed through the space, bouncing off the chandeliers and statuary adorning the ostentatious display. Men in tuxedos and women in ball gowns dotted the balcony.

"Better a brute than a sleazebag." He shot me a grin and continued dragging me.

"I hate attending these things with you," I said louder than was necessary.

"Good, because we're leaving." Emmett slowed as we stepped onto the grand, white marble staircase. He was considerate of that, if nothing else, even though my stilettos were as comfortable as bare feet.

I scanned the room below us and located Rav. Taller and broader than most of the other guests, with deep-olive skin and slicked-back, wavy black hair, he stood out from the crowd. And yet somehow blended in at the same time—one of his specialties. I swept two fingers across my nose. He raised a full champagne flute in salute, and he was gone.

When Rav moved, the man behind him looked up at me. I gripped the railing when my eyes met his. So blue I could see them from thirty feet away. Blue as the sky at sunset. Like the

Winston Blue diamond. His hair was dark-blond, styled in a medium quiff, and he sported enough facial hair that it wasn't a beard but was definitely intentional. Lips so sensual I felt their curl deep inside.

The evening might have gone differently if Thomas looked like that. Probably not for the best though.

Emmett's face appeared in front of me. "What are you doing?"

"Sorry, my shoe landed funny." I resumed my progress down the stairs behind him. *Focus*. "Twelve minutes to the hour."

"You never space out."

"And you never take more than one minute after I give you the code phrase," I shot back.

A slender, dark-skinned woman in red brocade and a tuxedoed man with matching accents stood at the base of the staircase, in our way. Emmett smiled at them and excused himself, then another couple, a pair of women, and we were almost at the exit.

"Emmett Reynolds!" came a deep voice behind us.

Don't react, Em.

Emmett spun us around, his scrunched brow quickly replaced by a wide smile. Blue Eyes. The two shook, and Emmett clapped the man's shoulder. "Mal? I haven't seen you in forever! What are you—"

The newcomer inclined his head and glanced toward me, looking pointedly at Emmett. "Who's the beauty with you?"

"My wife." He wrapped an arm around my waist and pulled me close. "Eloise."

Instead of taking the offered hand of greeting, I folded my arms. Ten minutes to the hour. We didn't have time for this. Rav was already on the move. "I thought we were leaving."

"We are, baby cheeks." He grinned, and I huffed rather than slapping the look off his face. Making a scene wasn't an option. "This is my old friend, Mal—"

Blue Eyes held up a hand.

Over his shoulder, I spotted Thomas coming down the stairs, studying the crowd. Looking for me? Or his father? I turned to face Emmett, presenting my back to his friend. Eyes narrowed, I whispered the one word that would snap his attention to me. "Broccoli."

Shit, he mouthed. About time. "Sorry, Mal, but we've got to go."

He grabbed me by the upper arm and yanked me the final fifteen feet to the exit. One of the staff took his information to the valet.

In a moment of weakness, I checked the glass in the front doors. It was dark enough outside to reflect the crowd at our backs. I was looking for Slobbery-Mouth, but what I caught was Blue Eyes staring at me. Not at my back, but locking eyes with mine in the reflection. My lungs heaved for real this time.

Dammit, he was gorgeous. But a distraction I didn't need.

He smirked at me, and a furious heat flushed through my body. Not good. I barged out and stalked across the granite landing, down the stairs, onto the circular cobblestone driveway. A black Ferrari rolled to a stop, and a valet opened the passenger door so I could slide in as Emmett did the same on the driver's side.

Once the doors shut, he revved the engine once—typical—and pulled out.

I rolled my eyes and checked the clock. "Twenty fifty-eight. Cake should be coming out in two minutes. Rav, you got that?"

His light French accent sounded in my ear as Emmett progressed down the long driveway. "Copy."

"Jayce, manuscript is still there and matches the specs we lifted from the safe company. Your carrying case will work. You're good in two?"

"Copy that," came a female voice.

"Per plan, the northern-most window is unlocked, and the library has been secured from the outside. Drawer is number eight on the schematic. Pull it out to see the keypad."

"Confirmed number eight."

"Code is..." I shook my head and looked at Emmett. "One-two-three-four-five-six-seven-eight."

Jayce laughed. "Literally the numbers one through eight?"

"Yup. The man's hand nearly landed on my holster so I could get that." Good intel was critical, but I hadn't planned on him being so forward, so fast. They usually took longer before their hands were on me. The clock on the dash switched to 8:59. "One minute."

Rav's voice came over the earpiece. "Sparklers on the cake are being lit."

"Jayce, you're a go."

Our car turned onto the main road, and Emmett hit the gas.

"Slow down, Em." I touched his forearm to calm the adrenaline likely spiking through him. He was always at its mercy. "If you're going as much as a mile over, every cop in a fifty-mile radius will want to stop you just to look at the car."

He exhaled, slowing to the speed limit. "It's a sin to drive this car so slow."

"You know what else is a sin?" I gripped his arm tighter.

"Watching some creepy rich guy make out with my big sister?" He made a face like he'd eaten something disgusting. "I hate that part, Scarlett."

Rav grunted his disapproval.

"You think I liked it?" Drool on my neck to learn one through eight. "And for the record, stopping to talk to that guy? Not only did the extra minutes risk our egress, but he announced your real name to the entire room and you reacted. Don't ever do that again."

"I'm in," said Jayce. "Room's clear."

"Meet you at the motorcycle in ten," said Rav, metal clanking in his background. Pots, pans, and the sounds of a kitchen.

Emmett kept his eyes on the road rather than hurling any witty barbs at me. He knew he'd screwed up and risked the op.

Part of me wanted to continue about how we weren't posing as a married couple, didn't have rings, and he'd risked the job that way, too. But I'd be wrong. Maguire was the kind of man who'd claim me for himself, if he so chose, whether Emmett had said he was a colleague, a date, or even a boyfriend. Husband was the right call.

That's why my brother was my number two. He understood people—read them well.

"Wheels up at the rendezvous point at twenty-two hundred hours." I released my grip and patted Emmett's forearm. "Stay safe. Don't anyone be late."

CHAPTER 2
MALCOLM

I STARED at the front doors, where Emmett and his fake wife had exited. "We have company."

"What do you mean?" came the low voice in my ear.

Before they'd vanished, my eyes had locked with hers in the reflection in the glass. No way that was his wife. I'd noticed the golden dress earlier that evening as she drifted from guest to guest.

Who wouldn't choose a statuesque stunner like her?

Emmett.

From what I'd seen, he preferred women without a fraction as much intelligence as flashed behind those big brown eyes. I wasn't a man given to poetry, but I might see fit to change for eyes like those. Let alone that body.

I'd smirked at her, which she'd answered by hurrying out the front door.

"Call it a hunch, but I think the other team we were worried about is going to beat us to the Codex—or already did."

"Shit."

"I'm heading upstairs. Get me authorization." I placed my champagne on a nearby table and strolled through the crowd, smiling at people who smiled back. This was the worst thing about working with a team—all the waiting and discussions and approvals.

The voice huffed. "You can't go up the main staircase now."

A redhead with skin stretched tight over enhanced cheekbones gave me a once-over.

I paused and kissed the air by her cheek, flowery perfume invading my nostrils. "It's been too long."

Events like this were full of people who either knew you or —if you'd secured an invite to the event—were sure they should. Very few questioned whether you belonged, if you pretended to be old friends.

"It has," she murmured, eyes glassy enough to betray she'd had more than one too many drinks. I pulled a flute from a passing server and handed it to her.

"Take the back staircase from the kitchen," came the voice in my ear. "The cake will keep the serving staff distracted."

I looked past the woman and gave a quick wave and nod to no one in particular. "Gene! How's the wife?" I looked down at the woman and excused myself with another kiss to her thin skin.

She smiled politely, and I scooted past her, past the groups mingling in the dining room where the hors d'oeuvres were situated, slowing in the short hallway to the kitchen. Three servers whipped by in rapid succession, held the doors wide, and the seven-tiered salute to Phillip Maguire's dick size wheeled out slowly.

The decorator had adorned it with the same giant 'M' as

the entryway floor. Just to be sure no one forgot who was paying. I ducked around a corner to not impede its progress, waited for the servers to pass, and made my way into the near-empty kitchen.

Not surprisingly, a house this size had a kitchen which looked like it belonged in a small restaurant. I knew the floor plan and could walk through it blindfolded, but it was hard not to slow down and appreciate that much gleaming stainless steel. I gave a confident smile to the three men sagged against the counter and was through the kitchen without difficulty.

The narrow staff stairway up to the second floor was at the very back, covered in worn, rust-colored carpet, a far cry from all the marble and crystal in the public areas. The first steps were casual, as if I belonged, changing to two and three at a time when I was halfway up.

I nodded to a woman in staff dress as I passed her, the chorus of 'Happy Birthday' carrying from the front of the house. Down the hallway, past a sitting room, a guest room, and I rounded a corner.

"Authorization to proceed to the library received," came the voice.

Little late for that. "I'm almost there."

The hallway was empty, and my hands landed on the door handles. I twisted down but met resistance. Locked.

Applause roared up the main staircase. The gallery above the lobby was only twenty feet away. I pressed an ear to the door but heard nothing inside. Once the clapping ended, they'd be cutting the birthday cake, still distracted downstairs.

I scanned the length of the hallway in both directions, listening. The woman I'd passed on the back stairs must have been the only one in this area during the party. I pulled lockpicks from an inner pocket and made quick work of the door.

A quiet click, and I eased it open. The library was lit by moonlight from the large windows on the opposite wall, reflecting off glass-enclosed shelves. I peered around the room, focusing on the dark corners as I entered. If another team was working this house, I couldn't move too fast. But no one was in the room. Nothing looked disturbed. Maybe I was in first. Maybe Emmett was actually a guest, and that really was his wife.

If so, he'd turned things around since we'd met.

"I'm in," I whispered.

Something slammed into my head. Something heavy. Hard. I stumbled into the door, closing it more loudly than I should have. Hopefully, the continued applause and laughter would drown it out.

The first thing I spotted when the room returned to focus was an elephant statuette on the floor next to me. I'd no doubt be sporting a trunk-shaped bruise by morning.

But it was the growl of a motorcycle engine outside that snapped me to attention. One window was cracked open. Whoever had gotten the jump on me was already down there.

I raced across the room, shoving the window open. Each movement sent a stab of pain through my head. One very tall story below me sat the motorcycle, a small woman leaping onto it behind a broad-shouldered figure. The smaller one glanced up at me as they sped away, a Codex-sized bag strapped to her back.

My stomach dropped. I'd lost. I hurried to the drawer where the manuscript was supposed to be, punched in the passcode, and found the drawer empty.

"Fuck." I rushed to the door.

"What?" came the voice.

"Hold." I listened at the door and was met by silence. The oval tube secured inside the lining of my jacket felt like an insult. I opened the door, watching, checking for the sound of anyone in the hallway, and slipped out. Two doors down, I ducked into a bathroom.

Prodding at the tender spot on the crown of my head, my fingers came away with sticky blood. That would have to be cleaned. The goose egg was already rising.

I couldn't leave this house empty-handed. What else was there? Jewelry in the bedrooms? A painting in the studio? Hell, take one of the vintage cars from the garage? That wasn't my style. I'd taken a job and fucked it up. The contract was for the manuscript, and the manuscript only.

But I was too late. "Either the other team got to it before us, or Maguire moved it."

Silence in my ear. That was never a good sign. They were consulting, deciding what to do. There were contingencies to be determined, which could include cutting me off.

Had Emmett traded counting cards in Vegas for bigger jobs? And who was the mystery woman with him?

"Malcolm." The voice had changed to a distorted one with a different accent. "Switch to the abort plan. Dispose of your comms and the container. We won't be needing your services anymore."

"Roger that." I ripped the receiver out of my ear before they could hear the stutter in my breath. Not needing my services could mean no more jobs from that team or being eliminated. I was good at what I did, so I'd find another job if I wanted one. That would have been the plan if we'd succeeded tonight, anyway.

I retrieved some tissues and wiped away the blood, sure to dispose of them down the toilet. Sure to take a few deep breaths before sneaking out of the bathroom and making my way through the celebratory crowd. This night could have gone worse; I could have been caught.

But I was leaving empty-handed, and that was almost as bad.

Maybe I'd track Emmett down and convince him to split the prize money for snatching the Codex. He owed me.

Unfortunately, I still owed him more.

CHAPTER 3
SCARLETT

OUR JET TOUCHED down at four in the morning, at a quiet airstrip an hour southwest of Halifax. Everyone had snagged at least a one-hour nap in the air, except for Rav, who only slept if the op stretched to three days. He didn't trust our safety to anyone else, and I wouldn't have trusted anyone but him to watch over us. Sure, he closed his eyes to let them rest, but his brain was still on, and no one ever snuck up on him.

An hour later, we stepped through the front door into the office, a buzz of excitement in the air. A skeleton staff was on-hand, doling out coffee as we entered.

A thin woman with thick, dark glasses and equally thick, dark hair pulled into a ponytail greeted me with a hug. "Manuscript?"

"Thanks, Brie." I handed her the case with a yawn. "How's the boss doing?"

Gabrielle was a touch shorter than me, a few years younger at twenty-nine, and dressed in a T-shirt and jeans, as always. Today's shirt sported an engineering joke which went far over my head. My baby sister and I had little in common other than our job and genetics, and some days I doubted the latter.

She exaggerated peering over her shoulder toward the glass-walled conference room with an impish smile that made me chuckle. "She's totally wired. I saw two espressos, which means she's had at least four. Hell, she picked me up two hours ago to get the scanner ready for this thing."

"I thought it only took—"

"Exactly." She rolled her eyes and strode toward the conference room with me behind Rav and Jayce. "I'll have it fired up in five minutes and we'll get a better look at this puppy."

"See you in a few." I gave a small wave as she veered off to the staircase leading to her lab upstairs.

Evelyn, the boss, stood holding the door open.

"Good morning, darling." She kissed me on the cheek and ushered me in, doing the same to Emmett, just behind me.

Her accent—slightly British, despite not being from England—was thicker than usual, the only clue she was as on-edge as Brie had indicated. Normally, she cultivated a local accent, no matter where we were, to keep her profile low.

But there was little low-profile about the sixty-seven-year-old stunner. She was an elegant woman with platinum-blond hair styled in a wavy bob and green eyes that scrutinized every detail around her. I'd grown up wishing I had her hair and eyes, but Em, Brie, and I had inherited Dad's brown everything.

I set my mug down and plucked a lemon Danish off the spread at the center of the large black table. It was good to be home.

"Excellent work, everyone." Evelyn closed the door and sat

with the team. "I've reviewed the recordings and want to highlight a few places we can improve."

She tapped a tablet in front of her, and the glass walls frosted over at the same time a big screen at the end of the room came on.

We discussed the drone surveillance, watched our entrance, and Jayce's rappel from the roof. We listened to snippets of the conversation I had with Slobbery-Mouth and had another laugh over the passcode.

Brie snuck in and took the seat next to me as the screen flipped to my exit with Emmett. "I still haven't found anything about the guy Jayce knocked out. He was on three security feeds we tapped into, but he must have known where the cameras were, because he faced away from them every time."

I hummed aloud. "It wasn't Thomas Maguire. He would have been downstairs with his father and the cake."

Rav pulled the tray of breakfast sweets closer to him and Jayce. "Possibly related to the gunman who was after Zac last weekend."

During the lead-up to the Maguire job, our tactical driver had tangled with what we assumed was another team that was after the Codex. They'd gotten some of the intel we'd needed and stolen his phone, but we still came out on top. Although Zac—who was supposed to be posing as my date for the party—was out for a couple of weeks with an injury.

Brie nodded at Rav. "I'll see if I can cross-reference with those street cams."

"Good job, sweetheart." Evelyn smiled at her baby, then resumed the video, skipping right over the interaction with Blue Eyes and Emmett's screw-up. Was she finally trusting me to lead the team? Had my criticism in the car been sufficient for her? Doubtful.

"Opportunity for improvement here." She paused the video and zoomed in on Emmett and me leaving. Good. He was going to catch hell for revving the engine. But she pointed at my figure on the front steps. "Rushing out like that brings unwanted attention, Scar. Be more mindful next time. Keep your emotional state in check."

Everyone nodded, and the presentation winked out. A lifetime of training couldn't hold my mouth closed. Brie nudged me before any words came out and my professional mask slammed into place.

"That was on me, Mum." Emmett rocked back in his chair.

I was never good enough for her. Not like precious Emmett, who even got away with calling her Mum in the office. He was so much like Dad—irreverent, charismatic, quick thinking—it was no wonder she favored him. But seriously? How many operations did I have to lead flawlessly—or close to it—before I got a Bravo Zulu? A pat on the back? Something more than 'Good morning, darling.'

Evelyn cocked her eyebrow at him, prompting for an explanation.

"Thomas Maguire was looking for her and egress was the best option." Emmett nodded at me, a faint grin dancing across his face before he turned to Evelyn. "She did exactly what we needed and had us out of there in no time flat."

A traitorous smile battled with my better instincts. He'd screwed up, I got the blame, but there he was, defending me. Almost—but not quite—admitting to his error. How could I complain about him when he was the only one who ever stood up to her for me? Brie was scared of everyone, so she clammed up when I received advice on my opportunities to improve. Rav listened like the trained soldier he was and provided support privately later. Jayce was likely too busy eating to hear half of what we were talking about.

Thanks, I mouthed to him.

"My turn!" Brie tapped her own tablet, and the screen displayed a blown-up copy of the manuscript we'd retrieved.

"It's gorgeous," breathed Jayce. The petite woman with tanned skin, broad shoulders, and short black hair leaned forward on the table. She maintained her gymnast's physique by working out a ridiculous number of hours a week.

Probably almost as many as Rav, whose khaki T-shirt stretched across his wide chest and flexed biceps. His arms were folded, lips tight, and dark eyes flitting from the screen to the door and back again. He'd pushed hard for the conference room to have one-way glass so he could watch the outside while we met, but Evelyn preferred the frosted, and it was her choice in the end.

"I didn't get a chance to look closely last night," said Jayce.

"Is it authentic?" I asked.

Brie nodded, tapping and swiping across the tablet. The image of the front zoomed out so she could present the back next to it. "This matches the photos we have from our client. But more importantly…"

With a few more taps, the colors switched. The muted beige background transformed into intense shades of blue, the dark text turning into glowing yellow and purple. At the center, shapes in an iridescent green became clear.

Everyone's heads tilted to make sense of it. At first blush, it was all squiggly lines.

"This is the mark they said to check for under x-ray." Brie zoomed in on the shape. "I don't know what it is, and the brief didn't say, but this is definitely the stolen Codex of San Marco."

Three waves with a circle between the second and third. A line underneath. This was likely related to that legend Thomas Maguire was talking about.

"Is it a cypher?" Rav leaned back, eyes narrowing in consideration.

"Confirming we recovered the correct piece and returning it to its rightful owner is our job." Evelyn tapped her tablet, and the screen switched to a project board. "Interpreting medieval manuscripts and secret codes is not."

Emmett pushed his chair away from the table and stood. "That's my signal to leave."

I shook my head. "The board's up. We're picking our next job."

He winked at me as he passed behind my chair, leaning down to give Evelyn a kiss on the cheek. "I trust ya, sis. Plus, I've got a hot date."

"It's not even five in the morning."

"In New York." He tapped the control by the door on his way out, removing the frost on the glass.

Rav's arms finally uncrossed.

"Why bother coming home first?"

He shrugged. "Better for US customs to see me arrive, isn't it?"

The company jet didn't always fly with official authorization. We used a network of private airstrips around the world when needed and knew precisely where to cross any border. He was right—there was no record of him being in the States in the last few weeks, so flying legally was one more step in concealing our activities.

I rolled my eyes. "Just don't get arrested, Em."

"He'll be fine, darling." Evelyn waved him out the door and brought up a case file on the screen. She was too easy on him. "First up, we have someone looking to retrieve this ring from an estate outside London. It's a fifteenth century English relic known as the Chalcis Ring."

On screen was a thick gold ring with soft edges and letters inscribed into it between crosses. It was far from modern and as old as the manuscript we'd just returned with.

As recovery experts, we handled all sorts of items. Often as not, our target was information, but it could be artwork, jewelry, cars, identities. Anything someone could steal from someone else, we could steal it back.

We found some jobs anonymously on the dark web, never sure who our clients were. As long as the target wasn't a government, a legitimate owner, or involved in organized crime, our team of analysts would consider it and present it to us, then we'd dig into the details. With one exception.

"It's a rush job," continued Evelyn. "Payment is commensurate, but they need it done within the next week."

And that was my exception. "Not nearly enough time."

"Wait for the details, Scar," said Jayce. She and Emmett were the daredevils, always needing to be reined in. But what could you expect from a former cat burglar whose signature was leaping off a roof and swinging through an open window?

"No." I stood, pushing back my chair. It was too early for this argument, and I hadn't had enough sleep. "Mum—"

Evelyn cut me off with a frown and one elegantly arched eyebrow.

"But, Scar, we haven't been to London in like a year!" Jayce put her hands on the table as though she was going to stand, too, but Rav put a firm hand on her shoulder.

I blew out a sharp breath. "My job is to keep you all safe."

Silence.

Jayce's gaze hardened, as did Rav's jaw.

Everyone's brains no doubt clicked back to the time I'd failed them all. When I hadn't protected them. And I wasn't ever going to let that happen again.

"One week isn't sufficient time to plan properly." An itch prickled the back of my eyes. I needed a good sleep and a glass or two of something strong enough to push the past into the forgotten recesses of my brain where it belonged. "And I think we should focus on above-board jobs for at least a few weeks to be sure the Maguire thing doesn't earn any blowback."

"The jet doesn't run on fairy dust, darling."

So get a smaller one. "I'm sending everyone home. We'll pick this up on Monday."

"Sweet!" Brie was out of her seat and halfway to the door before I moved. Her sense of self-preservation was far stronger than Jayce's and my mother's. But odds were she hadn't even been to sleep yet and was just heading back up to her lab anyway.

"Good idea." Rav stood, and Jayce followed his lead. They left while Evelyn and I continued eyeing each other.

"Mum, you know how I feel about—"

Her tight face brightened without warning. "Coming for dinner tonight, darling?"

"It's not like we're hurting for money and need to grab every crap project the analysts find."

"So, no to dinner?" Her fake smile and the repeated invite were the closest she'd ever come to an apology.

I rolled my chair in against the conference table and leaned on the top. "Why didn't you say anything about Em talking to that guy?"

"Being point means you get all the glory and all the blame. You know that." Her unsaid words were just as loud. 'Toughen up. Stop whining.'

Deep breath, Scar. "I'm heading home. I need to shower that creep off me and take a nap. And the girls are coming over tonight, so no dinner."

"Say hello for me." She turned a cheek for me to kiss, which I dutifully did.

CHAPTER 4
MALCOLM

Saturday was a new day.

And with it, a new job.

A woman with long blond hair opened the hotel suite's door. She wore a black dress so tight it must have been painted on, sky-high stilettos, a polished smile showcasing very expensive teeth, and was holding a tablet.

Behind her, the sound of intensity and the smell of money.

"I'm Malcolm Sharpe. I believe you have a seat for me?"

She tapped the tablet, her long nails clacking against the screen. "Of course, Mr. Sharpe. I see your funds have already been transferred."

The friendly buy-in to the game was fifty thousand and, win or lose, I intended to gain something more important than money—intel or clients.

"If you'll follow me?" She turned and walked through the entryway, and I followed, the door closing behind me. No visible security, but the game's manager undoubtedly had cameras watching her table.

The main room of the suite was large, with pale-blue walls, heavy brocade curtains nearly blocking out the noon sun from the floor-to-ceiling windows. A patio door slid open, then closed, and a man in a sweat-streaked gray polo stepped inside. Doors led off in three directions, while couches and chairs upholstered in cream and black lined the side walls.

Four more women in the tight black dresses watched the game, while three men in dark suits stood vigilant along the perimeter.

At the center of the room... my target.

The green-felt oval table with thick brown leather rail was surrounded by nine chairs, plus the dealer. Five chairs were occupied, and some of the men and women wandering around were likely the other players.

Poker didn't hold the same thrill as breaking into Phillip Maguire's mansion, but it paid bills. I almost pulled my hand out of my pocket to feel the lump on the top of my head. That job had gone horribly wrong. If I'd been able to go up to the library when I originally wanted to, instead of being told to slow down and wait, I wouldn't have been surprised. I would've retrieved the Codex and gotten it to the rendezvous point.

But that's what happened when you worked with other people. They screwed up and you suffered the consequences. I preferred to work alone and depend on myself. All the successes and all the failures were no one's but mine.

That's why I normally worked as a private eye. Just me, my business, and clients who came and went.

As the hostess gestured to a seat across from the dealer, the men on either side of it looked up at me. The heavyset one with gray hair gave me a once-over and grunted, returning his focus to his chips.

The other—holy shit, it was Emmett Reynolds—smiled. "I don't see you in... what's it been since that Celtics game? Six months? And now it's twice in two days?"

"Will the coincidences never stop?" I slid off my jacket and hung it on the back of my chair. Surely, he didn't have the Codex with him, but would it be nearby? Did I still have a chance to get it? "Did the game bring you down from Boston?"

"A friend of mine's in Miami and I was thinking about joining him."

"Playing your way down the eastern seaboard?" I took my seat, the chips appearing in front of me before I landed in the chair.

"You know..." His gaze drifted to the ceiling theatrically and returned to me. "That's not a half-bad idea."

After being cut loose from the crew at the Maguire mansion and realizing I wasn't about to chase Emmett down for the Codex, I'd considered drowning my sorrows at a pub or five in Boston. Instead, I'd received an invite to this game I'd been hearing rumors about for months and hightailed it south. A few hours of shut-eye in the very hotel where we were playing, and I was good as new.

The hostess lingered near the door, as though more players were on their way. Word on the street said this game continued around the clock until Monday morning, with revolving staff and an assortment of players. The table was half-full, and from the smell of the room, several people had been there since before I'd arrived at the Maguire mansion.

A clean separation from last night's team was what I

needed. Hiring on for the occasional contract had its perks. People used fake names, sometimes you met your employer and sometimes you didn't, and you were free to leave once the job was done. Although our failure to obtain the Codex also meant no payout. I'd wasted a month in preparation. Risked revealing myself when I lifted a phone from someone with the case's schematics. Endured the loose cannon they'd saddled me with, who ended up in jail a week before the event.

It had to be Emmett Reynolds, didn't it? Fate kept bringing the two of us together, and he was the closest thing I had to a friend, other than my landlord, and that was only because moving was a hassle. No, the Codex was gone. I wasn't about to con him out of it. Not him.

The bartender—an older woman with lined skin and a *don't mess with me* attitude—came by with drink and cigar selection as the dealer began tossing out hole cards.

The first hour was mostly losses, investments in the bigger game. It was a time to learn tells, watch for tics, and get a feel for the level of skill at the table. Were they gamblers? Or were they poker players? Emmett was clearly the best at the game itself, reading the others with the same mastery I'd noticed in him when we'd met three years ago.

One man boasted incessantly about a tech firm he was getting off the ground. Another spoke about a play he was holding auditions for. And another claimed to be writing the next great American novel.

Emmett encouraged each of them, toasting every good hand, and quietly nursing his drink. The stakes steadily rose, and the conversation turned away from idle small talk towards more serious matters. Emmett's attention shifted to the man opposite him. "So, what do you do for a living?"

The question was casual, but the glint in his eyes betrayed his true intent. The two of them were the only ones left in the current hand, and Emmett was either trying to lower the man's defenses or searching for a tell.

The man's smile was wide and genuine. "Venture capital. It can be risky, but it pays off when you get it right."

Emmett nodded thoughtfully. "Do you trust your gut or your statistics more?"

"Start with the stats." The venture capitalist put his hands behind his chips and shoved them to the middle. "Then end with the gut."

"Interesting." Emmett peeked at his cards, a wry smile emerging before he slid them facedown toward the dealer. "Fold."

"No way!" The tech guy nudged my shoulder and laughed. "I was sure your buddy had it."

Something told me Emmett had the better hand and folded to keep the rest of them guessing. Show them some false tells, pretend he had the winning hand, then fold at the end so they'd question him when the stakes got big enough.

The dealer collected everything, chips were moved, and congratulations given.

"You don't lose often, do you?" I said to my old friend.

He straightened his stacks of chips, which already contained roughly a quarter of my original buy-in. "Often enough to keep it interesting."

The flutter of the shuffling machine signaled the next hand would begin soon. Men who'd wandered off during the dance between Emmett and the venture capitalist resumed their seats, ready for another round.

After my cards slid across from the dealer, I peeked at

them, happy with what I saw. Time to start the actual game. "Say, Emmett, I don't see your wife here."

He snorted and checked the big blind.

"Not your wife?" I hadn't been able to shake the memory of her since I first spotted her at the party. The gold dress had hugged some miraculous curves, and her legs went on forever, but it was her eyes that stuck with me.

"Still chronically single, Mal?"

"Married to my work, my friend." I wouldn't say no to a little fun on the side, but anything beyond that was liable to get messy. Women were fickle, and relationships were unreliable. My own baggage was enough of a burden to carry. "But I'm always on the lookout for a set of legs like that."

"Trust me, buddy, she's so far out of your league you'd get whiplash trying to find her league."

The man to my left—the tech braggart—chuckled. "Sounds like someone I need to meet."

"So, not your girlfriend, either?" I called and tossed in my chips.

Emmett took a genuine sip of his drink as the other players added their chips to the table. "Drop it, Mal."

If there'd been even a hint of heartbreak or agony in that comment, I would have stopped there. But since there wasn't, I pressed on, a ridiculous need to know more overcoming me.

The dealer burned a card and dealt the flop.

Two queens and a king, giving me a boat full of queens. "How about this? If I win this hand, you give me her phone number."

"Done." The answer came so swiftly, it was clear—he had a hand he was certain would win.

I wasn't the only one who picked up on his reaction. Everyone else at the table—except for Broadway—folded.

My hand was good, and based on the flop, his only chance at beating me was pocket kings or if the next cards gave him something better. He'd checked pre-flop instead of raising, so there was no way he had the kings.

He must have been bluffing. He was too clever to give away his hand with that fast response.

There was a pounding at the door and the hostess hurried out of the room, moving faster than she had since I arrived. Tech Guru leaned back in his chair to see through to the door. His eyes widened and he scrambled out of the seat.

Not good.

And her protests of "I'm sorry, but you can't—" which were cut off by a squeal, were even worse.

The game was legal as far as I knew. No money went to the house, no obvious drugs, and the eye candy watching hadn't offered themselves to anyone. For all intents and purposes, it was nothing more than a game between friends. So it wasn't law enforcement.

Two of the guys who'd been plastered to the walls reached under their jackets, but not fast enough.

Three armed men in clown masks barged in, handguns drawn. The latex masks covered their entire heads, each sprouting different colored hair—red, green, and blue.

"This is not a robbery," growled the one with the red hair to the men easing their hands from where their pistols were no doubt concealed. "We'll be in and out before you miss five minutes of your lives."

Green hair continued, as he and blue hair trained their sights on Emmett and me. "You two are coming with us."

We hadn't seen each other since last fall. Both received invites to a private game in New York when we happened to be close enough to make it. Less than twenty-four hours after we were both at the Maguire party. No way it was a coincidence.

"Mind if we finish out this hand?" I said, ordering my body and voice to remain calm, despite the gun inching closer to my face. "I've got a big bet riding on it."

Green hair stomped around the table and jabbed the gun against the side of my head. *Thanks for showing me you're the one with the temper.* "Our boss wants to talk to you."

"Anyone interesting?" *Shut up, Malcolm. This isn't your dad you're talking back to.*

Emmett's hands raised and he bowed his head. "I'm pretty sure you don't want to do this."

Red's gun swept across the room, ensuring no one moved. If there were cameras on the table, it was capturing them. Would they have a panic button? Would the hostess have alerted someone on her tablet?

More importantly, if anyone came in response to a distress call, would it result in rescue or bloodshed?

Probably the latter.

I lifted my hands and leaned away from the gun, but Greenie followed the movement. "I'm coming. You with me, Emmett?"

"May as well." He shot me the wink he always did when we were about to get in trouble. "My sister only warned me against getting arrested. Anything else is fair game."

Greenie moved fast, smashing the butt of his gun into the side of Emmett's head, knocking him to the floor.

"Jesus fucking—" Emmett's hand flew up to his head and

when it came away, there was blood on his fingertips. He blinked slowly, as if he couldn't believe what had just happened.

"This is not a joke!" shouted the clown, cocking his arm for another. "Move your ass! Now!"

"Okay, okay." I eased from my seat and helped Emmett up, steadying him when he closed his eyes and swayed.

The other two continued watching the room, guns swiping back and forth, ensuring no one got any smart ideas.

I should have stayed in Boston.

CHAPTER 5
SCARLETT

Laughter filled my kitchen. Kelley wiped her eyes, taking deep breaths before finishing the story about her husband's barbecue mishap the night before. "And he just shrugged at me. Eyebrows singed, the fire extinguisher stuff covering the deck, and all the man does is shrug!"

I pulled the baked brie out of the oven, the scent of warmed maple syrup overwhelming my senses. Add in the blueberries surrounding it and some seedy crackers on the dining room table connected to the kitchen, and my mouth was watering. "Good thing you're here tonight, then."

"That calls for the Sortilege!" Jenn hopped out of her chair and grabbed the bottle of maple whiskey to pour us all a couple of fingers. The flush on her cheeks from the first glass of wine practically glowed against her pale skin and dirty-blond hair.

"Water for me," said the very pregnant Kelley as she pushed her springy black coils back from her face. "With ice. Little man's like a portable oven."

"I'll take hers." Heather held out her glass, already halfway to too much.

Jenn poured, and I placed the brie at the end of the table with the other snack bowls.

Game night with the girls. I'd lived in this town on Canada's East Coast since I was twelve, and these three had been my best friends the whole time. Elementary school, high school, and university. First loves, group dates, and heartbreaks. Marriage plus kids for one. Marriage plus divorce for another.

Through it all, we ensured we saw each other at least once a month. My job and family provided a skewed view of reality, but my friends kept me grounded.

"How was the conference, Scar?" asked Heather, already polishing off her glass. Good thing Kelley was driving her home. Two months off a divorce that no one saw coming—except her ex—and it showed.

Jenn began dealing our cards. "Where was this one again?"

"Boston. And not interesting unless you're into disaster recovery systems." I pulled up a four and an eight, making a vomiting noise. "These cards suck."

Jenn laughed. "You've got the worst poker face in the world."

I shrugged and took a sip of my whiskey, savoring its sweetness over the light burn of the alcohol. They had little idea what I actually did for a living. I didn't con them, cheat them, pretend to be what they wanted. With these girls, I was just me. The only lie between us was the part of my job that pushed—and sometimes broke—the boundaries of legality. They knew I was in recoveries but thought it was limited to things like phone calls, coordinating with various police forces, and tracking down cyber thieves.

Heather tapped her cards as they came to her. She never checked until the full hand was dealt. "No hot security guys sweeping you off your feet?"

"I told you already. It was work, not playtime."

Jenn focused on dealing, keeping her voice neutral as she asked, "Emmett sweep anyone off their feet?"

Kelley snorted a laugh. "Still? You've been in love with him since tenth grade!"

I opted for another vomiting noise.

But Heather, eyes not quite able to fix on me, continued. "Seriously, Scar, you haven't so much as gone on a date in two years."

She's drunk. Ignore it. She's projecting her own pain.

Jenn nudged her, voice quiet. "Stop."

Heather shrugged and picked up her cards, dropping one in the process. "You've got to get back on the horse some—"

Kelley leaned back abruptly, obviously kicking Heather under the table. "Stop it!"

"I'm worried about her, that's all." Heather grabbed her empty glass, eyed it a moment, then swiped Jenn's. "That man was not worth two years of celibacy."

My heart took a sudden, unavoidable tumble. I stared at her, but the pop of yellow on the wall behind her called to me. Begged to be looked at. Absorbed my peripheral attention.

Noah and me at Niagara Falls in our ridiculous yellow ponchos.

The day he'd proposed.

Over the last twenty-three months and four days, I'd gradually gotten rid of the pictures and mementos. But I didn't have anything to take up that space on the wall. It had to be the right size, the right color. Besides, every time I reached for it, his eyes met mine out of the photograph and I had to leave him there.

"I know, I know, don't speak ill of the dead, but does no one here remember how passive-aggressive he was? I mean, remember when he skipped Christmas dinner with her family?"

"It was Thanksgiving," said Jenn. "Emmett was pissed."

"He was, was he?" Heather winked at her, and Jenn's cheeks flushed.

Noah had his moments, most of them being in conflict with my mother. He'd been my number two at the company. That blow-up had been a day after we'd returned from an op where he'd miscalculated a hand-off and we lost the painting we were after. Mum didn't hold back when we made mistakes, and Noah had barely spoken to her for three weeks.

Like everyone other than Emmett, he couldn't stand up to her in person. Noah had chosen to skulk off and avoid family dinner instead of facing the music. Even still, he loved *me*, no matter how messy my family or our work got. He loved my brain and my skills and we made an amazing team.

Heather continued as though she were on a podium giving a speech. "What about Rav? That sexy beast could—"

Kelley cleared her throat. "How about we go back to harassing Jenn, who's still crushing on Scar's brother?"

They laughed, but all I could do was twist my head down to my shoulder. Curled my arm in close so the sweater's hood rode up just enough that I could smell him. Two shirts and this sweater left. Then even his scent would be gone. Maybe then I'd take that photo down.

Noah's death was all my fault. I should have kept him safe. But our comms went down, he wound up in the car behind me, and by the time I saw him lose control, it was already too late.

I missed him so much.

Deep breath.

Never again. Never fall in love with someone in the business again.

Kelley nudged me with a foot. "You in or not?"

I pushed the memories aside and threw a quarter into the kitty. He'd come up twice in one day. First at work, now tonight. Not a good sign. "Anyone want wine? I feel like opening a— "

My doorbell chimed, and everyone's brows furrowed. I lived in a friendly area on the waterfront, but people didn't just come to my door after the sun went down.

"You order pizza or something?" asked Heather.

"No." I pulled out my phone and launched the home security app Brie had written for each of us in the company. One car pulling out of the driveway, one person at the front door.

Kelley leaned over to look at the wide chest and squared jaw standing outside. "I don't care what he's selling, let that man in."

The hair on the back of my neck rose. It was Blue Eyes.

But it couldn't be.

"Is it Emmett?" asked Jenn, the blush on her cheeks deepening.

How did he know where I lived?

I stood so quickly I nearly knocked my chair to the floor. Something wasn't right about this, and my friends weren't getting in the middle of it. I put on my professional face—no matter how much I hated showing it to them—and said calmly, "Get your stuff, girls. You're leaving."

"Let me see him." Heather reached for my phone, but I dropped it into my sweater sleeve faster than she could react. "I want to meet this guy!"

I looked Kelley square in the eyes once she'd stood. "Back door."

Her eyes widened, hands curling around her belly.

"Don't worry, Kell. He's just a friend."

Drunk Heather, on the other hand, raced from the dining room and through the foyer to the front door, like it was some game. I wasn't fast enough to stop her. She unlocked the door and swung it open.

I paused, waving Kelley and Jenn toward the back door before continuing to the front. At least I could keep two of them safe if this was as bad as I feared.

Heather gave him a once-over so obvious I could tell she was doing it from behind her. "Well, hello there."

"I'm sorry, I must have the wrong house. I'm looking for —" He stopped when I joined her at the door, a tight smile gracing his lips. The fall of his shirt and pant legs said there was no gun unless it was in his back waistband. But there was something underlying the smile and it wasn't good.

The faded jeans and navy-blue Henley were a far cry from the tux last night at the party. A casual look, as though he belonged in this neighborhood. But polished brown Oxford shoes and an Omega watch. This man did not belong.

I maintained a neutral expression. He was an intruder. A danger to be evaluated, no matter how hot he was. What next? Play it up for the girls? Pretend he was a boyfriend or a late-night booty call, so they'd leave me to him? Or a protective stance? Get in between him and them? "This is a surprise."

"Sorry for dropping by unannounced, but I saw Emmett this afternoon and he asked me to say hello." His deep voice rumbled inside me, lighting up pathways better left dim. "Any chance we can talk?"

"I'll talk to you," said Heather, wavering slightly. The alcohol must have hit hard when she launched from the table. She thrust a hand out to shake, miscalculating and slamming it into his stomach. She batted her eyelashes. Maybe it wasn't an accident. "I'm Heather."

I lowered her arm before Big Blue could introduce himself, swiveling her toward the living room and the rear door without taking my eyes off him. "Kell needs your help getting home."

"Me, too!" came Jenn's voice from the back of the house. Good. At least they were listening.

Heather careened into me as she spun and said in a stage whisper, "Do you need condoms?"

"Just go. I'll call you tomorrow."

"Fine! Fine!" She waved her hands as she went, mumbling something to Kelley and Jenn as they hustled her out.

They were outside, rounding the house. They'd be safe so long as I kept him distracted. "Why are you here?"

"I really am sorry for interrupting your party, Eloise." He smirked, mischief lighting up his eyes. So blue under the porch light. Tonight, they were a deeper shade, like a moonlit ocean. Like the Hope Diamond. "Or should I call you Scarlett?"

I curled my toes, even though I wasn't wearing shoes, and I blinked slowly, showing only my work face. Calm, detached, observant. "Alright, you say Emmett asked you to stop by. Why?"

He folded his arms and leaned against the doorframe, crossing one ankle over the other. The smile tightened, almost to a grimace. "Your friends are probably still watching, you know. They'll be disappointed if you don't invite me in."

"Very true, but I don't make a habit of inviting strange men into my house."

He nodded, reaching for something behind him.

Gun? Knife?

I inched one arm back, ready to intercept whatever he was planning to surprise me with.

But no, it was only a phone. He unlocked it, swiped a few times, and passed it to me. "I was told to bring you this."

It was a video, starting on Emmett, tied to a chair, with three men in clown masks. My heart sank. No amount of training prepared me for this. Blood streamed down the side of his face and from his nose. His eyes were swollen.

A splinter of ice crashed down my spine. I sprang back, swinging the door shut, but Blue Eyes slammed a hand into it and slipped in.

Fuck. I threw open the foyer closet and grabbed the Glock from its hiding spot over the door, pointing it at him. I always stashed this gun with a round in the chamber. "Who the hell are you?"

"My name is Malcolm." He didn't budge. Didn't come any closer. Didn't flinch. Simply gestured at the phone. "And I'm not here to hurt you. Just watch it."

A layer of dread settled over my heart as I held the phone up next to the gun and hit play, keeping my eyes on this man who claimed to be here at my brother's insistence. "Back up."

He nodded and moved farther into the living room, putting enough distance between us he couldn't grab my gun. Giving me more time to watch the video.

Emmett's voice shook when it started. "Scar, I'm so sorry."

The clowns all had different colored hair, and the one with curly red stepped forward. His clothes were black, as were his gloves. Pale skin around his eyes. Caucasian. Compared to Emmett's size, the man looked to be just shy of six feet. Thin with long limbs. Maybe a hundred and fifty pounds. Probably not the one beating Em.

Red Hair spoke in a distorted voice. "We want the Codex. We know you have it. Give it to our courier or your brother dies. You have twenty-four hours."

The video zoomed in on Emmett's face, his bloodshot, swollen eyes flicking back and forth, then boring into the camera. "Trust Malcolm. Please."

The image faded out, and I extended the gun toward Malcolm. Their courier and yet a man Emmett told me to trust.

Twenty-four hours. What was I going to do?

Whose side was Malcolm on?

I instinctively scrunched my toes, the movement pushing Mum's lessons through my brain. There were plans to make. A team to call in. These clowns would not get away with taking my brother.

"Scarlett," Malcolm said, raising his hands in a gesture of surrender. "We need to talk."

CHAPTER 6
MALCOLM

STEP ONE. I was inside.

Step two. Scarlett had watched the video.

Step three. Get the gun off me. Four in one day was four too many.

"Okay, so talk," she said.

This wasn't how I'd expected the next meeting with her to go. If I'd known she was going to pull a gun on me, I wouldn't have worked so hard to have Emmett give me her phone number. Mind you, if Emmett had given it to me and he'd introduced us, things probably would have gone better. "He and I were at a poker game in New York—"

The gun relaxed slightly. What it was in reaction to, I wasn't sure.

"All above board, until those three showed up. They came straight for him and me, hauling us out of the hotel suite where the game was being held."

"Whose game was it?"

How did that matter? "They held guns on the entire

room. Our hosts weren't behind it. And even if they were, I don't know how they linked us to this Codex they want."

She was good. Not a flicker of emotion crossed her face. Only caution, an extended gun, and sharp questions. And no hint she knew what the Codex was.

"They said Emmett was at Phillip Maguire's party to steal it."

"Really?" Her aim retrained on me. "You saw the two of us on our way out. Did you see us carrying whatever they were talking about?"

I nearly held my smirk at bay. "I don't know about him, but your dress wasn't hiding anything."

Still no reaction.

"Not that it matters, because Emmett confessed."

"He's never confessed to a single thing in his life."

"There's a first time for everything."

Her eyebrow quirked. Considering her lack of response until this point, that was a question, and a controlled one at that.

"He told them you could get it for them." That information hadn't come easily. He'd resisted, and they'd taken a couple of shots at me for good measure, but when they threatened to take fingers, he caved. "I have a feeling they're serious."

"You were there?" She held up the phone with the video paused at the end, on Emmett's face. "When they did this—you were there?"

"I was."

"And what did you do about it?"

I dropped my hands from where they'd been raised. "They flew me up here on a charter jet, so they know I've arrived. They told me they'd call in an hour and a half to check in.

Maybe we should focus on getting the Codex instead of on this interrogation?"

Her attention flitted to the front window and back to me, as though expecting someone to be waiting outside. "Why'd they send you alone?"

"Funny enough, I didn't get the villain monologue." *Stop taunting the woman with the gun, Mal.*

She stared at me for a few beats, then grabbed a set of keys from a hanger by the door. "I don't have the Codex. Not here. I assume they're calling on your phone?"

"That's what they told me."

"So my options are to tie you up and leave you here while I deal with this or bring you with me." She paused again. Still not betraying a single thought in that gorgeous head, but speaking volumes, all the same. Scarlett was a thinker. She was working through a plan and wasn't certain what the outcome was yet. Every pause was an opportunity for me to influence that plan.

"Considering you need to hurry, and I'm sure you want to continue the interrogation, I think option two's the better one." Plus, it would give me a chance to study her further. The sweatshirt hadn't been what I was hoping for, but she pulled it off nicely.

She circled the gun in my direction. "Turn around. The only way this happens is if you're zip-tied and hooded. You try anything funny, and that cute little face is going to get real messy."

Cute little face, really? She may not have shown many emotions, but she was susceptible to one of my greatest strengths. I turned around and placed my hands behind my back. Was a smartass comment appropriate or not?

Before I could decide, she shoved the gun against my shoulder and the zip ties were on me. A lick of pain shot through my side—where the clowns had gotten in several good shots before they realized Emmett's team had taken the Codex, not mine—as she wrenched them tight. Great. This wasn't a simple home zip tie. It had a double cuff.

"Those are a bit more professional than I expected."

She nudged my shoulder with the gun. "Out the front door and to the silver Audi."

I did as I was told, giving her time to lock up and do something with her phone—likely setting an alarm—before I walked ahead of her to the car. "Aren't guns illegal around here?"

She said nothing until I was seated on the passenger side. With the gun still trained on me—this woman had serious trust issues—she gestured for me to do up my seatbelt, then hold my hands toward the armrest, where she secured my zip ties to the door's pull handle with another zip tie.

She pulled a thick black winter hat over my head, leaving it just above my nose. She did it with a great deal more care than I would've expected, given the gun and the ties. It only took long enough for the scent of patchouli and some flower that wasn't roses to wash over me. It was subtle, possibly a shampoo instead of a perfume.

"You don't think this will look odd to people who see me sitting in the passenger seat? You could just leave me without the hat."

She closed my door and got in the driver's side. "I don't like strangers."

"Really? I hadn't noticed."

"I'll trust you more if I know you can't grip the steering

wheel, find the right opportunity to nudge me with a foot, or think you're somehow going to get the gun away from me." The engine revved, and she pulled out of her parking space. "Right now, I have to think about my brother. You know what happened to him. You were there. Which means I need you."

"And your brother suggesting that you trust me didn't help?"

"You're still alive."

Yeah, a friendlier introduction would have gone a long way.

"We've got a fifteen-minute drive. The first thing you need to explain is how you know my brother."

If I could have seen, I would've stared out the window so she couldn't see my face. "He got me out of a jam in Vegas a few years ago."

"What kind of jam?"

"Not the illegal kind, if that's what you're thinking."

"Of course not." Her words didn't convince me she believed them. "Why did they send you?"

"Instead of Emmett?" I snorted a laugh, which was met by a smack to my shoulder. With her hand, not the gun, so that was progress. "Because you wouldn't give two shits if they were holding me in exchange for him. They knew Emmett and I were friends. I don't know how they knew that or how they knew we'd be at that game, but they did. No doubt they expected I'd do their bidding to ensure he got home safe and sound."

"How do you know Phillip Maguire?"

"I did some work for him a few months ago." I shrugged, unsure if she noticed. "He really appreciated it and invited me to the shindig."

"What kind of work?"

How many answers could I give here? What would she believe? What would convince her to trust me? Maybe the truth? "I was investigating one of his business partners, who he believed was cheating him. Turned out he was, so they removed him from the company."

She grunted in assent. "So you're, what? A cop? A PI?"

"The latter. I wanted to be a cop or in the military when I was a kid but wasn't cut out for it." I blocked out the memory pushing its way to the forefront—my dad's face when I gave him the news. From the time I was three and he was teaching me the alphabet by NATO's phonetic letters, he'd expected me to follow in his footsteps.

"Who invited you to the party?"

"That's not the kind of thing a gentleman talks about."

"You're a bit of an ass. Has anyone ever told you that?"

I stifled my laugh. One more reason I didn't do teams. "Pretty much every day."

We'd sped and slowed, turned left and right repeatedly, rose to highway speeds, and paused. The fifteen minutes was almost up, when she made a turn and drove slow enough we must have been in a parking lot.

I hazarded a guess. "We here?"

The car rolled to a stop, and she shifted gears before turning it off. "I'll be around in a sec."

This wasn't going as smoothly as I'd hoped, but she'd neither left me at home nor had she shot me. I knew to take my wins where I could get them.

The door opened and she pulled the hat off. She sliced the zip ties with a pocketknife, stuffed it into an invisible pocket in her tights, and stepped back, giving me room to get out. Where was the gun? "Can I trust you inside?"

We'd parked directly in front of a long, nondescript row of two-story office buildings. Gray stone, floor-to-ceiling windows, and cubicle walls hiding what was inside.

"I suppose that depends on where we are?"

"You're right." Her lips tightened. Finally, some emotion peeking through. "My brother said I should trust you, so I suppose I'll have to do that if we're going to get him home."

"I'm not the bad guy here."

She headed for the building without looking back. The tights and sweatshirt look was a far cry from the gold dress last night, but in some ways, it was even better. "Close the door and stop staring at my ass, Malcolm."

I was liking her more and more with every second.

She used her phone to lock the car door once I'd shut it. Another swipe across her phone screen resulted in a buzz from the door into the office. She held it open and waved me in first. "You're going to sit in that big meeting room over—"

"Scar? That you?" a female voice called from somewhere inside the cavernous space. The cubicle walls lined the outside, while the interior of the office was full of desks in tight quads, a second-floor mezzanine at the back, and a glass-walled meeting room directly beneath it.

Scarlett replied, "What are you still doing here? It's eleven o'clock. Shouldn't you be in bed?"

A thinner version of her appeared at the railing to the mezzanine. Hair pulled up in a ponytail, with oversized glasses and another sweatshirt. Emmett had never mentioned having *two* sisters, but they looked too similar to be anything else.

"Will and I were just working on a software update for some—who's that?"

"New client." Scarlett inclined her head into the glass-walled brig. "Take a seat. I'll be back in a few."

I pulled out a leather seat from the meeting table. At least it would be a comfortable wait and maybe I could grab a few minutes of shuteye.

"Give me your phone." Scarlett held out her hand, and I dutifully passed the goods over. "And your last name?"

"Why?"

"I trusted you enough to walk into this office. But until we've vetted you, that's as far as it goes." She cocked an eyebrow. Another one of her questions. "Last name?"

"Sharpe."

"Alright, Malcolm Sharpe. If we disprove anything you've told me in the next ten minutes, you're going to wish Emmett was the one they sent to see me. And trust me, Brie can learn everything we need in a quarter the time of a normal human being."

CHAPTER 7
SCARLETT

I LOCKED the door behind me, used my phone to cut the power to the meeting room walls so he couldn't see out, and instructed every muscle in my body to *not* sag against the wall or blow out some ridiculously deep breath. This morning, all I wanted was for Mum to tell Emmett he'd screwed up.

What was the last thing I'd said to him? Did I tell him to behave himself? Not get arrested? Don't lose too much money? Those were the condescending things I always said when he flew off to Vegas or Monte Carlo or wherever the hell the best game would be.

Despite that, he'd told her I did a good job. I was so fucking petty, and now he was stuck somewhere in New York, bloodied and beaten, waiting for me to save the day.

The deep breath burst out of me, and I stepped away from the door so Malcolm couldn't hear me. I'd controlled myself the way I'd been trained since the moment he showed up, but every tick of that frustratingly sexy jaw while we were in the car had posed a challenge.

Not to mention his cologne. Bergamot, like Slobbery-

Mouth Maguire, but with a hint of vanilla instead of pineapple. It set my thighs on fire.

Between my brother and his friend, I was losing it. I tucked my hands into the front pouch of Noah's old hoodie, the calm that came with his scent settling in. An equal sense of betrayal threatened to choke me. Two shirts to go, then I could move on. Everything else was work until then.

Brie bounded down the stairs from her lab. She whispered, "He's not really a client, is he?" as if he could have heard her from inside the closed meeting room.

Next office upgrade: holding cells. "What time is it in London?"

She shrugged. "Will's mom had one of her episodes that woke him up, so he figured he'd get to work on the drone we've been tweaking. I got a ping he was checking out my code, so I hopped on a chat and... you know. Here I am."

I could have hugged her for how excited she was to be collaborating with her best friend. Instead, I was about to destroy that mood. "Let's go up to your lab."

Brie was our computer whiz, but Will was our gadget guy. He'd been in London for the past eight months, taking care of his sick mother. Evidence of his absence littered the room, from his empty desk to his shelves Brie refused to fill. She'd been spending more and more time in her lab working with him than before, even though it was remote. She'd always been a night owl, but with him four hours earlier than us, she'd taken to arriving at the office by four or five in the morning.

The plush sofa at the back of her giant workspace called to me, but if I sat, I'd crash. The nap this afternoon hadn't been enough to make up for the trip to Boston, the party, the escape home, the meeting... and Mum wanting us to take on another job with insufficient prep time.

"I've got some bad news, Brie." I rolled my neck, inhaling the old scent which still clung to the sweater. She wouldn't take this well. For how much Emmett and I excelled in the family business, she'd failed at everything required for field work. She was brilliant, but she was a feeler, unable to separate work from reality. The way my heart climbed up my throat almost made me think I had some of that in me, too. "Emmett's in trouble."

She snorted, waking her computer to reveal Will's smiling face.

He yawned and ran a hand over his wavy brown hair. "Everything okay, Brie?"

"Yeah, it was Scarlett and a client." She leaned to the side so the camera had a clearer shot of me. "Apparently, Em's in trouble."

"Just an average Saturday night around there?" He laughed.

"Unfortunately, no." I touched Brie's shoulder, and she looked up at me, her joking face falling. "Some guys broke into a game he was playing and kidnapped him."

Brie gasped, shuddering so strong I felt it. "Kidnapped?"

"The guy downstairs was with him, but I'm not buying his story until we've cleared him."

Will nodded, but Brie's mouth was still hanging wide.

I squeezed her shoulder, a lifetime of lessons on how to calm the churning in my stomach running through some part of my subconscious and almost working. "This is no different from Friday night. We were all in danger the moment we approached that house, but careful planning got us out safely."

"What do the kidnappers want?" asked Will.

"The Codex."

"It was already shipped, wasn't it?" he said.

With a nod, Brie turned to her desk. Will remained full screen on her third monitor, while her central one switched to our secure tracking system. "Courier came for it at three this afternoon. It could be in London by now."

Dammit. "Getting it back from the courier or the client isn't an option without ruining our reputation."

Will's focus was somewhere offscreen. "Why'd they think he had it? We bypassed the Maguire security feeds around the library, didn't trip any of the alarms, and you had a clean exit."

To them, everything had gone off without a hitch. To me? I'd been replaying every tiny failure. Losing intel, losing Zac, a staff member who'd questioned me going into the library, the delay with Malcolm, my emotional response to him, the revved engine... Mum's voice echoed in my head as the list grew, reminding me of both where I'd messed up and that I had to focus on the present moment. "What if the guy who took Zac's phone got information—"

"Not likely." Brie blew a raspberry. She switched to a new window and pointed at a grid of characters that made no sense to me. "Zac's phone was destroyed the second whoever lifted it turned it on."

"Fine. Then it could be the gunman who went after him, someone who recognized me from the recon at the architect's office, or—"

"Or we missed a camera at the Maguire mansion somewhere." Brie tapped her keyboard in thought.

"Or someone shared a selfie on social media," added Will.

I pulled Malcolm's phone from one of the hidden pockets in my tights. "We'll do a full Lessons Learned session later. Right now, we need to focus on the fact that Emmett's kidnappers want something we don't have. They're going to call in an hour, and I need to figure out a plan."

"Where does the guy downstairs factor into this?"

Will's jaw set. "I'm calling Rav."

"You'll do no such thing." I held the phone up. "It's too up in the air for Rav to do anything but get pissy. The guy's name is Malcolm Sharpe. He claims to be a PI and an old friend of Emmett's who was taken with him."

"Why'd they let him go but keep Emmett?"

I gave them a summary of everything Malcolm had told me. For Brie's sake, I kept my words measured and factual, despite the nerves careening around my chest that I still hadn't gotten control of. "With all the coincidences or mistakes required for those kidnappers to know we took the Codex and for them to find Emmett, my assumption is Malcolm's in on it. I need you two to tell me the odds of that. Hack his phone, research his identity, and let me know."

Brie swiped the phone and placed it on a docking station, windows and command lines already flying across her screen. "I'm creating a new VPN for this, Will."

"Got it."

I strode to the rear of the room, past a work table covered in electronics, a mini treadmill she sometimes pushed under her pneumatic desk, and stopped in front of the sofa. "And I need it before the kidnappers call in an hour."

"Consider it done," said my super-smart little sister.

Instead of slipping down for a few minutes of rest, I veered over to Brie's whiteboard. "You need any of this?"

She craned her neck, squinted at the board, and pushed her oversized glasses up. "Nope, it's all yours."

I began erasing, plans and options and strategies flitting through my brain. If I wrote them down, I'd be able to wrap my hands around them. I'd be able to figure a way out of this and bring our brother home.

CHAPTER 8
MALCOLM

THE DOOR WHIPPED OPEN, and I looked up just in time to catch the phone hurtling toward me.

Scarlett marched in with the other woman behind her. "This is Brie."

Brie nodded, tapped on the tablet she was carrying, and the large television at the end of the meeting room flicked on. The left half of the screen contained video feed of a man in his mid to late twenties with brown hair and eyes, while the other half was my driver's license, three of my PI licenses, and a photograph of my passport.

"And that's Will," said Scarlett, pointing to the man on the screen.

I gestured to the painting I'd been admiring. "This looks remarkably like a piece that was stolen from a museum in Miami about five or so years ago?"

Scarlett continued, unphased by any of my words. "Military brat, grew up moving from country to country around Europe, went to some of the best prep schools in England and the US."

"I don't suppose it *is* that painting?"

"Only one arrest, when you were twenty-three for drunk and disorderly, and your PI licenses are... What was it you said, Will?"

The man on the screen said, "Real."

"I could have told you all of that, if you'd asked. I'm on your side here."

"But what I don't understand is how a private investigator from New York gets himself an invite to a high-end closed-door poker game?" Scarlett pulled out a chair to sit, and Brie did the same. "Emmett flew all the way down at five in the morning. He doesn't do that for small personal gains. What was the buy-in? Thirty thousand? Fifty?"

I leaned on the chair in front of me, taking some pressure off my injuries—my painkillers were wearing off. "Nothing more than a business investment. I'm not some cheap back-alley gumshoe you'd see in a movie, pissing into a jar. My clientele come from money, and you'd be amazed at how loose some people's lips can get when they're drinking and playing cards with you. Lose a few hands, and they feel superior. Win a few hands, and you're one of the gang."

"And that's how you get clients like Phillip Maguire? And why you have PI licenses up and down the East Coast?" She'd introduced me to her two colleagues and hadn't thrown me out on my ass, so she was leaning toward trusting me. With someone else, I might've guessed it was a desperate attempt to keep me around because of the kidnappers. But I was pretty sure Scarlett Reynolds hadn't experienced desperation in at least a decade.

"Yes. And it keeps my options open."

Scarlett folded her hands and leaned on the table. "What would you do in my shoes?"

"Trust me." And I could think of a few other choice thoughts, but saying any of them out loud wouldn't garner me any favors.

"I meant beyond that. Let's assume I believe what you're telling me. You happen to show up at the same game Emmett does. Possibly invited by the same person, but maybe not. Three armed men come in, take you and my brother. They beat him and leave you untouched, trusting you for some reason, and hoping you'll convince me to hand over some item Emmett claims we stole from Phillip Maguire. What would you do next?"

Not quite untouched, but I had a sneaking suspicion she'd accuse me of injuring myself to gain her favor if I told her that part. I looked at the man on the screen, who must have been watching me from a camera hidden in the television. Then to Brie, who continued tapping away on her tablet. "Obviously, I'd give me the Codex."

Scarlett's eyebrow quirked again. That was the *tell me more* prompt.

"Except you won't, will you?" I should have talked to Emmett more about her. Figured out what made her tick before I flew up. Because no matter how good I was at reading people, she was giving me next to nothing.

She was mistrustful—evident by the fact that she kept a loaded gun by her front door, let alone how quickly she'd pulled it on me and rushed her friends out of the house. She was cautious—she used the cuffs and secured me to the vehicle. And she was calculating—it was all questions and trying to figure me out.

Emmett was nothing like her. He was loud and brash, not to mention a risk-taker. He liked everyone and everyone liked him. She was definitely the oldest.

I sat in the chair and folded my arms to mirror her, attempting to gain some psychological connection. "You claim you don't know about the Codex, but I'm betting you do. Emmett told them as much. But if you won't hand it over, that either means your brother's life isn't worth much to you…"

Brie's face pinched. Emmett's life *was* worth a lot to them. She was more emotional than anyone else in the room, and she knew it. She also telegraphed it by the way she kept her head down.

"Either that or you don't have it."

Scarlett undid her folded arms and clasped her fingers instead. Interesting. Was she intentionally moving out of the position I'd shared with her? "Go on."

"Your next play would be to offer them money."

"No."

I waited a beat, but she didn't explain. What was she doing?

Of course.

She wanted me to go through suggested actions, in case I slipped up somewhere and revealed that I knew everything. That's why she'd shifted her arms into a different position than mine—she was trying to unbalance me.

"Alright, your next option would be to contact the police. You're hoping I know where they're keeping Emmett, or maybe you're even thinking that you can trace their call. Then you alert the authorities."

Brie looked at Scarlett from the corner of her eye. "Good plan."

I stood and paced the length of the table. Movement gave me power—maybe that would work with her. "No, it's not a good plan. Three masked gunmen with more information than they should have. If you call the authorities, the next question is how long would a standoff last? Would they be able to save Emmett? Is there a chance he gets shot in the process?" No, if she was as smart as I suspected she was, that option was off the table. "You're not going to call the authorities. Your next choice is money. How much was the Codex worth?"

"Three point four million."

"And you say you don't have it. So, do you have the money?"

The corner of Brie's mouth slid up for a fraction of a breath before she contained it.

I had to pay more attention to her while I talked to Scarlett. "I'll assume money's not an issue for you. So, if the authorities aren't an option and you have the money available, go with money."

Scarlett leaned over to peer at Brie's tablet. "Who invited you to the poker game?"

No indication if I was right at all? Why go through the whole exercise? "I don't reveal my sources."

Her gaze shifted to me, just as impassive as the last hour. "Money isn't the next step. You told me those gunmen came into the game and targeted Emmett *and* you. It wasn't a coincidence. They took both of you for a reason. The first step in finding out that reason is tracking down whoever invited you. Because the odds are that person invited my brother, they're tied in with the clowns, and no matter how this plays out with Emmett, it will not end well for them."

I flipped my watch over and tapped the face a few times. "They're going to call within the next five minutes. We can talk about that after. I want to know the plan, so I don't sound like an idiot."

Brie's shoulders bounced in quiet laughter, and Will—giant head on the television—couldn't hide that he'd bit down on his lip.

Scarlett though?

Nothing.

"What if they ask you to steal the Codex back?"

"We didn't steal it."

"Fine. What if they ask you to do a different job?"

"When you say job, what does that mean to you?" Scarlett gave me so little to go on. Open-ended questions, eyebrow raises, and not a flicker of emotion. As a man whose entire livelihood was about understanding what made people tick, this enigma was steadily becoming my nemesis. Or the sexiest fucking thing I'd ever encountered.

I scanned all three faces in the room. They did all work together, right? Was the setup in the office with all the professional-looking desks just for show? Or were Brie and Will part of a legitimate business, while Scarlett and Emmett—plus whoever hit me on the head with the elephant—part of the covert element? The illicit element? "Emmett said the company is called Reynolds Recoveries. He said you recover stolen goods. So by *job*, obviously I mean recover something else that was stolen, other than the Codex."

Was that the right answer?

Before I could find out, my phone rang.

CHAPTER 9
SCARLETT

LAST WEEKEND, I'd arrived in Boston with Zac and Rav. Our plan had been to secure blueprints for the Codex's location and for the security measures surrounding it. Our mission had been planned within an inch of its life, like always. The way I demanded.

But the mysterious other team was a variable I hadn't expected. After they stole the schematics for the Codex's case from us, we'd snuck into the safe company that'd designed the case and retrieved the plans Phillip Maguire had commissioned. We'd also discovered a duplicate set of plans, drawn up for an organization called the Fenix Group. It left me wondering: Was there more going on? Was there another codex somewhere? And was the other team involved in Emmett's kidnapping?

They hadn't gotten close enough to see me—and even if they had, I was in disguise. Unless they'd somehow gotten into the Maguire mansion, made me, and then saw Emmett and Malcolm's interaction before we left?

No one on my team had talked—I trusted each of them with my life.

As much as I hated to agree with him, Malcolm was right. Again. We had to negotiate and buy time, then we could figure out who was behind everything. Money came first.

Brie attached a cord to her tablet and passed the loose end to Malcolm. "Plug that in. It'll let us trace the call."

Malcolm hesitated. "But I already know where they are? Why do you need that?"

"You know where they are, so long as they haven't moved." I pointed at the cord. "Plug it in, then answer."

He did as asked and answered, "This is Malcolm."

The same distorted voice as on the original video came over the phone. "Do you have the Codex?"

"No." He flashed those light-blue eyes at me, eyes that no doubt caused knees to give out all over the world. They must have served him well as a private eye, if that was all he really was. Something still niggled at the back of my brain, telling me there was more to him than that.

I put up a hand before he said more. "This is Scarlett Reynolds. Emmett is my brother."

"The legendary thief, herself?"

Jackass clown. "I'm not sure what you've heard, but I'm a recovery agent. And what I want to discuss with you is recovering my brother."

Brie tipped her tablet toward me, showing her trace narrowing in on New York City. Will, meanwhile, was on mute, attempting to undo the distortion so we could get the sound of his real voice.

"The price is the Codex."

A jackass and stubborn. Great.

I leaned forward, a knot twisting in my stomach, and I stared daggers into the phone. If only Emmett had listened. If only he were less of a gambler. Less concerned with fun times and fast money. "Before we discuss this any further, I need proof my brother's alright. Your courier showed me the video, and he was in bad shape."

"Trust us. He's in no worse shape than—"

"I don't trust anyone. Let me hear him or you can call back later."

There was silence, followed by a jostling sound, then a groan. The knot loosened a little when I heard Emmett in the background. He was still alive and speaking clearly, which meant a lot.

"Scar? That you?" The same panic laced Emmett's voice as in the video.

Tamp it down. Hold it back. Stay in control. "It is. Are you alright?"

He scoffed, and I could just imagine his sheepish look. It was the same one he always gave me when Mum caught us doing something wrong as kids. With a mother like Evelyn, we never got away with anything, although she encouraged us to try.

"Are you as alright as you could be under the circumstances?"

"I'll say yes to that one."

The kidnapper I'd been talking to returned to the call. "Now that you've heard him, let's get back to business. Your brother is alive, and you're going to give the Codex to our courier. You will not follow him back here, put any trackers on it, or—"

"We don't have it," I said. "But I know the estimated sale

price was three-point-four million, so I'm willing to pay that for his release."

"No."

My gaze rose from the phone to meet Malcolm's. His breathing had increased, revealing more stress than his face did. No sweat at his hairline, no tremble in his hands, no fidgeting. He was calm and restrained, other than the visceral reactions most people had a difficult time fighting. He did, however, raise his eyebrows at me, likely to say, 'I thought you weren't going to offer them money?'

"Then what will you accept, other than the Codex?" I checked Brie's tablet again, as her map zeroed in closer and closer to a target. "Insisting you get it won't accomplish anything, because it's already on its way back to its rightful owners. And if you kill Emmett, the only thing you'll get is a need to look over your shoulder for the rest of your life. So, what's it to be?"

"Rightful owners?" Someone else was speaking this time. Still a distorted voice, but it felt more like the one who was actually in command. "I doubt that very much."

The Codex had been stolen from the British Museum over a decade ago, and one of their wealthy benefactors who wanted it back had contracted with us. Who the clowns thought it belonged to wasn't a debate I was interested in.

Art and cultural items could be claimed by any number of interested parties. If the museum had obtained it illegally from some other source—conquest, Nazi loot, sold by a thief—the original owner could use the legal system to get it back. If that failed, they could come to us.

But we only worked with people who had legitimate claims. People who were recovering items, not stealing them.

"Five million." How far would I go for Emmett? How much money could we get on short notice? I could only access so much at one time without having to tell my mother. And the moment she found out about this, all hell would break loose.

"We don't want money, Ms. Reynolds. But we have a proposition for you."

One more check of Brie's tablet showed me that the tracing had paused. Software glitch or were the clowns cleverer than I'd expected?

"There's another item we want. If you bring it to us, we'll release your brother."

Malcolm shrugged. Son of a bitch. That shrug may as well have been him saying, 'I told you so.'

I closed my eyes, feeling for my heart, forcing it to slow. *Zen state, Scar.* "What is it?"

Dear God, don't let it be a premium item like the Mona Lisa.

"An insignificant item. A ring which is kept in a safe by a man who is not its owner. Something in your wheelhouse. A recovery, yes?"

Brie shook her head and pointed at her tablet. The trace wasn't going to work. I gave her a curt nod and she switched to some other app. "I'll need all the details before I can confirm it's even possible."

"I'm sending the information now."

Malcolm's phone buzzed, and before he could grab it, I did. The text message had an attachment on it, and I clenched my teeth when I opened it.

Fuck.

I tilted it toward Brie, then tossed the phone to the center of the table.

The clown's distorted voice chuckled. "Your twenty-four hours is now one week. Everything we have is in the attachment. I'm sure you're more than capable of creating your own plan."

Malcolm's brow furrowed as he examined the details on the phone.

I scrunched my toes inside my sneakers, the only movement I could make that wouldn't reveal the torrent of rage and frustration flowing inside me. The only way I could get any of the anxiety out of my body. "I still need time to go over this. Give me a chance to read it and figure out if it's doable."

The problem was, I knew it wasn't doable. I knew there wasn't enough time. Because it was the Chalcis Ring. Exactly the same case Mum had brought to my attention at the debrief this morning. I'd already said no to it once, but I couldn't this time.

All I needed was twenty-four hours to get ahead of the clowns. We needed a plan, and we needed it fast.

If I was going to bring my brother home, I was going to have to do the impossible. My team members were some of the best in the business, but I didn't like last-minute jobs. Last minute led to risks, which led to people getting hurt, arrested, and killed.

"One week. The ring for your brother's life." The call ended abruptly.

Malcolm continued scrolling on the phone while I fought the desire to be sick.

Brie said, "I couldn't narrow them down to more than a

five-block radius. And in the Garment District, five blocks is a lot of people."

"The game was in the Upper East Side, and they questioned us there," said Malcolm. "They've moved him, so I can't help pinpoint them."

"I can work with the filters to unscramble the voice," said Will. "Want me to focus on that or help with whatever case they sent you?"

"Will, track down information about the other players at the poker game. Malcolm will cooperate and provide as much as he can." I glowered at him, silently making every threat I'd wanted to make on that phone call. "That includes the name of who invited you, the names of every person you know from that room, and every second of what you can tell us about what happened."

Malcolm's eyes softened. "I want to bring Emmett home as much as you do. You did your research and confirmed I told the truth about what I do for a living. Your brother trusts me. So should you."

If only it was ever that easy for me. Trust had to be earned, not begged for. "Brie, we're going to review this file, and I need you to pull all the stops. Use whatever resources you can."

She lifted one finger in that way she did, like a nervous schoolgirl asking the teacher a question. "I know you won't be happy about this, but..."

I raised my eyebrows, waiting as patiently as I possibly could for her to get over the nerves of whatever had to come out of her mouth. We had to get going, not hem and haw.

"I got a call from Zac this morning."

She was right. I had a good feeling I knew what she was about to say, and I wasn't going to like it.

Will blurted out, "It's fantastic news, Scar. I think the great idea."

I turned my glower on him—he was lucky he was in England. "Let me guess. Ashley wants to come work here?"

Brie may have been nervous to tell me, but the sparkle in her eyes gave her away. That woman had stolen my getaway driver. If Zac had been with me last night, Emmett wouldn't have been there. He wouldn't have talked to Malcolm, he wouldn't have been revving his engine, and who knows what else he wouldn't have done.

And there was one thing for sure. If Zac had been at my side last night, the kidnappers wouldn't have taken Emmett this morning, because they wouldn't have had any idea he was linked to our recovery of the Codex.

Ash could burn in hell.

"She still works for the FBI, so she's of no use on this job." The rest, we could argue about later. I stood from my seat. "We need to call the team in. I want to talk this over with Rav, Jayce, and Declan. Then we'll figure out our next steps and call in the support staff."

I pulled out my phone, staring at it for a blink. The biggest question of the night was whether to keep Malcolm in the loop.

We were down two of our core team members. I'd have to either bring in a contractor or use the one sitting across the table from me. As a private investigator for people as wealthy as Phillip Maguire, Malcolm would probably be a help.

The problem was, I wasn't sure if I trusted *myself* to make the decision. Was I swayed by Emmett's plea in the video? Or was it those forearms and their corded muscle? The strong jawline? The brilliant-blue eyes?

Or was I just way too tired?

CHAPTER 10
MALCOLM

Scarlett and I sat at a small round table in the office kitchen, a mug of coffee in front of each of us. It was strangely normal. Brie was working upstairs, and from the excited chatter drifting down from her lab now and then, she must have still been on her call with Will.

"Are they an item?"

She stared at her mug. "Brie and Will? Nah. They've been best friends since they were, I don't know, nine? Maybe ten? They did every school project together, from elementary all the way up through university. They skipped social events instead of school—to play video games. They built their first computers together."

"And they work for the family company together?"

"Family?"

I took a sip of my Americano. It would be hours until I needed the jolt, so there would be more in my future. "Emmett said it was a family business. He never mentioned having more than one sister, but when the two of you were sitting next to each other, I noted some similarities. So, I'm guessing either sisters or cousins?"

"Sisters." Her gaze lifted to meet mine, and a sliver of fatigue showed on her face. A little in the squint of her eyes, a little just in how she didn't snap at me. "Fair warning. I haven't decided whether you're in or not."

"You've downloaded all the details about the Chalcis Ring from *my* phone. Whether or not you let me help your team, I'm going to do something about this. Emmett may not be my brother, but he's my friend." One of the few I had. "I expect we'd both be more successful if we worked together."

"He never mentioned you. How close could you possibly be?"

"Like I said, he got me out of a jam." I held the cup under my nose, inhaling deeply. I didn't do commitments, which was exactly why Emmett and I were good friends. We simply kept running into each other, fate bringing us together a few times every year, and we got along. No promises, no plans to *do something* together like buddies. "This is about repaying him."

Her gaze roamed over my face and my arm with the coffee. If it was any other woman, I'd think she was checking me out. With Scarlett Reynolds, the look was cataloging my strengths and weaknesses. "No favors left on the table for someone to call in later?"

Should I shift to sound more empathetic or worried? No, any show of weakness might give her an excuse to force me back to New York. Maybe tell her how I recognized the painting in the meeting room? No, that was my ace in the hole if everything else failed. Go slow, hold the big details back until they were needed. "Something like that."

"My head of security's going to have a chat with you. He'll decide whether or not you come with us."

"So you've decided to get the ring?"

She lifted her cup to her lips and drank slowly, not responding until the cup sat on the table again. "My team's safety is my top priority. I don't think one week is enough time to do a proper job, but if everybody puts their heads together and we can come up with a plan, I'm willing to try."

"You kind of have to, don't you?"

A chime sounded, likely a door notification.

"The team's arriving." Scarlett stood with her coffee and headed for the hallway toward the main office. "Come with me."

When I rounded the corner, I had a view of the front door. The first one coming in was a behemoth. To the uninitiated, he might look like a soldier. Tall, muscular, walking with an almost unnatural level of confidence. But his dark, shaggy hair was just a little too long. His posture a little too relaxed. His eyes, though, told the real story. This was a man who had not only seen death but caused it. Sniper? Special forces? Whatever he was, he was no doubt the head of security I was going to chat with.

Scarlett detoured into the meeting room and waved us in.

As requested, I followed.

She cradled the coffee mug and nodded toward me. "Rav, this is the guy you need to talk to. He's apparently a friend of Emmett's, and I'm debating whether we should take him. The team's down by two, and we don't have time to bring in—"

"Call Zac back in," he said in a voice that invited nightmares. Deep, ominous, lethal.

"Until his hand heals—let alone his thick skull—he's of no

use. Malcolm's a PI, so hopefully he has skills we can leverage. Either way, I want your opinion on whether he's an asset or a liability."

"Of course." He swung the door shut, then sat and gestured to a seat across the table. Unlike Scarlett, he had an accent. French. French-Canadian, more specifically. "We'll only be a few minutes."

The chime sounded again, and Scarlett headed for the door. "Don't kill him unless you have to?"

My heart thunked against my ribcage. *That was a joke, right?*

"I'd prefer to be out there with Scarlett, making a plan to bring her brother home. Instead, I'm stuck in here with you. What questions do you think I should ask?"

I got to lead my own security interview, too? Or it was another test, like Scarlett asking what she should do about Emmett. "You should ask if you can trust me, and I'll say that you can."

He nodded. "That seems reasonable. What do you think of Scarlett's ass?"

I shook my head to clear it. That must've been his accent. That wasn't an actual question.

"Because my priority is to keep it safe. Do you understand that if you betray her or this team, I will kill you?"

Again, that couldn't have been an actual question.

"And if not me, I have a list of men who will receive your name, and if I'm not able to do it, one of them will happily do the job for me. Are we clear?"

Emmett had always seemed like an easy-going guy. Granted, there was usually alcohol and cards involved, but his family company was far more intense than I was expecting.

"Clear. And I can't say I blame you. But the truth is, I want to help."

He nodded and stood, crossing the room to open the door. "Come on in. Malcolm's joining us."

Was it really that simple? Or had the two wonder kids done some more research into my background? They couldn't have gone too deep, otherwise that meeting would've gone in a different direction. Either that, or the threat against my life was genuine and he trusted that I valued my skin.

It was probably a combination of both.

A woman entered first. Petite with short, wavy black hair and olive skin, moving with the grace of an acrobat. Her shoulders and thighs were thick. She placed both hands on the armrests of her chair and lifted to curl her legs underneath herself. "Hey, Malcolm. My name's Jayce."

Next, a man roughly my height, with a long, lean body and sharp hazel eyes. He looked like a swimmer or a runner. Distance skills. He nodded at me. "Declan."

Brie entered the room with her tablet, and the television flipped on to show Will's face.

As Scarlett joined us, still nursing her coffee, the door chimed. Everyone checked to see who else was coming in.

The first thing I saw was the platinum-blond hair, then the impeccably tailored light-blue suit. The closer she got, the clearer her age became. From far away, thirty. Then forty, fifty, and possibly even in her sixties. Perfect makeup, perfect posture, and carrying a baker's box in one hand with a crocodile skin clutch in the other.

Scarlett muttered, "Who called her?"

Brie shrugged but didn't look at her sister. "Sorry. I thought she should know."

Scarlett placed her mug on the table and leaned close enough to whisper to Brie, "She shouldn't have known until we were already in the air and had some semblance of a plan."

The woman swept into the boardroom and hit a panel by the door, causing the walls to frost over again.

"Evelyn," said Rav. "It's two in the morning. We don't need that."

"Sorry, habit." She slid the box onto the table and waved at it. "I stopped by Russo's for some sweets. Thought we could all use a bit of sugar at this hour."

Scarlett took Evelyn by the elbows and kissed her cheek. "Mum—"

This was her mother? Blond hair and green eyes to Scarlett's brown and brown. The Reynolds siblings must have taken after their father.

"Evelyn, Russo's is not open at this hour."

"Darling..." She patted Scarlett's cheek tenderly. "Everyone's open for me."

Scarlett shook her head. Either she was warming to me and letting her defenses drop or she was just too tired to keep them up. Or her mother was someone who could get a reaction out of her no matter what. Interesting.

Jayce drew the box toward herself, selected a sugar-dusted croissant, and kept the box as though it were all for her.

Evelyn slipped out of Scarlett's grip, and her eyes landed on me. Landed on every inch of me. From my hair all the way to my toes. There was the similarity—the assessing gaze. "And who is this stunner?"

I stood and held out a hand to shake. "My name is—"

"Malcolm." Evelyn's face cooled, and she looked me up and down again, even more obvious than the first time.

"Emmett's PI friend who left my only son with a trio of kidnappers, I believe?"

If this was the lion's den, she was the head of the pride. There was an edge to her that reminded me of Rav. This woman had even more secrets than the rest of the room, no matter how innocent or elegant her exterior.

I took my seat. "They weren't going to let him go."

Her eyebrow quirked in that same manner Scarlett's did.

"My coming here was the only way to ensure he lives."

"Of course." Nothing about the tone of Evelyn's words made me believe she meant it. "What do we know?"

Scarlett walked to the far end of the room and stopped next to the television. "Yesterday afternoon, Emmett was kidnapped in New York City. Malcolm was with him at the time. The kidnappers wanted us to return the Codex of San Marco, but given it's already in transport back to London, I told them we couldn't get it. I offered them money, but they demanded we do another job instead."

Will's face moved to the bottom corner, and a photograph of a ring appeared. Solid gold, with a thick band. Engravings covered it, but everything was soft at the edges, as though it had been buried for hundreds of years.

She pointed to the ring on the screen. "This is the Chalcis Ring. It's currently in the possession of Hugo and Camilla Albrecht in Oxshott, England. It's what the kidnappers want."

Evelyn leaned forward. "Isn't that the ring I brought up yesterday morning?"

Scarlett nodded. "I didn't think it was a good job then, and I don't think it's a good job now. But with Emmett's life depending on it, we'll have to make it work."

Jayce's nose wrinkled. "What's so special about that ring?

It looks like something we could easily reproduce. It's just dull gold and—"

Brie tapped her tablet and the image shifted to a closeup of some markings—crosses and letters. "We haven't tracked down any history or provenance for the ring, but Will suggested he might visit a couple of museums to get their thoughts on it."

Scarlett leaned against the wall and crossed her arms. "This isn't one of our normal jobs. There won't be any payment, and we're not even going to spend the time to find out who the ring really belongs to. Whether we're stealing it from the rightful owner or not, this is about Emmett. Not my conscience. I understand if any of you choose not to participate, for whatever reason."

Evelyn snorted. "*I* won't understand."

"On top of all that, we're going in without all the information. I don't like how much of a risk this is, but I'll go by myself if I have to."

"You'll have me," I said.

Rav's eyes settled on me, his earlier threat repeated silently. "So I definitely need to go."

"And me." Jayce took a cookie from the box she hadn't shared. "I was just saying yesterday morning I wanted to go back to London."

Declan waggled his long fingers. "And no offense to Jayce, but if there's a possibility they have something more complex than she can open, you'll need me. This isn't like last weekend, when you could fly me in with a week to spare. I'm coming, too."

The photo on the big screen shifted to a manor house of

—if I had to guess—thirty thousand square feet. Covered in pale stone with Corinthian columns and rows of tall windows.

"This is our location. They're holding their daughter's wedding reception in one week's time with over two hundred attendees. There's a chance we can get in before that, using the chaos of final preparations as cover, but it's just as likely one or more of us will be attending. Go home and pack. Standard equipment plus black-tie wedding attire. Anything you don't have can be sourced once we're on the ground in London." Scarlett tapped the television with a knuckle, and the image switched to one of Emmett from the video.

Jayce and Declan tensed. This must have been the first time they'd seen it.

Evelyn didn't flinch. That was her son with the bloody, swollen face. This was a strange family, and my curiosity just kept growing stronger.

"This is our goal," said Scarlett, scanning the team. Her eyes paused on me, a flicker of doubt disappearing as quickly as it had appeared. "The jet is wheels up in one hour. So pack fast."

CHAPTER II
SCARLETT

Our overpriced company jet sat up to sixteen in plush leather seats and could sleep seven in fully flat beds. Split into three small cabins with one private suite at the back, purchasing it was a battle I'd fought Mum on for months. At long-range, she could fly us from home to anywhere but Australia and New Zealand direct—high-speed flight cut out parts of Southeastern Asia and Africa. Given the range and the sleeping arrangements, I'd eventually conceded.

Malcolm and I sat across from each other in the aft cabin. Four seats on our side, another two across the aisle, and a folding table which could cross the width of the plane. Said table was covered in printouts from the original dark web proposal for the Chalets Ring recovery, which matched the information from the clowns perfectly. They must have been behind the dark web request.

There were a lot of starting points, but everything lacked detail. We had the name of the Albrecht's architect, but no floor plans other than a hand-drawn sketch of the main floor. The name of the event planning company, but no guest list.

Brie and Will fed information to our tablets as they found it, but it wasn't coming fast enough.

I'd been right to decline the job when Mum brought it up.

After the first hour of flight, Jayce and Declan had converted the seats in the forward cabin into two single beds and were sleeping. Rav was setting up the divan in the VIP cabin as well. Strange. He wasn't normally one to sleep during travel, beyond leaning a chair back and closing his eyes.

Malcolm yawned, flipping between documents on his tablet, which was flat on the table. "We should try their insurance company. Even if the ring isn't legal and off their books, we could find some details about their security measures. Alarm discounts, notes about jewelry in safes—"

"No, we already decided." I matched his yawn. Get more coffee or not? We still had four hours on the plane. "Architect first. We need the floor plans."

"Will can get the insurance information while Brie's pulling up the other details." He was on my last nerve. Beyond my last nerve. Every suggestion I made, he countered. Every reasonable decision, he thought he could shoot it down.

"You work alone, don't you?"

He leaned on the table and dropped his head into a hand, blinking those stormy blue eyes at me. "The way you say it almost sounds like an insult."

"I'm in charge of this team. The sooner you accept that, the smoother everything goes."

"You don't like being challenged."

"No, I'm tired."

He shrugged one shoulder. "So go to sleep. The rest of the team is."

Rage burst through every inch of my body, and before I could stop myself, I slammed a fist on the table.

Malcolm straightened, his brows drawing down, then winging up as his gaze flew toward the open doorway to the rear-most cabin. Hopefully, worried about Rav overhearing an argument.

Breathe, Scar. Just breathe. Don't lose control. "I let you come with us because I needed an extra resource and you said you wanted to help. Well, if you're going to help, you'll need to play by our rules. Otherwise, you can fuck off around London on your own and do whatever the hell you think will help Emmett get home safely. But if you can't play with the team, you're nothing but a liability."

He turned off his tablet and started gathering papers, stacking them in the original order they'd come in. "It was a woman."

He worked alone because of a woman? What did that have to do with this argument?

"Three years ago, Emmett and I met in Vegas playing poker. We were sitting next to each other at a table and hit it off. We had a few meals together, a couple rounds of golf, and made our way from one casino to another." He attempted to suppress a yawn while he tapped the pages to straighten them. "On day four, my luck was riding high, so before we cashed out and left for dinner, we stopped at a craps table. I rolled the dice a few times, my luck continued, and my stack of chips grew to over fifty thousand."

Part of me wanted to know how far in the hole Emmett had been or how deep into the stack he'd been counting when they met, but the wiser part refrained. He was an adult and had control of his finances. He'd never gotten in serious danger because of his risk-taking, so I'd stopped nagging him about it years ago. Until yesterday. When someone used a poker game—his weakness—to lure him in.

I felt Rav's big frame in the doorway behind me, attempting to lull me into a feeling of calm.

Malcolm glanced up at him and continued. "Some women in impossibly short dresses joined us, insisting they become our good luck charms."

"Typical." Not that I could say much. I flaunted my body on almost every op we ever did, either to bring attention to me, or just to keep it off my face.

"We took them out for dinner after that."

"And discovered they held PhDs?" *Stop being so catty.*

Malcolm laughed quietly, shaking his head. "Not quite. But we did discover one of them had a boyfriend. A very large, very mean boyfriend."

"And this is the point at which Emmett saved your life?"

He pointed at me and winked, that same curl forming in my belly as the first time I'd seen him at Maguire's party. "The guy tossed me out of the restaurant, hit me a few times, and that's when Emmett came to the rescue."

"Don't tell me Emmett actually hit someone?"

"I offered the guy money, thinking that was why his girlfriend came after me in the first place—that I was her mark. But he didn't pause until Emmett said he could get the guy an invite to a special game later that week. One he hadn't even told me about."

My younger brother knew a lot of people and knew how to get them to introduce him to even more people. It was a blessing and yet a curse at times. "Bet you were glad you weren't working solo that night."

"I don't know what would have happened if he hadn't been there or if he hadn't convinced the guy to leave it at a busted lip, bruised cheek, and a broken rib. But it wouldn't have been good."

"I can understand why you want to help. But where in all of that story is a reason for Emmett to tell me I can trust you?"

"Because we're friends."

For as much of a risk-taker as Emmett was, and how many people he got involved with, he did have an excellent judge of character. Maybe there was more to it, but I had what I needed to know. Malcolm owed Emmett—probably his life—so he wasn't there to screw us over. Unless he was lying about everything, but I had a feeling he wasn't. I rested a hand on top of the stack of papers, which included the starting point for our heist. The item, the location, and the time.

My eyelids drifted closed. I was so damn tired.

A warm hand landed on top of mine and gripped it. Rav must have been— I opened my eyes and it was Malcolm. Something deep inside of me reacted, like it hadn't reacted in years—dry throat, thudding heart, shivers deep in my core.

Those big blue eyes threatened to swallow me. "I promise, I'm on your side."

I forced my body to pull my hand away, my heart wanting to leave it there. I wanted a friend, a partner, someone to share the burden with me again. Emmett had always been my second-in-command, but Noah had been my support. When I left a debrief and wanted to scream or cry because Mum told me I'd done something wrong, Noah had been there. Every time I had to fake my way into a party or some office, Noah was at my side. Now, it was just a revolving door of Emmett, Rav, Declan, Zac, and random contractors, all slipping into Noah's shoes for a mission and then out of them again.

They were all capable, but Noah had been my rock. And I hadn't even gone back for him.

I curled my toes, pushing it all down. "I know."

"Scar," came Rav's voice, surprisingly gentle for such a big man. At least, it would surprised anyone who didn't have a past with him like I did. "I made up the bed in back for you."

"No, I have more—"

Rav put a hand under my arm, forcing me up. "I'm responsible for security, and you being this tired is not a risk I'm willing to take. It's Sunday morning now, and it will still be Sunday when we arrive in London. Step one is to go to the architect on Monday. That means you can sleep for the four hours until we land. We can finish planning as much as possible once we're on the ground."

Malcolm was right—I didn't like being challenged. But Rav was doing the job I'd given him, and if I argued, Malcolm would know he was right. That was *not* happening.

"You two should do the same." I straightened, collected my tablet, and patted Rav's shoulder before I left. I slid the doorway closed behind me, so they wouldn't know I was going to stay up and review files anyway.

I sat on the bed, the Egyptian cotton sheets and freshly fluffed pillow calling to me even more than Brie's couch had last night. After the Maguire party on Friday, I'd napped for a half hour on the flight home. A few more hours Saturday before the girls showed up. Nothing since then. I laid down and propped the tablet up on my chest.

For all my time lecturing Malcolm about working alone, *I* was alone. I didn't have anyone to call. Three best friends who didn't know what I genuinely did, my brother had been taken, and my sister was probably on the verge of breaking down, with work being the only thing keeping her solid. My mother would tell me to toughen up.

Nothing in my world mattered as much as this team's safety. If they saw how scared I was that we were going to fail, it would shake their confidence. All the weight was on my shoulders, like always.

Maybe I could close my eyes for a couple of minutes. Set an alarm so it wouldn't be over thirty. Then I'd touch base with Brie and find out if there was any news.

I let out another yawn.

London in four hours. We had hotel rooms booked under fake names, and Will had arranged for vehicles. Everything we needed for arrival was ready.

Yeah. Thirty minutes should be fine.

CHAPTER 12
MALCOLM

THE BIG MAN remained next to me as the door to Scarlett's private cabin closed.

I hooked a thumb over my shoulder to the mid-cabin. "I think I'll lie down on the couch and catch some shuteye."

Rav's glower landed on me, pinning me in my seat. "We didn't finish our conversation earlier. I think this is as good a time as any, don't you?"

"No, you were pretty clear back in the office. Cooperate or die, wasn't that it?"

"I didn't tell you to cooperate. I told you not to betray the team. I'm going to go one step further and say don't screw with her." He slid into the seat Scarlett had vacated and folded his arms on the table. They were like fucking tree trunks.

Ink peeked out from under the cuff of his short sleeve T-shirt, but not enough to make out what it was, except to know it wasn't an armband tattoo. Maybe that would give me a clue what kind of special forces he'd been.

The look in her eyes when I gripped her hand had been

unexpected. The ice queen possessed emotions after all. "I wasn't trying to do anything like that. I'm trying to help."

"You use this word a lot: *Help*. I'm not sure you know what it means." He unfolded one arm long enough to point to the cabin where Scarlett was resting and tucked the arm back in. "She's the best at what she does. If she says architect first, then that's the best play. You may have good ideas—I understand you have investigative experience—but this is what she does. She's trained her whole life for this."

Trained? Or was she groomed? Maybe that was the difference between her and me. I'd been groomed for a military career but rejected it. She'd embraced the role she'd been assigned. "What's the story there? Emmett mentioned once that he worked with his sister, but I wasn't expecting two sisters in different roles. He never mentioned his mother being part of it either. If Scarlett's the boss, what does that make Evelyn?"

"Other than the owner?" The corner of his mouth twitched. "The mascot even?"

"And what about you? Former SEAL? Ranger? Delta Force?"

"As the saying goes, if I told you, I'd have to kill you." His smirk ratcheted up higher. Hopefully, it wasn't because the prospect of injuring me excited him. "I worked with some of those organizations. That's all I'm going to say."

"Why'd you leave?"

He tapped a button on the console under the window and a lid opened, revealing bottles of water. He pulled one out and offered one to me, which I declined. "Have you come up with any theories on how the clowns connected you and Emmett? Or how they knew where to find you?"

"To be completely honest—"

"Which I would hope you are about everything?"

"Of course." I should've taken the water. My throat was getting dry. "Was there any indication that another team may have gone in during the Maguire party?"

The big man nodded. "The library doors were locked before Jayce went in, and she said someone picked the lock. She hit him on the head with some little statuette."

Reminder to self: don't let any of them near your head and don't mention your goose egg. "My theory is that the other team spotted Emmett at the Maguire party and knows what your team does. They follow him the next day, planning to take him and force Reynolds to hand over the Codex. They break into the poker game and see him sitting next to me, a friend he was talking to at the party. And they change their plan—they now have an extra resource."

"And maybe they assume you were working with us?"

I barely talked to Emmett at the party. How would they have known we were anything more than casual acquaintances? "Maybe?"

Rav twisted off the top of his water bottle and took a sip. "There were also two men that came after us while we were doing prep last weekend. We're assuming they were working with the man Jayce knocked out. And you're right—it's likely the clowns are involved with them, since we got the Codex and they didn't. The FBI took one of them into custody, but the other was smarter. He stole one of our phones but didn't get any information from it, so that's not our link to how they found us either."

We'd been a ragtag team, with no loyalty between members. It was all about the money or the adventure. I was smart and had avoided cameras when I approached the Reynolds team. But the guy that got arrested? He was a loose cannon, running around Boston, waving his gun with no thought to his safety or his life outside of prison. Fortunately, he didn't know enough about me to put me at risk.

Whoever hired me did, but not him.

Was it too late to tell anyone at Reynolds the truth? Or would they throw me out of the plane if I did?

Definitely the latter.

I was in too deep now. I had to get to London with them, help them steal the Chalcis Ring, and secure Emmett's release. My debt would be paid, and no one would be any the wiser that I'd been on the other side of the Codex heist. Or that I'd been the one who'd stolen their driver's phone.

CHAPTER 13
MALCOLM

What a difference a full night's sleep made. The few hours on the plane helped, but once we checked into the hotel, it was back to planning. Eventually, everyone surrendered to exhaustion and went to their separate rooms. Part of me was surprised they didn't insist Rav watch over me for the night, to ensure I didn't breathe the wrong way.

But I'd gotten the message. If I wanted in on this job, I had to change my tune. No more arguments, just follow Scarlett's lead. That included a Monday morning full of shopping, since I didn't have the required attire for our visit to London.

She'd used it as an excuse to spend a ridiculous amount on shoes at Alexander McQueen and a new handbag at Stella McCartney. Although I couldn't argue with the result. The suit I wore to the architect's office was a simple lightweight, navy-blue wool. But hers? The silver-tipped shoes peeked out from under slim pants and a long tailored jacket with a simple hook closure. Underneath that jacket, she wore a sheer lace tank top. The ensemble threatened to reveal something precious if she moved too fast.

If the architect was into women, they didn't stand a chance.

"Mr. and Mrs. Stone?" The receptionist stepped out from behind her long black desk. "If you'll follow me, I'll take you to one of our meeting rooms."

The office was all clean lines, angular furniture, and stark black-and-white photographs. It was structure, constraint, and restrictions. Scarlett fit in perfectly.

"You certainly called at the right time," said the receptionist over her shoulder. "We had a last-minute cancellation this morning."

"You hear that, honey? Perfect timing," purred Scarlett, a sound which settled a bit too low for comfort.

Instinctively, my hand reached for the small of her back, begging to feel the curve of her waist, of the smooth slope to her ass that was hidden underneath the jacket. *Focus, man.* We'd discussed levels of physicality, and they were to be used only if absolutely required. Walking behind a receptionist who wouldn't have seen the move didn't fall into the *required* category.

I halted my hand and considered shoving it into my pocket. "Absolutely perfect, my love."

That also wasn't supposed to be the nickname I used for her.

The devil on my shoulder shrugged and I continued. "We just flew in from Boston this morning and are leaving for Tuscany in three hours."

Scarlett glared at me from the corner of her eye. She'd been clear I was an untested resource and was acting as arm candy exclusively, since we didn't know enough about the architect. Her plan? We'd spend a few meals together in public, where

I'd prove I could stick with a cover story. Then, she'd decide if I could open my pretty little mouth.

But now that we were in the architect's office, all bets were off. She was going to see what I was capable of, whether or not she wanted to.

Her plan may have revealed that she found me attractive, but I was no one's arm candy.

My hand finished its trek and landed at the small of her back, which caused her to arch away from it. I slid it all the way around her waist, to her opposite side, and pulled her close. Her musky perfume mingled with the patchouli in her shampoo, and I nearly planted my nose in her hair. "We have a little love nest in Tuscany and want to build another here."

In her sky-high heels, she was almost as tall as me, so I couldn't miss the look in her eyes. The one that said she was considering whether to slap me, stomp on my toe with one of her weaponized shoes, or scorch me with her fiery gaze.

The look was gone almost as fast as it had appeared, replaced by a loving smile. She'd only slipped out of character for a second, but it was worth it after how she'd dismissed me and had her guard dog growl.

My inner angel nudged me, a reminder that there were more important things to focus on. Something about this woman scrambled my brain, but I wouldn't screw up the mission.

"Mr. White's the best." The receptionist opened a door into a glass-walled meeting room. "I'm sure he'll be able to design exactly what you need."

I pulled out a plush leather office chair for my lovely wife, Mrs. Eloise Stone, and she ignored it. Instead, she walked to the far windows to take in the view.

"Can I get you anything while you wait?" asked the receptionist. "Coffee, tea, water?"

"Coffee, please. Milk and sugar-alternative for both of us." Scarlett gestured vaguely and the other woman left. "Brie, you copy?"

"I do," said her sister over my comms. Their technology was top-notch. The earpiece was invisible, unless someone literally stared into my ear canal, plus they'd granted me one of their custom phones. It looked like a run-of-the-mill store-bought smartphone, but it had required a half-hour of instruction before I was allowed to turn it on.

If it got lost, there was an embedded GPS chip with its own power backup. And if it was stolen, it would leak a chemical that ate the phone from the inside out so no one could trace it back to them or get information off it.

No wonder the one I'd snatched from their getaway driver self-destructed the moment I'd taken it out of its Faraday pouch last weekend.

I joined Scarlett at the window and leaned close to whisper, despite us being alone in the room and the entire team listening in. "I'm just trying to sell it."

She scanned the bustling city—no, she was scanning the faint reflection of the room. "They have us in a meeting room with no computers, instead of an office."

Bric had only needed five minutes to bypass the security of their cloud-based booking software. Apparently, it wasn't the first time she'd come up against that particular program. All it took was one quick call to the office to cancel on behalf of their noon appointment and a matching call to the man who was supposed to be coming in. That hack had been simple, but it had only provided scheduling data, which wouldn't give us a floor plan.

Now, Scarlett had two drives—one USB and one microSD, depending on what was available—in her new handbag, and we were hunting for a computer to plug one of them into. Brie would take care of the rest.

But no computers meant no USB or SD access.

"Step one," she murmured, "if he doesn't bring a computer with him, convince him to."

"Step two, distract him while we"—I placed the hand on her back again—"insert whichever tab into whichever slot."

"Step three." She moved closer, canting her head and batting her eyelashes at me. "Don't throw Mr. Lucius Stone out this window."

Brie snorted.

"Is it too late to switch my name? I was thinking maybe Maximus?"

Brie laughed again.

"Mute yourself if you're going to keep that up, Gabrielle. And you." She removed my hand from her back. "Behave yourself."

"Mr. and Mrs. Stone?"

At the sound of the architect's voice, Scarlett seamlessly moved from reproach to cover and slipped her fingers into mine. "Bruce White?"

"Pleased to meet you." Under his arm, a notepad and the laptop we needed. "If you'd like to take a seat, we can discuss what you're looking for."

We walked hand-in-hand to the table, where I took every opportunity to touch her. Positioned her chair with one hand and held her arm with the other. Stroked her shoulders when she sat. Pulled back her hair from her shoulder as though I were going to kiss her cheek or neck.

A kiss would have been a bridge too far. I had the same goal as her in the end, and attempting to throw her too far off her game wouldn't help either of us.

"There you go, muffin. Now why don't you tell Mr. White what you're looking for?" I pulled my phone out and addressed Bruce. "You don't happen to have a Wi-Fi password? I have some emails to check."

He smiled and nodded, scratching something on his notepad before tearing it off for me. "Here's the password for our guest network."

"Swing and a miss," said Brie. "They won't have anything valuable on a guest network, so it's safer if you don't connect."

"Thanks." I settled into the seat next to Eloise-Scarlett and did my part as dutifully distracted husband, scrolling absently through a deluge of fake messages and websites pre-loaded onto my phone.

The receptionist returned with our coffees, which were sadly pale and sweet-smelling. "Can I get anyone anything else?"

We shook our heads and she left, closing the conference room door on her way out.

Scarlett placed her bag on the table and fanned her hands out in front of herself. "I want something reminiscent of old English manor houses. Stone and columns and lots of tall windows across the front. Box hedges."

"Indoor pool," I muttered, not looking up. The dark web proposal had provided enough information that we could access public satellite images of the house. It also included a few notes about special features. "The weather isn't predictable enough here for outdoor exclusively."

"But it has to be close enough to amenities. Not isolated out in the sticks like a real manor house, but in a community with like-minded neighbors."

"Nearby golf course would be good."

Scarlett turned to me. "Honey..."

I glanced up and caught her lips tightening. That was the *Shut up* sign. "I love it when you take charge, honey muffin."

"He has an annoyingly large car collection, so something that allows him to show them off is probably in the cards, too." The proposal had mentioned a small showroom for vehicles, so hopefully that would get us closer to our target.

Bruce hummed aloud, clicking keys and swiping a finger on his mouse pad. "Not to be crass, but what's your budget?"

"Thirty to forty million, but if you have something that makes me extra happy, he'll go higher."

I nodded absently.

"You're a lucky woman." He paused while Scarlett made a noise of assent.

I sensed his eyes lingering on me and looked up, only to catch him quickly averting his gaze. Was my focus on the phone bothering him? He knew I was the one with the money so wanted to cater to me? Or—my, my. The architect preferred men. Scarlett's lacy top wouldn't accomplish anything here, unless he batted for both teams.

Bruce stood and crossed to the television. He returned with a small USB device, plugged it into his computer, and his local display lit up on the wall. "I have a few ideas, but the easiest would be to show you some homes we've designed that may fit the bill."

"Brilliant!" Scarlett clapped her hands as she swiveled toward the monitor with Bruce, but she must have realized the same thing I already did. There was only one USB slot in that laptop. If Bruce was using it to broadcast to the television, it was off the table for us. The SD card was still in play and would be less conspicuous if we could get close enough.

Brie said in my ear, "Will, we need to install something on their phones that can piggyback off a Bluetooth signal instead of using drives."

"After the drone's ready?" said Will.

"That drone's never going to be—"

I cleared my throat to silence them so I could pay attention to the room.

"Sorry," whispered Brie.

The architect cycled through images of homes, large and larger. Bricks and stones of all shades covered them, from red and rectangular to grays and blues which resembled giant river stones. Bruce would recite some undoubtedly rehearsed notes about each and move on to the next.

Scarlett's excitement waned after the sixth *No*. "What's that triangular thing called? Over the front of the entry?"

"A pediment?" he asked.

"Yes! A pediment! I want one of those, too. And I want it white, so it's reminiscent of a Greek temple." She was leading him by the nose. If this process took much longer, she'd end up giving him the address. We *did* have the right architect, didn't we?

"One... minute..." Bruce clicked his tongue and squinted at his laptop, tapping the mouse pad over and over. "Here it is. This might be more to your—"

"Honey!" Scarlett spun in her chair to swat my knee. "That's what I want."

I shifted my hand with the phone so it was on the conference table, pointing toward the television. Brie had remote access to everything on that phone, so she could grab images from the camera.

"I like it, sugar butt." I smiled at my fake wife, who returned the gesture with such warmth I would have thought it was genuine, had I not been a victim of her frosty reality. In case Brie hadn't flipped on the camera to watch yet, I said, "Do you have blueprints?"

"All of our designs are bespoke, Mr. Stone." He flipped to an image of a grand central staircase in an entry hall oozing with white-and-gold marble. "But I have some photos of the interior which might help illustrate how exceptional the ceilings and windows are. Plus, it will—"

Scarlett swiveled her chair to watch the images, knocking her coffee cup into her lap. She shot up, waving her hands in a panic. "Shit! Shit! Shit!"

I bounded to the shelf under the table and grabbed several tissues. This hadn't been part of the plan. At least, not a part I was aware of. Before I could dab at her suit, she swiped the tissues away and did the job herself. As much fun as toying with her had been, wiping coffee from her lap might have landed me a black eye.

Bruce stood and rounded the table to us. "Let me take you to the toilets where you can clean up."

She shook her head, slowing in her process of cleaning the formerly stunning outfit. "Just point me the right way and you can show Lucius some more of those photos."

"Of course." He led her to the door and opened it, providing directions.

Scarlett had just left with both of the drives in her purse. What was I supposed to do now? As she made her way down the hallway and Bruce returned to my side, Scarlett's voice sounded in my ear. "I'm not getting a device near his laptop. I need another option."

I remained standing, staring after the spot where she'd disappeared. I'd just switched from the arm candy to the distraction.

Brie said, "You've only got ten minutes left in your meeting. It's not enough time for me to hack into a locked machine *and* find what I need in their network."

"So I need to find one that's unlocked, right?"

Bruce sat in front of his laptop. "Did you wish to continue?"

Not only was I arm candy and a distraction, I didn't even warrant a 'Sorry, Malcolm, change of plans. I'll be right back.'

"Everything's locked or occupied," whispered Scarlett. "I'll have to get someone away from their machine."

"Ask him about security." This voice was a male one, without Will's faint London accent or Rav's obvious French one, so it must have been Declan, the safecracker.

"What about your coffee?" asked Will. "Can you spill it on him so he leaves you with the laptop?"

"No," said Declan. "Just ask about security."

"Use the coffee!"

There were too many voices in my head—Scarlett's conversation with Brie, Declan asking questions, Will providing guidance.

I flipped open the button of my jacket and made my way

to Bruce's side of the table, discreetly turning off the earpiece in my ear. I settled on the table with a hip next to his hand. Flirtatious, but it could still have been perceived as me trying to get a better look at his computer, rather than using the television. "I think we're lucky she had to leave. I wanted to discuss security concerns with you."

Bruce looked up at me, his pupils dilating. Yes, the close proximity was working.

"I have certain... possessions which I need to keep safe. Does your firm have experience in integrating security measures into a house like this?"

He nodded, not taking his eyes off me. Maybe I was too distracting. If he was staring at me, he wouldn't show me anything on the laptop. "As a matter of fact, the owner of this stunning house requested a safe room for ultimate security."

I leaned closer to Bruce, shifting to look at his laptop monitor. "Where? The house is literally covered in windows. Surely, it's not hidden in the house's core?"

He shook his head. "It presented a challenge, but I'm quite pleased with the end result."

"Basement!" I snapped my fingers and rounded on him, attempting to drag him along in my excitement, to a point he'd confess something he shouldn't. "Tell me you dug out a level below the house and put it in there?"

"No." Bruce waggled his eyebrows. "He wanted it close to what mattered most to him."

Shaking the finger I'd been pointing at him, I said, "It's got to be the bedroom."

His professional demeanor all but vanished, and his gaze roamed over my shoulders.

I folded my arms, emphasizing the breadth of my chest, as

that appeared to be what he was interested in. "I mean, that's where *my* most important things are."

At the moment Bruce's mouth opened—about to spill the beans, for sure—Scarlett burst into the room with a rather pissed-off looking receptionist.

I shot off the conference table, making it appear as though I'd been doing something I shouldn't with Bruce. "Everything alright, sugar lips?"

The receptionist braced herself against the door, holding it open with her back. "I really am sorry, Mrs. Stone."

Was someone watching the room? Had they seen the play I was putting on?

"I wasn't—" began Bruce.

His receptionist put up a hand and mouthed, *Bob*.

Scarlett marched right up to me, her mouth a firm line. "I don't believe we'll be dealing with this company, honey."

I gripped her elbows—this was exactly a scenario which warranted physicality—but she shrugged away from me. "Of course."

She quirked a brow, waiting for whatever ridiculous pet name I'd pull out that time. Something was wrong though, and taunting didn't feel right anymore.

If she was insistent on leaving, it meant she'd either gotten the information we needed or someone had caught her. She hadn't given me the operational safe word, so it must have been the former.

But what happened? Why was the receptionist apologizing to Scarlett? And what was bob?

CHAPTER 14
SCARLETT

DESPITE DOZING off for far too long on the plane and theoretically sleeping last night, I was exhausted. And Blue Eyes was tweaking the last nanometer of the last nerve in my entire body. I marched across the street and clicked the unlock button for our little London-sized SUV, so I could tell it from the two others parked nearby.

I slid into the driver's seat, my foot demanding to hit the gas and leave him behind.

"You got the blueprints?" Malcolm asked as he shut the passenger-side door behind himself.

"You're off the team." I gripped the steering wheel gingerly, as though I weren't about to explode. "You can work comms with Will, but—"

"Don't be ridiculous."

I put up a hand to stop him. *Keep it together, Scar.* "You *never* shut off your earpiece. Ever."

"I couldn't work with all of you nattering in my ear."

"If you'd been listening and nodding to him, like you were supposed to, it wouldn't have mattered how many people were on the line." My speech was quickening, anger and frustration begging for release.

"Sometimes, you need to improvise."

My hand flew across the small distance between us, and he flinched like I was about to hit him. But I ripped the earpiece out of his ear and shut mine off.

"All you need to do is to listen and follow the plan," I ground out. "It's obvious why you and Emmett are buddies—you're as irresponsible as he is. You're fucking everything up."

"Listen here, ice queen, I'm not fucking anything up."

He was fucking up my feelings. Every time he got close to me, touched me, it wasn't like working with the other guys. There was a different instinct behind what Malcolm did. Something primal about his hand on my back when no one could see it—when it wasn't a calculated move to convince someone we were actually married.

Men pawed me all the time, and I let them because it got me what I needed. I knew where my lines were and never crossed them, but so help me... goddamn Malcolm Sharpe was screwing with every line I had.

I swallowed, battling with what felt like a wad of cotton blocking my throat.

'Tears are a tool, darling,' my mother had told me at the tender age of twelve. She hadn't repeated those ridiculous words until after Noah's death. I had one month to grieve, one month to sell the lie to my girlfriends about the cause and about whose ashes we buried, then it was back to work. 'If you can control them, you can control anyone around you.'

"Hey now..." Malcolm's soft voice mirrored his soft touch on my thigh. "Don't do that."

And now he was fucking up my self-control. A Reynolds

woman didn't cry. "If we don't stay in constant contact with the team, people wind up dead."

"I'm fine."

"This is not about you! You selfish, arrogant, little prick." I swiped a palm across my eyes and threw his hand off my leg. *Tears are a tool. Tears are a tool. Reynolds women don't cry.* "If you'd kept your earpiece on, you would have heard I needed backup. That's why we go in together. We're a team."

He reached for me again, like he was about to hug me, and I shoved him away.

"And stop touching me. There's no one here to see it, so it doesn't matter." Although the staff could have been watching, waiting to see what happened when my husband found out that one of the employees had cornered me after I tried slipping the USB into his computer. I'd flipped his suspicion into an unwelcome come-on, which the receptionist had walked in on.

From her reaction, it was clear I wasn't the first client he'd propositioned.

Malcolm's spirit of self-preservation obviously clicked in, and his irritating little turned-down brows straightened. "Okay, what did you find?"

I tossed his earpiece to him before turning my own on. "Nothing."

The son of a bitch smirked at me as he put in the earpiece. "You didn't get us blueprints for the house?"

Rav snapped, "Tabarnak! Rule number one—"

"I know." Malcolm put up his hands as though they could see him. "But I found out they have a safe room."

Declan said over the comms, "Did you get any details about it? Location? Biometrics?"

"I probably could have, but we got interrupted."

Nothing on his face or in his tone revealed the truth—that my little escapade with Bob, the handsy architect, screwed up what Malcolm could have gotten for us. Fuck. I was out here berating him while I was the one who ruined his smart move.

"I got him to narrow down that the safe room is not off the bedroom, in the house's core, or in the basement. He said it was close to what the homeowner finds most important."

"What does that mean?" I said, forcing my heart rate back down.

Malcolm shrugged. "Do we have an opportunity to meet them? Maybe if we can find out what's important to them, we can figure it out?"

We had a sketch of the main floor from the clowns, plus knowledge of a safe room hidden somewhere in the house. Would they store the ring in there? Would they have other safes where they might keep it? It was a medieval antique, so not likely someone would wear it.

We needed more information, and we had little time to get it.

Jayce piped up from the command center. "I could go in tonight and do some reconnaissance?"

I held my eyes back from rolling. "Jayce, we don't know what their security system is like yet. That's too much of a risk this early."

Malcolm said, "Surveillance is usually the right step at first. We don't know enough about the homeowners. Plus they may have guests staying with them for the wedding. We should find that out first, maybe spend a couple of days trailing them? Establish patterns, and maybe, if we get really lucky, find out what matters most."

I nodded at him. Part of me wanted to continue arguing, but that was my foolish side. The side that never got to express my emotions and felt surprisingly alive around this annoying man. Either way, I had to focus on Emmett.

"Time for the drone?" blurted Will.

Brie groaned. "It's not ready yet. I still have code changes for the nav system."

"We'll talk about it when Malcolm and I get back." Unless I shoved him out his door and I talked to the team when I got back alone. "I'm shutting off my earpiece now. We'll be about an hour. Order some delivery, would you?"

The communications were flooded with a discussion of where to order from, whose preference was more important, and that Jayce wanted to get out because she was already stir-crazy.

I could almost understand how Malcolm found it overwhelming.

He handed me his earpiece for storage in a false lining of my handbag. "When you work alone, no one questions your decisions or tells you what to do."

Mum was right. As team lead, I had to take all the praise, but suffer all the consequences. "You did a good job in there. The truth of the matter is..." *You can do it, Scar.* "You got more information out of him than I did."

Before the corner of Malcolm's infuriatingly sexy smirk rose too far, I added, "But you also didn't know that when I tried to distract one of their other workers, he got physical with me."

His jaw clenched. Guilt? Or some macho bullshit reaction? "That was the Bob the receptionist was mouthing about?"

"Yes. And I didn't get the USB into his computer." One or two more of the muscles in my body tensed at confessing the failure out loud. "I understand you're not used to working with a team. But if you're going to help, you need to meet us at least halfway. There are ground rules that you do not break."

"Like not giving you a hug when you're…" He gestured vaguely at my face.

I cocked an eyebrow at him. If he uttered the bald-faced lie that one molecule of moisture had leaked out of my treacherous eye, I'd definitely push him out and leave him.

"When you're happy to see me?" He grinned, which vanished when I didn't return it. Malcolm was obviously used to women caving to him at every turn—and men, if Bruce White was any indication—but this was a job. One that wasn't over until Emmett and everyone else was home safe.

I pressed the ignition and let out a long sigh. Maybe I could confess more to Malcolm, since he wouldn't be around long. What did it matter what he thought in the end? "I'm scared."

His hand headed toward my leg again, but I didn't flinch this time. He was, however, smart enough to stop himself. "About Emmett?"

"Yeah, and about this whole job."

He settled back in his seat, arms folded and body canted toward me. "You don't strike me as the type who's scared of anything."

"The ice queen, right?"

He shrugged a shoulder. "I'm guessing ice princess would be more accurate?"

Bingo. 'Reynolds women' only included Mum and me. Somehow, Brie got free of those expectations. She was more than happy buried behind a mountain of screens and code, which left me to lead the family business. I'd never seen a tear from Mum unless she was getting out of a speeding ticket or on the couple of jobs she did with us when we opened the company ten years ago.

Not even at Dad's sentencing.

"We lost a team member a couple of years ago after some problems with our communications." A shudder ran the length of me, and the vision of Noah's car going off the side of the bridge was as clear as day again. *Calm. Breathe.* "When you cut out like that, it distracted me, and I got caught sneaking around his cubicle."

"How could you even tell I was gone with all those people talking?"

"I guess we've both been trained to work in different conditions." I turned to face him. In the afternoon gloom, his eyes were almost gray, like the Wittelsbach-Graff Diamond. "But I'm serious—what I *can't* work with is a lone wolf who thinks he knows better than the rest of us."

"Okay, deal." He unwound one arm and held his hand out. "I still want in. I still want to help."

I shook his hand. His big, strong hand with the firm grip, which had been on my back, my arm, my shoulder, my waist. Heat should not have been pouring through me at that moment, but it was. There were more important things in the world than my lack of a love life.

"Maybe we need our own safe word?" At the quirk of his lips, I hauled my hand out of his. "You know, for when I'm being too much of a lone wolf."

The heat traveled upward, into my chest, and a little into my jaw. Son of a bitch. "You have no control, do you?"

"All the control I need." He recrossed the arms and settled back as I pulled into traffic. "Now, what's with this drone? Will keeps talking about it."

"He built it before his mother got sick and he moved back here." I let out a little laugh, remembering when he unveiled it to a chorus of 'That's it?' from the entire team. "Brie likes to tease him about its size."

"And we're using it tonight?"

I shook my head. "We'll go back to the hotel, eat, and review the floor plan sketches. Go over more contingencies, and I'm sure Declan wants to talk about the safe room. Jayce will want to talk about ingress points. But tomorrow morning will be for surveillance, including the drone."

CHAPTER 15
MALCOLM

THE REYNOLDS TEAM didn't do things small. For them, surveillance was more like a police operation than a private investigator. Will's decked-out Sprinter van looked like a camper van. Fold-up bed in the back, bathroom with ceramic toilet and shower, four leather chairs at the front, and a fridge and kitchenette.

But once the window shades went down, he hit a few buttons and screens withdrew from their hiding spaces behind cabinets. The bedframe converted into a desk with the primary display, where Brie's yawning face appeared.

"Morning." Will smiled at her, a sheepish look which didn't seem appropriate on him. He was a few years younger than me and wore geeky shirts like I'd expected—Star Wars jokes both yesterday and today—but he was as tall as I was and obviously worked out as regularly as I did.

Brie held up a steaming mug. "It sure is!"

Rav was out following the husband, who was playing a round of golf with his son-in-law to be. Declan followed the wife for brunch with her daughter and bridesmaids. I should have been doing one of those jobs. No matter what any of them said, I had more experience trailing people.

I was a patient man, but since our experience with the architect, Scarlett hadn't let me out of her sight. I'd made a few jokes about it last night, but her frosty exterior persisted all evening. Not a glimpse of the woman she'd revealed in the car.

Scarlett slid in next to Will. "You happy with the nav system update?"

"As happy as I can be." Brie yawned again. It was ten a.m. on Tuesday morning in Oxshott, the village south of London where our target lived. For Brie, that was only six. "I uploaded everything three hours ago and took a nap."

I sat in the driver's seat, swiveled around to face a fold-out table with a wall-mounted screen showing Brie, the group at the back of the van, and me.

Jayce was on her feet by the sliding van door. She paced from the door, between the counter and the bathroom opposite it, past the tiny fridge, to the desk. Then back to me at the front. She'd made comments about being cooped up at least a half dozen times last night, and this morning she was such a ball of energy, she seemed about to explode.

The others didn't appear fazed by her movements.

Coffee, donuts, and silence. Binoculars. And many hours of calm. That was the surveillance I was used to. Not a van full of people, screens detailing everything, and the thief-acrobat, who couldn't stop moving.

"Can you pop the skylight?" said Scarlett.

Jayce, who was at the back of the van, launched up on the desk and popped open the light above her. Before Scarlett got in another word, Jayce had hauled herself out through the opening, vanishing onto the roof. She moved fast. There were a few noises above us, and she hung down with her head and one arm extended. "Give me the little guy."

Brie put a hand on her face to stifle a laugh, while Scarlett frowned.

"Don't call it that." Will pulled a small box out from a cabinet under the desk and opened it. He gingerly withdrew a little black something, no more than two inches in diameter.

I stood from my seat and walked the length of the van to see it in person. The drone was tiny. It looked like a child's toy, not something that Brie was updating the nav systems for at three in the morning, let alone what this big van was concealing. "That's it?"

Flames practically erupted in Will's eyes, and Scarlett almost laughed.

Will turned it over, so the four blades were on the bottom. He jammed his finger at tiny pieces I could barely make out as he talked. "It has two cameras, can stream to us wirelessly over a four-kilometer distance, has onboard storage for ten hours of video, can compensate for any wind up to thirty kilometers an hour, all while being small enough it won't trip any security designed to ignore a hummingbird. And all you can say is, 'That's it?'"

Jayce, still hanging from the roof, snapped her fingers. "Then give it to me so you can prove it's as good as you say it is. Because if it's not, I'm going into the house."

Scarlett glanced up at her. "No, you're not."

As she took the drone from Will, Jayce smirked at Scarlett. "I'm already outside. How are you going to stop me?"

Scarlett's eyebrow rose. Nothing more.

"Okay, okay, but this drone had better work." She rolled back up to the roof, and Will tapped a few buttons on his keyboard, bringing another display up on the big-screen. Brie and Will chatted back and forth, checking systems, starting the rotors which made a high-pitched hum above us, and lifting the drone a few times. Another window appeared on the monitor, displaying Jayce and our parking space.

We'd pulled the van into a small wooded parking area which led to a walking trail half a mile outside of the gated community where the house was. The goal was to fly the drone up and over the trees, and then around the house to check for security cameras, ingress and egress points, and to film the interior.

With only a rough sketch of the main floor, we needed more. And Jayce was right. If this didn't work, someone was going to have to go inside.

As far as this team knew, I did all of my surveillance from outside. Legally. With how much Scarlett had mistrusted me from the beginning and Rav's warnings, I hadn't told them about some of my less-than-legal jobs. Like the one that had taken me to the Maguire mansion last Friday night. But the truth was, if they needed someone to go in, I could do it. Maybe not as stealthily as Jayce would be able to, but I could talk my way into almost anywhere.

I returned to my seat at the front, most of my screen taken up by the two video feeds from the drone. One below, and one ahead.

The drone rose quickly, avoiding tree branches and leaves with no effort. Will was an excellent pilot. The drone moved remarkably fast given its size, in a near straight line despite the mild breeze. The camera feed included details of air speed, temperature, and direction.

Within ten minutes, it arrived above our target.

We'd reviewed enough satellite images of the house that the view of the roof was unremarkable. The basic floor plan was a hundred-foot long rectangle, by sixty feet deep. Front door at the south, pool to the west, tennis court to the east. The garage extended from the front on the western side, while turret-like rounded rooms decorated the back and sides of the main floor. Two dozen people milled about the backyard, despite the owners not being home. A few women in suits, while everyone else wore black pants and light-blue shirts.

"Event planners," said Scarlett. "I recognize the uniform from the Blue Luxe website. They're measuring. Probably putting up a tent for the reception."

"In this weather?" Jayce's head popped through the skylight. "I'm sure men in tuxes will be warm enough, but evening gowns?"

"They'll have patio warmers. Probably a lot of them scattered around the yard." Scarlett stood, offering her a hand. "Come down and watch."

Jayce's head descended, and she eased herself in a slow roll down to the desk. "There's a walkway all around the roof."

Scarlett took Jayce by the waist and eased her to the floor. "They'll likely have at least one security member including that on their route, if not permanently manned."

I watched the three team members as much as the video feed. They'd gotten in and out of the Maguire mansion before me. The security was higher than at the Albrecht house, but Scarlett would have ensured they were perfectly prepared for that job. Who would have expected I'd end up working with them?

Had it really been a coincidence that Emmett and I were invited to the game the clowns crashed? Were we both the targets, because they didn't know which team had gotten the Codex? If that were the case, Emmett's confession saved my life, so I owed it to him twice over. And if all that were true, but I'd gotten to the Codex first, I wouldn't have had a team to rescue me when the clowns showed up on my doorstep.

Teams. I held back the eye roll. It was just as likely my unknown boss on the Codex job was behind the clowns.

Maybe there was something to be said for working with a group like Reynolds. People who had your back. People who threatened anyone who risked that team. Not that any of it mattered. I had a job to do, I was going to do it, and then I'd be done with them.

Rather than sit by myself, I stood behind Jayce, watching the video feed over her shoulder. "Will, you said you'll be able to use this video to create a three-dimensional dollhouse?"

"Yep." He lowered the drone, so it flew in line with the third floor, dotted with dormers jutting out from the mansard roof. There were four suites with walk-in closets and private bathrooms, each with at least three windows, and two with balconies which connected to a walkway that led around the perimeter. "Brie's been training an AI program to take the 2D images and extrapolate room sizes. We should be able to use the 3D printer back at my place to construct a scale model, too."

Brie nodded on the screen. "If I bring that online now, will it startle your mom?"

"No. One of her friends took her to a market since I was going to be out. We're good for a couple of hours, at least."

"Alright, bringing the printer online now."

Yeah, I needed to get one of these vans. Even just being able to walk around in it, instead of moving from seat to seat while I watched a house or an office. It was even narrow enough to fit into a regular parking spot. And given how many construction companies, delivery companies, and other small businesses used Sprinter vans, who'd ever suspect one in a busy city? I'd need decals to pose as an electrical company or something outside of the city though.

As Will finished rounding the uppermost floor, I said, "The architect told me the safe room was near—"

Scarlett held up a hand. "Slow down. He only told you about one security element. We want to find the safe room, but we're also looking for prime real estate for wall safes and possibly to find standing safes. Then it's a matter of chance and educated guesses to figure out which one we focus on."

There it was again. Don't let the new guy make any suggestions. Maybe I should've taken Jayce somewhere, so we could do our own recon. Scarlett was too slow. Too cautious. It was already Tuesday, and the party was in four days. She was treating this as if we had all the time in the world.

Will piloted the drone to the next floor, peering into whatever windows had open blinds or curtains, which was almost all of them. The house itself was quiet. All the activity was outside and the only people roaming inside were cleaners. The second floor housed the primary suite and an enormous closet, with an en suite that rivaled the spa in our hotel.

My research showed that the owners were worth just shy of a billion. They owned three homes in other countries and their business dealings were legit. At least everything I could find on them sounded legit.

The drone floated up and farther back, avoiding security cameras as it moved. They were mounted on the corners of the house, trained on the yard. Motion sensors wouldn't register the drone, and any video feed would likely only see a small, black blur and assume it was a bird.

The primary suite took up half of the second floor. Two other bedrooms and an office completed the level.

Jayce pointed at the screen. "Can you move back? I want to get a better view of the office."

Will did as she asked.

She leaned forward. "You don't have a zoom on that thing, do you?"

"Keep going," said Scarlett. "He's got video of the entire room, so we can review it in greater detail when we're done. There's no reason to increase our chances of being caught by sitting here too long."

Yeah. Way too cautious.

Jayce's shoulders slumped theatrically. "Why am I even here?"

"To keep you out of trouble?" I nudged her back. "Same reason I'm here."

A muscle ticked in Scarlett's jaw. Revealing her emotions around me? She was thawing. However, she didn't respond beyond that, except to glower momentarily at Jayce, who was laughing.

Will moved the drone in, close to the house. The view wobbled slightly. "The wind is hard to accommodate for so close to the building."

Brie said, "I was afraid of that. I'll have to add something in the next update."

There was a sharp rap at the side door and a man's voice called out, "Hello! Anyone inside?"

I bolted to the door, waiting for the signal.

"Boss alert," whispered Scarlett. "Take over the drone, Brie."

Will hit a pre-programmed set of keys on his laptop and the screens switched to display local maps, weather forecasts, and video feeds from nearby trees. Cover established. We were bird watchers.

I slid the door open and smiled at a man with warm skin and light eyes, wearing a local police officer's jacket and peak cap. "What can I do for you, officer?"

He peered inside, no doubt evaluating potential threats, then gestured to the front windows. "There's no overnight parking allowed here."

Scarlett stood from her seat by Will and edged past Jayce. "We're doing avian migratory research."

I hooked a thumb over my shoulder, toward the screen on the wall behind the driver's seat. "It's easier to monitor the cameras without the sunlight."

The officer looked up at the cloudy sky.

"Daylight, I mean." I stepped back. "Some local birders reported sightings of a Montagu's harrier, which is—"

He put up a hand and shook his head. "This is a car park, not a research station. I'll need you to move along, please."

"Of course." I nodded, smiling at the team to ensure the officer didn't come in to inspect anything. Although the video feed of the nests were live ones and Will could likely have spoken at length on the cover story. "We'll pack our stuff up and be gone within twenty minutes."

"If I find you here in a half hour, I may have to cite you." The officer tipped his peak cap. "Have a good day."

I slid the door closed as Will hit the button to bring the drone video back online.

The bottom camera was dark, the front one obscured by leaves. It was suspended a couple of feet off the ground.

Will's face and shoulders fell.

"Sorry," murmured Brie. "The wind was too much."

He looked up at her, their two sad faces mirroring each other. "At least you got it into a bush instead of the middle of the lawn or on one of the patios."

"We have to... you know?" Brie gave an exaggerated grimace.

"No." Will pointed a finger at the screen. "We were streaming all the data, so it doesn't contain anything sensitive. We don't need to destroy it. Maybe I can recover it later?"

Energy sparked through Jayce, and she practically bounced. "My turn?"

All gazes turned to Scarlett, who nodded. "We'll have to call the guys and see if there's time today. Otherwise, we need to figure something out for tomorrow."

Jayce's eyes grew wider the longer Scarlett talked.

"But yes, Jayce, you're going in for reconnaissance."

CHAPTER 16
MALCOLM

THAT NIGHT, I stared out the window at the darkening city, the sun already having set and leaving nothing but gloom. Will's feed from the drone was processing through Brie's AI program, generating a 3D model. The team had transitioned from chatting to bickering, the stress of the last few days wearing them down. It had taken eons for them to agree on a plan for tomorrow—Scarlett, Jayce, and I posing as event planner staff to get access to the house—and once that was done, Scarlett ordered everyone to bed.

The days were long, the nights too short, and we only had three days left for planning.

I paced away from the window to sit on the bed and stare at my phone charging on the side table. Would the kidnappers call again before the party? How was Emmett holding up?

There was a knock at my door.

It was after Scarlett's imposed curfew, so it wouldn't be anyone from her team. I hadn't ordered room service, and it was too late for housekeeping. Likely a guest at the wrong door. The knock came again, so instead of waiting for them to realize their mistake, I stood from the bed, made my way down the short hallway, and peered through the peephole.

So much for curfews.

I undid the safety latch and swung open the door to a smiling Declan.

"Thought you might be a little lonely?" He held up two bottles of Stella Artois in one hand, earning him the title of my new best friend.

Another of Scarlett's rules: no alcohol.

"I don't suppose they're twist-off?"

He shook his head. "There should be a bottle opener in your kitchenette."

"Aren't you risking some level of wrath by coming here? Both after curfew and with alcohol?"

"Scar, Rav, and Jayce travel together on almost every job. They only bring me along for special events." He put the bottles down on the tiny kitchenette counter and rooted around in the drawer. "Kinda makes me warm and fuzzy having you around, so I figured I'd embrace the moment."

"Special events?"

He waggled his fingers before pulling a bottle opener from the drawer. "Anytime they need the magic fingers." He handed me the first open bottle. "Or the magic brain."

I took the cushioned chair by the desk and gestured to the couch for him. "What do you do other than open things?"

"Keep things closed."

"Anyone ever tell you that you're cryptic?"

"Another one of my specialties."

I took a swallow from the bottle, appreciating the malty

sweetness and hoppy bitterness. "Is this a social call? Are you really flying under the radar, or is this another test?"

He inclined his beer toward me. "You're a straight shooter. I like that. Don't see much of it in this business."

"That's not an answer."

"No, it's not." He eased down on the couch, pulling one ankle to cross over his other leg. "We don't usually work with people we have so little information about. Scarlett and Evelyn have good instincts, and Rav didn't kill you on sight, so I have to assume you're on the up-and-up."

Don't clench your jaw, Malcolm. "I want to bring Emmett home just as much as the rest of you do."

"Not as much as Scarlett does."

So much for the warm and fuzzy. "She doesn't trust me."

"Her trust is difficult to gain. But if she's taking you in with her to the Albrecht house tomorrow, that means what you did at the architect's office impressed her."

"She has a funny way of showing it."

He took a swig of his beer and sat back, scrutinizing me.

"She told me I was off the team after that."

"Scar's... How can I say this delicately? She's a hardass, but she needs to be. I can't remember when she wasn't like that, and we've known each other since grade six."

She'd told me Brie and Will had been friends since they were little. Now this. Reynolds Recoveries wasn't just a family business. Was it all family *and* friends? "How long have you been working for them?"

"Evelyn opened the company the day after Scar and I graduated university. I wasn't involved before that, but I'm certain some of their family vacations"—he made air quotes—"weren't just vacations."

I'd already figured out Scarlett's mother had groomed her for the role from a young age. But had she done the same to Scarlett's friends? "And you joined right away, too?"

"Founding member. Evelyn encouraged me to study..." He smirked and pointed his bottle at me. "I figured you for a wily one."

I held my hands up in mock surrender. "I just like to know who I'm working with."

Hiring on as a contractor with a team usually entailed getting to know roles and responsibilities, not people. Once you got to know the people, your guard was down. You let too much out. Put yourself at risk.

Too much team bonding and you were liable to get attached.

And what happened when you got attached? People left. Or your father moved you to a new country and you had to start all over again.

"You probably should've picked a different team." Declan was already halfway through his beer. This was going to be a short visit. "We've had six newbies on the team over the last two years and none of them have lasted more than a month. Usually, they only make one job."

"I'm not looking to be a member of this team long term."

"You know what the problem usually is? Everyone's terrified of Scarlett."

That was hardly surprising. The woman had looks, brains, and an almost supernatural level of control. Not to mention how fast she could draw a gun and the way she could coat you in ice with a stare. "She's not particularly welcoming."

Declan threw back the last of his beer. "There are some big shoes to fill on our team. I know you're not interested, but it was good to see someone stand up to her. She gets so stuck in her own head about what she's doing and about keeping the rest of us safe that she doesn't always make the right choices."

Was this a chink in the Reynolds Recoveries armor? Dissent among the ranks?

"Just make sure you only do it at the right time. Continuing to battle with her just because you think it's entertaining or to stroke your ego is going to get somebody hurt." He stood and made his way to the kitchenette counter, where he placed his bottle. "And if it ends up getting Emmett killed, Rav is going to do his thing, which you do not want to see."

"I'm not going to—"

"Never said you were." Declan turned to face me, his cocky smile back in place. "I'm just giving you a friendly warning about the lay of the land. This team is a family. We have been for a long time. And I'll be damned if we don't bring Emmett home safe."

"Then I suppose I should say thanks." I stood and walked him to the door.

"Also, I'm guessing Scarlett didn't tell you that Brie and Will finished checking into the other players at your little poker game."

She hadn't said a word, either good or bad about it.

"Somehow, they got their hands on a surveillance video from the game and she watched your interaction with the clowns. She pulled the kids off that line of investigation, which means she doesn't suspect you were behind it, at least." He opened the door, pretended to tip a hat at me, and left without another word.

Tomorrow, I was going into the Albrechts' manor house with Scarlett and Jayce for reconnaissance. Apparently, including me in that mission was a bigger step than I'd realized. During our planning session, Scarlett had advised that I was to remain quieter than at the architect's office.

But based on what Declan said, I might have more latitude than I expected.

CHAPTER 17
SCARLETT

WEDNESDAY MORNING, Malcolm, Jayce, and I got out of the SUV in front of the Albrechts' house. We each wore black cargo pants and light-blue, button-front shirts embroidered with the B and L of Blue Luxe Events.

Will's mother's embroidery machine had made quick work of the shirts. We all sported exact replicas of those worn by the men and women we'd watched measuring the backyard for the tent and other decorations yesterday.

"How do people wear these things every day?" Malcolm blinked incessantly—almost as frequently as he'd complained about the need for colored contacts. The blue shirt had lit up his eyes so brightly, there was no way any woman within a fifty-foot radius wouldn't immediately recognize him the next time they saw him. That was a risk we couldn't take.

"Brown suits you," I said.

Jayce snorted quietly to my other side. She'd wanted to see him in hazel, but pale eyes were too similar to the blue, in case he had to join us at the party. If I had my way—and I typically did—he'd be our driver that night, so the eyes wouldn't matter.

But his irritation with the contacts was too much to pass up, after how much he'd screwed around during the architect visit. Served him right.

"Better than the red suits you," he grumbled.

My wavy mass of fiery-red hair was a showstopper. No one would remember anything about my plain face—the hair would be the first and only thing anyone would describe. Since I *was* going to be attending the party, the misdirection was important. The thick-framed black glasses I wore would help, plus they had the added benefit of a camera built into the frame. The recording they'd send to Will would help clarify anything the drone missed. "How's the camera signal?"

"Perfect," said Will.

The pea gravel driveway crunched under my far-too-sensible flats. A stream of women in high heels would descend on this house in three days—ruining their beautiful soles and heels. Of course, most attendees could probably afford to throw out any pair they wore after a single night, so the only downside was the hassle of balancing over the gravel when they arrived.

"Do we know yet if they'll have valet service?" I asked.

"I'll find out," said Rav over the comms. He was doing his own recon today, meeting with some old friends he'd served with on overseas deployments who were now in private security. If one of them was working the party on Saturday, they'd be a significant asset. "Signing off now."

"They're sitting down for brunch." Declan was following the Albrechts, who were attending a wedding party brunch in the city center. That gave us at least an hour and a half to get in, survey the house, and get out. "I'll be on mute, but I've got the video feed on my phone."

"Speaking of which—Brie, Will, keep the chatter down today, okay?" I was used to carrying on multiple conversations at a time, listening to them in my ear while having a full discussion with the person in front of me.

Malcolm, not so much. And even though he pissed me off, he'd shown he was an asset, and I had to swallow my feelings and help ensure his success as part of the team.

As we neared the front door, Malcolm and Jayce fell into step behind me. Her job was to scout for ingress points and identify any areas the drone may have missed. His was to stay with me, stay quiet, and flutter his eyelashes when needed.

Pale Cotswold stone covered the house. The front door, facing south, was flanked by two Corinthian fluted columns on each side, echoing the columns which stood at the corners of the building. Tall windows with decorative stone arches over them lined every wall.

Two of the third-floor rooms, built into the mansard roof, had balconies with stone balustrades, which resembled the columns at the front and corners. From those balconies, there was access to a narrow walkway around the home's perimeter, except for the space over the pediment at the front. If there would be any security personnel up there, they wouldn't have a full circuit around the house. They'd have to start at one side of the pediment, trace the walkway around the full perimeter, then turn around and retrace their route.

As we took the last few steps to the front door, I put the final touch on my costume: *Panic mode.* I tightened my muscles, drew up my shoulders, and widened my eyes before rapping on the immense door. "I hope someone's home."

"I can't believe you did this," hissed Jayce.

I knocked again, harder. "Please be home, please be—"

The door opened to reveal a young woman with her long blond hair pulled back into a ponytail. Cleaning gloves and white sneakers.

Bingo.

"I'm sorry, but—"

"Oh my god!" I flung my hands out in front of me, nearly sending the clipboard in my hands flying. "I'm so happy you're here! We need to get in to do our estimate."

The woman's brows furrowed and she looked blankly at me. She started again, "I'm sorry, but—"

"We're with the Blue Luxe clean-up crew." Irritation wafted off Jayce as she stepped forward, arms folded. "We were supposed to be here with the rest of the team yesterday to do our estimates, but *someone* got the schedule wrong."

"Stop," I said from the corner of my mouth.

"I'm sorry," said the cleaning woman, "but the homeowners aren't here right now."

"That's okay." I shook my free hand, telegraphing my stress to her. "If you could just let us in, we'll be so quiet you won't know we're here."

She shook her head, giving me a rueful smile. "I'm not allowed to let anyone in."

"Shit," I muttered, putting a hand to my head.

Jayce snorted. "You are so fired."

Malcolm stepped forward, inching his way in front of me. Let the eyelash fluttering begin.

"I, um..." The cleaning woman looked up at him, obviously holding back a smile.

He dipped his head toward her while Jayce made a quiet

sound of disgust. He lowered his voice—not to a whisper, but to make it seem like they were having a private moment. "We were supposed to be here yesterday with the rest of our team, but we had a scheduling mix-up. My colleague is right though. If it gets back to our boss that we either didn't get our estimate done or even that we were a day late, at least one of us is going to be looking for a new job. Is there any way you can help us out?"

She glanced inside the house, chewing on her bottom lip. She was thinking. That was something we could work with.

I took a half step forward, coming into contact with Malcolm's arm. To display a little more anxiety, I gripped his bicep as if it were the only thing stopping me from shaking all over. "We just need to see the areas where the party is going to be. We'll evaluate the rooms, I'll skip the measurements and eyeball it, but we just need to see the space we'll be cleaning up after the party."

The lip worrying ended abruptly. "You'll be cleaning up after the party?"

I nodded quickly. "Full-service event planning."

Her shoulders relaxed, and she smiled at Malcolm. "It took me two days to clean up after their last party. It's a relief they're having someone do it for me this time."

I added to my mental to-do list: Hire someone to actually do the housecleaning at the party. This poor woman didn't need to suffer for us.

She stepped backward, opening the door farther. "I'm supposed to be out of here in forty-five minutes. The party will only be on the main and lower floor, and outside. I'll take you on a quick tour, if that works for you?"

Jayce said, "We can see ourselves around."

"I don't think that'll work." The woman grimaced. "I shouldn't be letting you in, as it is. But this way I can show you which rooms will be open to the guests and which ones won't, so you won't be wasting any of your time."

I threw my gaze heavenward, expressing relief, while also checking the roofline for cameras. "Thank you!"

She stepped out of the way and waved us in.

The grand hall was enormous. White marble, more white Corinthian columns, and a split staircase with a railing that looked like it was spun from gold. Deep-brown marble inlays traced the edge of the floor, matching the wooden double doors off either side. The hall was open to all three floors, with railed balconies overlooking.

"My name is Bethany." As she closed the door behind us, she took off one glove and swept her hand across the space. "All the guests will come in through here and be funneled into any of the rooms on this floor. There's going to be a rope across the stairs, so that's only for family and overnight guests. To the right we have a water closet at the front, then the library, and then the drawing room. We can peek in each of those quickly."

Nothing would be hidden in the grand hall, but the other rooms were up for grabs. Jayce was chomping at the bit to explore, but if we were getting a tour, we had to stay with Bethany.

The library had tall windows on two sides, with upholstered window seats in each. Four matching chairs sat around an ornate table with bankers lamps and a globe. The books in this room were for show. Long stretches of matching black and gold tomes, either legal texts or ancient encyclopedias.

Small statues, gold urns, and marble busts decorated the open spaces on the shelves.

There was only one painting in the room, our most likely bet for a hiding place. But why keep an ancient medieval ring in a safe in this room?

That wouldn't make sense.

Bethany led us through the drawing room with its three separate seating areas and piano, the dining room with its table for twelve, and the family room and kitchen. It was all the same opulence, yet somehow homey. With each room, I made notes on my clipboard, sketches and random statements that were for cover, not for actual research.

Jayce peered into the pantry. "There's a door that goes out the back of the pantry. Where does it lead?"

Bethany squeezed around her and closed the door. "Second kitchen, laundry, and boot room. The guests won't be going back there."

The drone video had shown us a glimpse of the kitchen, but not those other rooms. They were candidates for the safe room and possibly storage areas. Based on the sketches we had of the floor plan, it also led into the garage.

"You've seen all the rooms up here. Do you need to go outside, or can we nip down to the lower floor?"

I said, "Our team has all the details on the exterior, so we just need interior spaces. Lower floor's perfect."

We followed her through the snooker room, back to the grand hall, and down the main stairs. The house was designed for entertaining. How often did the Albrechts hold parties here?

The stairs led us out into a reception area with a round couch in deep purple, between a glassed-in gym and a wine room. A media room sat directly below the library, with oversized lounge chairs and a large screen for viewing. Underneath the drawing room, dining room, family room and kitchen, was an indoor bowling lane.

"There's a bar kitchen over there, and they'll have finger food out during the reception. The cigar cupboard is upstairs and that will be limited to the snooker room, but there will probably be a lot of food around here."

Part of me wanted to go back to the architect's office and try for the plans again. Downstairs, there were too many places to hide things. Upstairs, it was all family space and windows. The upper floors were much the same, open to the grand hall and windows in every room. Hopefully, the drone's laser measurements and any video from today would be enough for Brie and Will's processing software to help us figure out where the Chalcis Ring might be.

Bethany led us back to the reception area at the bottom of the staircase and into what I could only call the water area. A fifty-foot keyhole pool with a skylight into the patio above it dominated the space.

"Depending on how late the party goes, the steam room, sauna, and the jacuzzi may get used." She led us along the tiled pool deck to another room with glass walls on either side.

Malcolm let out a low whistle and practically plastered himself against the glass. "Please tell me we'll be cleaning over there."

The room itself was nothing special. A lounge with a couple of couches, more shelves with various statuary, and a wide-screen television. A doorframe opened to a circular staircase heading upward. But through the glass on the far side, we could see into the lower floor garage. It was more showroom than storage, with three vehicles on display, and no exits.

Bethany chuckled and pulled open the first door to the lounge. "No, Mr. Albrecht has a special team who comes in for this. They've already prepped the cars for the party."

"Will the guests be allowed in there?" Malcolm's breathless whisper wasn't part of the act.

I didn't know cars, but I knew luxury. I recognized the Ferrari GT, similar to the one Emmett had driven us in last weekend, a Rolls-Royce two-door sedan, and a Velatti roadster. "How does he get them down here?"

Bethany opened the other door, granting us access. The floor was white marble, like most of the house, with the same dark-brown marble trim around the edge. But beneath the Velatti—which sat directly next to the lounge—the brown inlay circled it. She pointed to the ceiling, where there was another round shape. "Car elevator. He rarely drives any of these and keeps them down here for parties. He maintains them in pristine condition so he can share his love of cars with his guests."

The architect told Malcolm the safe room was near something precious.

I gestured to the far end of the underground display room. "What are the doors back there? Do they lead out?"

"You don't need to worry about those rooms. Those are the power plant."

Power plant. If it was self-contained, that would be a good space for a safe room. And they definitely wouldn't allow any guests down there. That was my top candidate so far.

Malcolm circled the Velatti, taking it in from every angle. It was almost like watching a kid on Christmas morning. Like watching Emmett get the skateboard he wanted or when Brie got the components to build her first computer. Wonder. Excitement.

I ran my hand through my hair. No wait, not my hair. *Shit, focus.* I was getting too carried away in his moment and almost forgot where we were. Fortunately, Bethany had, as well. Her eyes were as plastered on Malcolm as mine were.

And Jayce?

I looked to my side. Other side. Behind me. Nowhere to be seen.

How far had she gone? Where was she? How much time did I need to buy?

As the energy began skittering around my stomach, I gave my toes one good scrunch inside my shoes and took a breath. She was a professional. She knew what she was doing.

"I'm getting it, Jayce," said Will.

Getting it? He must have meant a feed. She must have been recording something on her phone. How much time did she need?

I took several quick steps, so I stood just behind Bethany and to her side. She could see the full car gallery ahead of us, but if she turned around, I'd be blocking her view and she wouldn't be able to see Jayce wasn't down there. "So, Bethany, is that everything down here? And the only ways up are the central stairs and the one in the lounge?"

"The stairs in the lounge will be roped off as well."

"Got it." I made more notes on my clipboard.

She flipped over her wrist and checked her watch. "By the end of the pool, there's another door that takes you out to a light well. It's just on the other wall from the garage and it provides access to a staff apartment. There are stairs at the far end, which come up to ground level at the far end of the garage. But you don't need to worry about that, because it will be roped off, as well. They want everyone using the main exits and entrances."

The architect had told Malcolm the safe room wasn't underneath the house. But if it was built into the power plant rooms, that wasn't *below* the house. Right? This was our best guess. Jayce and Declan would have other opinions, other options, but this was one. How would we get in and out of here? Guests would be allowed in this showroom, in the glass-walled lounge, and in the pool area. One door into the car gallery, plus the car elevator up, unless there was a secret door at the back of the power plant.

Bethany might not know about it, but it made sense.

How were we going to figure it out in three days' time, unless we came back in or hacked into the architect's system?

"We should get going," said Jayce, suddenly next to me.

I hadn't heard her approach, per usual. Had she found something? Or had she just seen everything she needed to see?

CHAPTER 18
MALCOLM

I WAVED to the pretty young Bethany before closing my car door, brain firing on all cylinders. We were still driving the small SUV Scarlett had rented, one of the most popular new vehicles in the area. She insisted on driving us everywhere, and considering it had been years since I'd driven on the left side of the road, I barely complained after the first day.

"You can pick your jaw up off the floor now," Scarlett muttered as she put the car in drive and pulled away from the Albrechts' house.

"Can I?" I'd contracted with a lot of very wealthy people, but that was a first. "I was six inches away from a Velatti Aereus."

"You what?" gasped Declan over the comms. "What color?"

"Midnight-blue carbon fiber exterior and the interior—"

Scarlett's jaw tightened. "Jayce, what did you find?"

"Don't tell me it was black." Declan was officially my best friend.

I cupped my ear and lowered my voice. "Didn't you see it on the video stream?"

"I was watching where Jayce went."

Will whispered, the excitement as clear in his voice as in Declan's, "Did you know Velatti monitors every one of them and has an electronic feed they can—"

"Would you three gearheads stop already?" Scarlett clenched the steering wheel, obviously fighting with her desire to hit me. And probably them, vicariously.

"Is there somewhere we can stop for a bite to eat?" asked Jayce. "I'm starving."

"Focus, people. I know this is a hectic schedule, but Emmett's life depends on us getting that ring." Scarlett pulled the car out of the small community where the Albrechts lived and onto a busier road. She drove as calm as if she were out for a leisurely drive through the countryside. "Jayce, you vanished on us. Where did you go?"

Sure, I shut my earpiece off for a couple of minutes at the architect's office and Scarlett was ready to confine me to quarters. But Jayce? No criticism, just curiosity.

One more reason I worked alone. Teams took time and commitment to build. Too much effort.

"Bethany stopped me in the pantry, but I figured the lounge between the pool and the car gallery was right underneath. She said second kitchen, which means hidden staff kitchen. I figured the stairs off the lounge went up there, because they always have stairs for the staff." She leaned forward, meeting Scarlett's furtive glances in the rear-view mirror. "They go up into the kitchen, but there's also a mud room, laundry, bathroom, and access to the main floor garage.

I sent some video feed to HQ from my phone, then ran up another couple of flights to see where the stairwell went."

"Anything interesting?" asked Scarlett.

"Not really. I think we already had everything above that kitchen on video, since the stairwell itself has windows."

Will said over comms, "But it helps build the full picture. The extra video takes care of a big blind spot in my measurements, so Brie and I can make a few tweaks to the digital model, then I'll get the 3D printer going this afternoon."

"How long will it take?" Scarlett asked.

"We've already got the model printed of the roof. I'll keep it running through the night, so we should have a full tabletop model of the bottom two floors ready by noon. The top two floors will be paper only, since they're less complex."

"Declan, they'll need your help with that."

"I'll head over there now," said Declan. "Signing off."

"Signing off here, too," said Will.

Scarlett held back a yawn. How much sleep had she gotten since the Maguire party last weekend? Emmett was taken the next day, and the circles under her eyes had grown progressively darker each time I saw her. "Rav's out for most of the day, so that leaves the three of us."

"What comes next?" I said.

Scarlett's gaze flicked toward me, then back to the road. "I don't suppose you brought a black suit?"

"Shopping?" Energy always bounced off Jayce, but with that word, it increased. I wouldn't have pegged her for the shopping type.

"I have the clothes I wore to your place and what we picked up on Monday morning." The kidnappers hadn't exactly given me time to return to my room and grab my suitcase.

"Contingencies." Scarlett turned onto the A3 highway. "Rav and I will pose as the guests, but you'll be driving. If they expect the driver to let us off in front of the house, we'll need you in something more chauffeur-appropriate."

"And food?" asked Jayce.

"Eat one of the granola bars in the bag." Scarlett gestured over her shoulder. "We're going to Harrods, woman. Focus on the Chocolate Hall."

Jayce grabbed Scarlett's shoulder. "Seriously?"

Scarlett smiled, one of the few times I'd seen her do that genuinely. It was almost enough to forget why we were all there and the pressure we were under. She was truly a beautiful woman, even with the crazy mass of red curls.

"Does that mean I can take these damn contacts out?"

"I don't know." Scarlett pulled her wig off and tossed it back to Jayce, who had the gear bag in the back. "The brown eyes seemed to work on Bethany."

The Reynolds team was going to forever remember me as the eyelash flutterer. Great.

CHAPTER 19
MALCOLM

THURSDAY MORNING, two days before the Albrecht-Bancroft wedding and our mission to retrieve the Chalcis Ring, Scarlett, Jayce, Declan, and I descended on Will's mother's house. She owned the upstairs floor of a modest duplex—maisonette was the appropriate term, I'd been told. We'd held all of our other meetings at the hotel, but the three-dimensional model of the house was ready and had to be kept private.

A kind-faced woman with gray-streaked brown hair greeted us at the door, arms wide. "It's been so long."

Scarlett accepted the first hug. "Too long."

Jayce held up a white box tied with string before her hug. "I brought your favorite chocolates from Harrods."

"Just as beautiful as ever," said Declan. "How do you do it, Mrs. Reaney?"

"Charmer." She grinned at him and pinched his cheek. "And who's this?"

"My name's Malcolm." I held out a hand, but she wrapped me up in her arms. "I'm new."

Mrs. Reaney put her hands on her hips, looking over my shoulder. "And where's Rav? Will says you don't go anywhere without him anymore, Scarlett."

"He's visiting a friend. He'll join us soon."

"Good." She clapped her hands and waved us in, up a flight of beige carpeted stairs in a tight hallway. "Willie's upstairs in his loft."

Her accent was slightly thicker than Will's, betraying a youth spent in England, but many years abroad. At the top of the stairs, she led us down a short hallway to the cramped kitchen, with a narrow staircase heading up. "Have you been here since we renovated?"

"No, Mrs. Reaney." Scarlett's face softened as she lay a hand on Will's mother's arm. "We haven't been here in a year, and you were just starting the loft conversion."

"Of course." She patted Scarlett's arm. "I remember that now. And who's the handsome one with the blue eyes?"

"That's Malcolm," said Jayce. "And I brought you chocolates."

Mrs. Reaney gave her a coy smile. "Not the ones from Harrods I like?"

"The exact ones." Jayce placed the box on the kitchen table between five untouched cups of tea. She undid the string, popping a green-and-white speckled bonbon into her mouth. "Eat as many as you want."

Scarlett's gaze swept across the three of us and flicked up the stairs. More shorthand that Jayce and Declan immediately acted on, climbing up to the floor above, and I followed them.

Mrs. Reaney continued talking with Scarlett. She explained about the renovation, thanked Reynolds for paying for the expansion, and asked whether Brie was in town. "My Willie misses her so much."

"She's still at home. We'll bring her the next time, I promise."

"You're such a good girl."

The upstairs was narrow, as though the room had been built into the attic space. Loft conversion. Of course. At one end, there was a giant white board on caster wheels and a rack of servers. Shelves stacked with bins were crammed between dormer windows and the 3D printer nestled in a corner. Next to a large-screen television, Will's two computers sat on a desk with six monitors.

A six-foot long table dominated the center of the room, half of it taken up by the house model, the rest covered in architectural diagrams.

When Scarlett had first mentioned Will's special drone, she'd said that he'd moved here after his mother got sick. The repeat questions, the confusion, and the excess of teacups—obviously Alzheimer's. And that was possibly why he worked out of the house so often.

Scarlett's mouth was tight when she finally joined us. "Will, can you get Brie on the line?"

The big screen on the wall switched from black to Brie's face. "Already here, Scar."

"Do you have a view of the model?"

"She's all set." Will pointed to a digital camera he had propped at the end of the table. "Are we waiting for Rav?"

"No." Scarlett waved her hand vaguely at the model, and everyone gathered around it. "High-level plan first. We'll have Brie and Will on standby, in case we find an access point for the security system or need other support. Jayce and Declan will enter covertly to secure the ring. Rav and I will act as married friends of the bride, doing lookout and running interference as needed. Malcolm will be our driver."

Relegated to the driver. Fantastic. I was never good enough, was I? If I told them about my side job, maybe they would have let me help more. Although maybe they would have sent me home. In a body bag. *This is about her lack of trust in you, Mal, not about your skills.* More like her lack of trust in everyone but her precious team.

One more reason working alone was better. She didn't have the flexibility I did. I could work with anyone. She could only work with the people in this room and a few others. What must it have been like for the contractors they hired? No wonder they went through so many. It wasn't fear of Scarlett; it was probably irritation at being dismissed so much.

Jayce pulled a wrapped chocolate out of her pocket and began twisting it open. "Which leaves the most important question—where's the ring?"

"Good morning, everyone." All eyes turned to the large screen with Brie's face, which was now split in two, showing Evelyn Reynolds on one side. It was only five in the morning for them, but she was bright-eyed, with immaculate hair and makeup. "I had a few things I wanted to discuss before you get into your planning session."

Scarlett straightened so much her spine practically snapped, and she clasped her hands behind her back. "Morning, Mu—Evelyn. I wasn't expecting you on the call."

Evelyn gave a curt nod. "First, I'd like to say thank you to everyone for working extra hours to resolve this issue quickly.

Brie hasn't left the office since Saturday, and I trust you're all committing yourselves as fully to our endeavor."

There were nods around the room and murmurs of 'Yes.'

"Scarlett, darling, I'll need you to review USB usage with Brie when you get home. If you'd been faster at the architect's office, you wouldn't have been caught and you'd have the blueprints."

She nodded once to her mother, her jaw as tight as her posture.

Evelyn Reynolds did not pull punches. She reminded me of my father—just with longer hair, lipstick, and pearls. "We'll also have to run a few scenarios on how to react when someone catches you. There were three things you said which I think we can improve on without inviting him to touch you."

"I didn't invite—"

"Of course not, darling. But the day we stop learning from our mistakes and improving is the day we hang up the hat and go home." Evelyn looked down, eyes flicking back and forth as though reading something. "Will, your drone was excellent. I'd like you to build a few more and ship them out here. Brie, once we're done with this mission, get back to improving the nav systems."

"Yes, Evelyn," said Will and Brie in unison.

"Jayce, kudos on your initiative yesterday. You were quick and stealthy, plus good thinking with sending the additional stream. Your footsteps were a little loud though, so either stop eating so much or wear different shoes next time."

Jayce rolled up on her toes. "I'll get new shoes."

"Declan and Rav..." Evelyn looked up, scanning her screen. "Where's Rav?"

Scarlett said, "Meeting with another source. He'll be here soon."

"Good. Neither of you have done much so far, so good job with that, I suppose." She waved a dismissive hand. "Now. Where's the blue-eyed wonder?"

Declan nudged me. "That's you, bud."

Evelyn's face was as impassive as Scarlett's. The ice queen and the ice princess. "I appreciate your quick thinking at the architect's office. From what I hear, you identified he was attracted to you, flirted with him, and got some information."

"Thank you, ma'am."

She cocked an eyebrow, and the resemblance between her and Scarlett became clearer. Their hair and eyes were different colors, but their bone structure and condescending glares were the same. "However, I can only say that's what I hear, since you shut off your earpiece. I expect you've heard this is one of our cardinal rules, and if you ever do it again, I'll recall the jet and fly over there to put three bullets in your chest before you have time to turn the earpiece back on. Am I clear?"

I had the overwhelming desire to stand at attention like Scarlett. "Crystal, ma'am."

"Good. I'd also like to state that you did an excellent job getting the team into the Albrechts' house yesterday. Apparently, flirting is your superpower. Use it wisely."

I nodded, rolling her words over in my head. She was about as good with the compliment sandwich as my father was. Two artificial kudos to wrap up the truth—I'd done a shit job at the architect's office.

Although everyone else got positives. No mention of Jayce running off without telling us yesterday. Nor of Brie losing the drone in the bushes. Criticizing the man who left her son in

New York with his kidnappers made sense. But why so harsh with Scarlett?

"Finally, we received word from our client this morning that the Codex of San Marco has not yet arrived, and the courier is not responding to messages."

Jayce let out a tiny gasp and Declan said, "Come again?"

What did that mean? Had the team I'd worked with in Boston tracked down the Reynolds courier? Or had the clowns gone after it when Scarlett said she didn't have it?

Evelyn continued. "I'll have to deal with it for now, but when you get home, Scarlett, I expect you to perform a full review of our transportation plans."

Scarlett's brow creased, the barest hint of a reaction. Surprise? Confusion? "Yvonne handles logistics."

Evelyn's expression hardened, her words clipped. "Yvonne might handle logistics, but you're the leader of this team and will eventually take over for me. I expect you to handle any issues that arise, and if that means learning something outside your comfort zone, so much the better."

Scarlett nodded obediently, and I could have shaken her. It was like watching myself standing in front of my father, absorbing one of his shitstorms instead of calling him out on abandoning me.

I couldn't help myself. "Sorry, ma'am, but..."

Evelyn's eyebrow hit me, the full level of her dominance weighing on me.

"Scarlett's doing an amazing job." I shouldn't have cared. But I did. She'd agreed to bring me and gave me the chance to help, despite her initial doubts and despite the constraints she put on me. Watching this strong woman wilt under her mother's criticism was just pissing me off. "Maybe we should focus on the mission at hand instead of—"

"Malcolm." Scarlett's eyes didn't leave her mother. "It's fine. She's right."

It wasn't fine, and Evelyn wasn't right. And neither was the way my stomach and jaw had tightened. I opened my mouth to continue, but Scarlett cut me off with a raised hand.

She pinned me in place with her big brown eyes. They weren't impassive and unemotional. They were intense and commanding. "We can talk later."

Later. Fuck that. I bet if I confessed about my attempt to get the Codex, everything would stop.

But then everything *would* stop.

We wouldn't talk about Emmett anymore, I'd be out on my tail, and then what? I didn't even know who I'd been working for, so the information would be as useless as I'd been at the architect's office when Scarlett needed me.

Declan's hand landed on my arm, and he tipped his head at me, the message clear: *Back off, buddy.*

I clamped my mouth shut. Declan was right, but the anger was still boiling inside of me, and I wasn't sure how to calm it down. Scarlett deserved better than this. She was a strong woman, pushing herself to the limit to save her brother, and she didn't deserve to be belittled by her mother. Certainly not right now.

Calm down, man. Evelyn isn't your father. Don't provoke her. "Fine. Later."

For half a breath, Scarlett's gaze lingered on me, her lips trembling, like she was holding back a smile.

"Relax." Evelyn clapped twice. "And back to your planning, everyone."

Scarlett's pose eased and she returned her attention to the model. Jesus Christ, she just moved on as if the conversation hadn't happened. No wonder she was the ice princess—she'd had a lifetime of dealing with an emotionally shut-off mother. "Our biggest variable Saturday night is the location of the—"

A deep voice sounded downstairs, along with the crinkling of a plastic bag. Rav had arrived. "Which would you like, Mrs. Reaney?"

"What's this one?"

"Pain au chocolat."

"You're such a good boy, Rav." Boy. Did that mean Rav was another member of the team who'd been with Scarlett since they were kids? Were all of their mothers aware of what they did for a living?

"Merci, madame." A moment later, the big man arrived.

Jayce ran to greet him. "Please tell me they're for everyone?"

"They are." He handed the bag to Jayce and scanned the room, stopping at the big screen. "Good morning, Evelyn."

"Rav," said Scarlett, not moving from her place. "Don't forget you're staying with me tomorrow night."

An unwelcome heat flashed through me. They were sharing a hotel room? They were sleeping together? Obviously, the entire team knew, otherwise she wouldn't have said it so clearly in front of them.

And why did this bother me? I had no claim on her. The two of us were as likely to claw each other's eyes out as share pleasant words. My fuse was short after the moment with Evelyn. That's all it was.

Rav shook his head as he neared the table.

"We'll be posing as guests, and I don't want our cover

blown because someone sees us coming in and out of different rooms."

I also shouldn't have felt relief that the shared room was all part of the cover.

Rav folded his broad arms and frowned. "I have good news and I have bad news. Which do you want first?"

"Always the bad first, Rav, so we end on the upswing," said Evelyn from her screen.

"I met with an old friend this morning who's in private security. There's going to be a lot of people worth a great deal of money there, so the Albrechts are hiring out. He confirmed there will be five men working the party. Unfortunately, two of them know me, but they aren't the type I'd trust to stay quiet when they see me."

"Use a disguise. We can—"

"Sorry, Scar, but I need to sit this one out." He placed a hand on her arm and dropped his voice. "This isn't a job where the risk is to a thing. This is about Emmett."

She looked at Will. "Do you have a tux?"

Will's eyes flew wide, and his hands darted up. "Hold on there. I don't do—I mean—I'm support, Scar. I can't—"

"Mingle?" The word sounded as dirty on Brie's lips as it likely would have on Will's.

Scarlett looked at me. If her mother hadn't been there, how many swear words would have poured out of her mouth? "I guess we need to head back into town this afternoon for a tux."

An almost sick level of pleasure pushed aside my earlier irritation. No longer relegated to driving. No longer the backup, but I'd be front-and-center. And I'd have her on my arm while I did it.

Not to mention I'd have her in my bed tomorrow night. "I'll move my things into our room first thing tomorrow morning."

Scarlett was quiet for a beat, not budging, barely breathing. "It's a two-room suite."

CHAPTER 20
MALCOLM

Jayce moved around the team, offering pastries to everyone. I declined and suggested she eat mine. Her eyes lit up and she grabbed a sugar-dusted scone with bits of red fruit popping out of it.

Scarlett passed on the food and turned back to Rav. "What's the good news?"

"That same friend will be working the door. He didn't have a guest list, but he gave me a copy of the invitation so we can produce two. Plus, he'll ensure you get in without issue." Rav took a bite of the croissant Jayce had given him.

"Evelyn." Scarlett pointed at the screen. "Do you have any contacts in town who can replicate the invite?"

"I do."

Rav continued. "It gets better. I told him we were on a rescue mission for a team member, and he offered whatever help he could provide. No one left behind." He hesitated only long enough to glower at me. The *You left Emmett behind* glower. "He's going to loan me his company's armored Bentley. No rentals required, and I can drive you straight to the front door."

"That *is* good," said Scarlett.

"Back to business?" Jayce licked some sugar off her fingers and gestured to the model. "The model's handy, but we don't know the value of the ring, so we don't know if they're more likely to store it in a small wall safe or a standing safe."

Declan covered his mouth, chewing on a cheese Danish. "It's a big, expensive house, but it's not Fort Knox. It's half the size of the Maguire mansion last week. There's only so many places available to hide something."

Jayce said, "If they're even hiding it."

"Let's start at the beginning." Scarlett gently lifted the roof level from the model and placed it to the side. "The kidnappers wanted the San Marco Codex, and when we couldn't deliver that, they demanded the Chalcis Ring. There was barely any hesitation when they switched from one demand to the next. Could there be a link between them?"

My job last weekend had been to secure the Codex. No one had mentioned a ring to go with it, but my mystery employer had only brought me on for the one job. If we'd come away with the manuscript, maybe that small team—me, the woman on comms, and the inside source who'd provided us with the camera locations—would have moved on to the ring. Or maybe they'd already had a second team working on this.

If so, would that other team be at the reception?

I still couldn't reveal any of that without Evelyn carrying out her threat. If Rav let me live long enough.

They wouldn't actually kill me, would they? They didn't

mention carrying weapons other than the one Scarlett had pulled on me at her house, so these were empty threats.

Right?

I couldn't give them the full truth, but I could ask the same questions I'd had when I started that job. "You said the Codex was worth over three million?"

Scarlett nodded. "Three point four million on the black market."

"Why so much for an old sheet of paper?"

"Thomas Maguire told me it was linked to a legend about an immense treasure."

"Could the ring *also* be linked to that legend? Maybe the kidnappers were after both items as keys to the treasure?"

"Hold on." Brie faced away from the screen, head bobbing up and down as she no doubt read from another monitor. "We did a little extra research into the ring's history. Turns out, it was stolen from a museum in Oxford."

Scarlett quirked an eyebrow. "Did you cross-reference that with the Codex theft?"

Brie nodded. "We did, but there didn't seem to be any link. It was three years earlier, and the methods didn't match. The interesting part I just learned is that it came from a horde buried in Chalcis, Greece, hidden during a siege in 1470, when the Ottomans took the city."

"Greece?" I said. "How would that tie in with the Codex?"

Brie turned back to the camera. "Because the legend is about St. Mark's Treasure, which is said to be buried in Venice. And Chalcis was a Venetian colony at that time."

Scarlett stared at the model as if it would give her answers. "But they don't have the Codex, so why would that matter?"

"Maybe they figure they'll still be able to get it somehow? Maybe they're why the client doesn't have it yet? Or maybe they think they can get whatever information they needed some other way?"

Scarlett's gaze shot up to meet mine and she snapped her fingers. "The patterns."

I'd been getting into a rhythm with her, but I was lost. "The what?"

"Brie, pull up your x-ray of the Codex." Scarlett made a beeline for the screen where the Codex appeared in greens and blues, with its lettering in bright yellow. Faded marks behind the letters, paler green, showed three waves with a circle between the second and third. A line underneath it all.

Rav said, "The cypher?"

Scarlett jabbed a finger at the image. "What if the code here is what they needed and they're thinking maybe Emmett saw it? Or they have a different approach to getting it? They could steal the x-ray data from the museum and not even need the Codex?"

All of those options made sense. "But why the rush on the ring?"

"Because they've got our attention with Emmett, and the wedding's a perfect distraction?"

"Or..." Time for a nudge along the truth road. "What if the second team you ran into at the Maguire mansion will also be at the Albrecht house?" Oh, the irony, since I was going to be there.

Scarlett nodded. "Good point."

Jayce swallowed the last of her scone. "Back to locations. If the ring is a key to this treasure, it won't be in a small wall safe with other rings and jewelry. It's going to be somewhere special. Like the safe room?"

Scarlett shook her head. "That's only *if* the Albrechts know about that link that *we* aren't even sure about. Brie, I'll need you to dig into the original thefts a little more. Maybe get someone on the ring's provenance and find out who the Albrechts might have purchased it from."

Her sister nodded. "Consider it done. I'm going to call Zac and see if Ash has any—"

Scarlett cocked that brow.

Brie rolled her eyes. "Scar, like it or not, Zac said she was involved with the Codex case for the FBI. She may not be able to give us all her details, but she can certainly point us in a few directions to speed up our progress."

"I received her resume this morning," said Evelyn. "Rather impressive young woman. She'll be an asset to the team."

Brie's face lit up, while the skin around Scarlett's eyes tightened. There was history there, but it wasn't the right time to ask about the story.

"Fine," said Scarlett. "Back to the matter at hand. Probabilities time. A man who puts a three-million-dollar car on display for his guests doesn't buy random medieval rings unless he's a medieval art collector. From the house decorations, I'm going to say he's not. Our best bet until we know better is that he knows or suspects it's related to something bigger and keeps it safe accordingly."

Jayce waggled a finger. "It might be a longshot, but there *was* that guy who came into the library just after I grabbed the Codex."

My heart stuttered. *Stay quiet, stay calm.* Jayce hadn't acted like she recognized me, so I must have been in the clear, but I still couldn't risk tipping any of them off about my role that night. *Just shut up and let them keep talking.*

Jayce continued, "What if Albrecht paid that other team to take the Codex?"

Scarlett paced to the table with the model. "Also possible, and it increases the odds we're looking for the most secure area in the house to find the ring."

"So, the safe room is my target?"

"Safe room first, if we can find it. Then, we target backward. The next best odds would be a standing safe."

Declan pointed to one of the floor plan printouts. "From the images we got with the drone, I suspect there's a walk-in safe just off the primary bedroom."

Jayce grimaced. "Going in there would be almost as high risk as walking in the front door. It's on the second floor, facing the rear of the house, where the party will be. They'll have the place lit up. If we're considering entry from the outside, I'd have to do it alone, and I've got a feeling a walk-in safe would need Declan's help if we don't have specs, and I can't risk a drill. Going through the inside hallways could be even riskier. The door to the primary suite is at the center of the house, right next to the railing that's open to the grand hall. There'd be no hiding, so if any guest were down there and looked up, they'd catch us."

Sometimes a big event was a blessing, sometimes a curse. "But we could come back the next day and check that out if needed?"

Scarlett blinked slowly, her self-control slipping. "Then we'd have the kidnappers to contend with. That would put us a day over."

Jayce moved next to Declan, studying the second-floor

plan. "We could go in before the party? Maybe during the wedding ceremony itself."

"It starts at eighteen hundred," said Rav. "The church is a half-hour away."

Scarlett leaned both hands on the table, staring at the model, everyone waiting for her to say something.

Not me. "Probabilities, right? If your best bet is a safe room, we figure out where that is and go in there during the party. We don't risk burning ourselves by going in early when staff and caterers will be swarming the place with last-minute checks."

Scarlett didn't budge.

I said, "The kidnappers won't do anything to Emmett if you're still going after the ring and need an extra day. If it were weeks, possibly. But not a day."

"Then where's the safe room?" Scarlett lifted the main-floor model so we could focus on the lower floor. "I think the most likely place is off the power plant."

I rounded to Declan with the sheets. "The architect said it wasn't in the basement. They didn't have to dig down to build it."

"Assuming he was telling the truth," she said.

"I know when people are lying to me."

"The architect said it was near something precious to the homeowner." Scarlett finally looked up, daggers in her eyes. "The cars are precious. It's got to be there."

That wasn't it. My gut told me it was wrong. The architect hadn't been lying to me. The floor plans and model were a distraction. I needed to think. Outside the box. What was outside the box? They hadn't dug to build it, so it wasn't in the basement. We'd walked through the entire ground floor and there wasn't anywhere to hide it there. The top two floors were all bedrooms.

Wait.

That was it. The top floors. "Where are we?"

Will's brow creased. "My mum's place?"

"No! We're in a converted attic." I placed the main floor model on top of the lower floor to put the pieces of the puzzle together. "Jayce, did you get any video of the ground floor garage?"

She pointed at the garage in the model. "It all went into the floor plan."

"Exactly." I took one of the floor plan printouts, as large as the model, and laid it on top. "This is a floor plan, not a ceiling plan."

As though figuring out my needs while I talked, Brie started a feed of Jayce's video on the screen.

"Pause!" I swatted Declan's arm and walked over to the screen. "The garage has a peaked roof. But not a peaked ceiling."

Scarlett joined me, placing a hand on my back. "Holy shit. There's a room above it."

"How do you get into it?" Jayce wedged herself in between Scarlett and me. "I ran up the stairs and came out where that room would be. There wasn't a door there."

Brie was already skimming ahead in the video and paused again at the moment Jayce had exited the stairwell on the second floor.

Declan clicked his tongue. "Nothing but a huge bookcase. Well done."

Scarlett turned to look at him, eyebrow raised.

"A huge bookcase tall enough to conceal a door," I said.

"Good job, wonder boy," drawled Evelyn. "Maybe we'll keep you around for a day or two."

They needed me, at least for another day, to be Scarlett's husband.

We gathered around the model, and Will placed the roof layer on top.

"Perfect." Jayce traced a finger from one side of the house to the other. "We scale the east wall, which is mostly concealed by the bushes around their tennis courts and trees. We cross the roof, make our way to the skylight at the top of that stairwell, pop it open or up or something."

Declan's nose wrinkled. "You know I'm coming with you on this, right?"

"Yup." She moved the roof model and continued following her path on the printed floor plan I'd sandwiched between levels of the 3D model. "We descend into the stairwell, figure out how to open the bookcase, and we're in."

Everyone was following Jayce's path on the plans, except for Scarlett, who gave me a smile. The real one. One that made me think that taunting her hadn't been fair. She wasn't the ice princess. She was a woman who was scared she'd lose her brother. She'd told me as much.

I smiled back, a strange warmth spreading through me. If nothing else, I wanted to help her prove to her mother that she was the strong, capable woman everyone around this table knew she was.

As quickly as the moment had started, Scarlett pushed the smile down and got back to work. "Alright, people. That's half our Plan A. Let's figure out how you're going to get out, and then we'll review every way this can go wrong."

CHAPTER 21
SCARLETT

Friday evening, we all strolled into the Lion's Head Pub together, down the road from our hotel. I'd been riding the team all week. Our plans were made. We reviewed and re-reviewed until they started getting punchy with each other, and we all needed a break. A little dinner out and then early to bed was the right call.

The two trips to Harrods, shopping for a suit and then a tux with Malcolm, helped me take a few breaths. A side trip into the women's luxury accessories section to pick up a crystal-encrusted Judith Leiber clutch for the party gave me even more breath.

But then we'd returned to the team, clothes and accessories for the party ready, and I couldn't calm their nerves. That's all it was. The bickering, the arguments about precise timing, the way Will and Brie kept their heads down to work on the programs and bypasses we might need.

There were too many variables. Too many unknowns. This wasn't how I ran my team, but there was no choice.

Just like there was no choice about finally going out for a bite to eat away from the hotel and Will's mother's house.

Before our butts hit the seats in the pub, Jayce snapped her fingers and pointed at Malcolm. "New guy pays for the first round."

I lifted a finger. I shouldn't have had to. "New guy buys the only round we're having tonight. Everyone needs to be at the top of their game tomorrow, so I'm enforcing a one drink maximum."

Jayce rolled her head back and flung her arms out in overdramatic fashion. "Fine. The new guy buys the one and only round, plus the food. Get me fish and chips and make mine a double."

"Do I need to make a list?" Malcolm chuckled and pulled out his phone.

Rav, Will, Dec, and I put in our orders, and Malcolm headed off without another word.

I took a seat on the booth side, on an old wooden high-backed bench that felt so worn it must've been at least sixty years old.

Jayce poked Rav in the chest. For anyone who didn't know them, it would've been a comical sight. He was nearly a foot taller than her, and probably twice as wide, but she cowered before no man. "I hereby challenge you to a game of darts while I wait for my food."

Will nudged her. "I'm the one you should be challenging. I'm the European champion."

"European champion?" She laughed.

"That's what happens when I'm the only one living in Europe."

"I call teams," said Declan. "And the champion is my partner."

Jayce and Will left with Declan, throwing taunts at each other. Hers were clever and quippy, Declan's were faux-cocky, while Will's were mostly delivered five feet over both of their heads.

I missed having Will at home with us. Remote technology made things easier, but he didn't get this sort of team bonding. The job was important—especially the job we were on right now—but doing it with people you knew like the back of your hand made everything better.

Not like Malcolm Sharpe. He was clever, fast on his feet, and had made all the right moves. No matter what I said to him.

And the way he'd stood up to my mother? Emmett was the only one who'd ever done that for me. Obviously, it was because he was new and didn't understand the hierarchy at Reynolds. It wasn't personal. He wasn't coming to my rescue like some white knight.

All the same, it changed something. I didn't have the time or brainpower to figure out what exactly, but something.

Rav settled into a chair opposite me and leaned forward on his elbows. "Do you want me to stay? Or should I mop the floor with the champion?"

In case I missed his point, he looked intentionally toward the bar, where Malcolm had gone. That was the *Do you need your big brother?* look.

I leaned forward to match him. "You are not seriously asking me if I need you to stay here for my protection?"

He shrugged. "I still haven't decided if I want to kill him or not."

A laugh burst free from me, and I shoved him with my foot under the table.

With a wink, he stood. "You can't tell all of us to take it easy for the evening and not do the same yourself. You're going to be the one mingling with the crowd tomorrow, so you need to be on your A game, too."

"Yes, boss." I shooed him off in the direction the others had gone.

Now that was a relationship no amount of digital technology could have replaced. Rav went with me on every single job, and I knew without a shadow of a doubt he had my back. In every way possible.

One word from me and he would've had Malcolm over his shoulder, asking whether he should throw him into an airplane or the Thames.

Maybe I should have forced Emmett to take Rav with him on his little *date* to New York. Kept him out of trouble.

No, my brother was a grown man. He was flippant and a risk-taker. But he was clever and always stood up to me—not just Mum—at the right times. Told me when my plans were stupid or short-sighted. And he always did it with either a laugh or a smirk.

My throat tightened. *We should still be planning. We should be going over more contingencies and more mitigation. More alternatives.* The team should have gotten over whatever argument they were having and understood that we had a bigger priority.

Reynolds women don't cry, Scar. Get your head on straight. Mum was right. I had to focus on our goal and work like it was any other job.

Otherwise, I'd get sloppy. And sloppy meant we lost

people. I balled up my toes to fight off the flood of emotions sitting just below my surface. I wouldn't lose my brother, too. He'd be alright.

"How goes the thinking?" A pitcher and five glasses on a tray landed on the table in front of me. "They'll bring the food over when it's ready."

I nodded, and Malcolm poured the beers.

"Where'd they all go?"

I gestured to the far end of the pub, past full tables and patrons milling about. People, smiling and chatting and having a good time. People with no idea who we were or what we were going to do the next day. People who were going about their normal lives while we infiltrated a wedding reception to steal an ancient golden ring. "Jayce can be a little aggressive. Will's gonna kick her ass."

"She eats like a linebacker."

"If you had her metabolism, you'd probably be the same."

Instead of taking one of the three chairs around the table, Malcolm slid onto the booth seat next to me. "I've been wanting to talk to you in private since Will's place yesterday but haven't had the chance."

He hadn't been subtle about it, nor had I been subtle about avoiding him since he argued with my mother and then discovered he'd be my date for the party. The concept was simple enough. But add the shared accommodations tonight, plus the intention to pose as a married couple, and it was a disaster waiting to happen. Not to mention the escalation of our levels of physicality to pull it off.

I'd posed with Rav on jobs before. We were comfortable together. We'd known each other so long we had the same tics and cues as a married couple. He knew where the boundaries were and knew when they needed to be crossed.

But Malcolm? I didn't want to admit to anyone—including myself—how many of the boundaries I wanted him to cross.

"Okay, so we're in private now. What do you need?" I pulled a glass toward me, no intention of drinking anything, but it would prevent me from fidgeting.

He shifted his body to face me and leaned one elbow up on the table. "Is your mother always like that?"

Of all the questions I'd expected, that was probably the last one I wanted. "What do you mean?"

"You know who my father is from doing the background check. You know I was in military schools and paraded around like the good general's son. I know a little about having a strict parent. But your mom is a real..."

So help me, he was about to get on my really bad side. "Bitch?"

He grimaced. "No, I was going to say hard-ass."

My muscles unclenched. "I'm just the ice *princess*, right?"

He took a sip of his beer, gaze falling to the one in front of me. "Not with your team though. You're more like a mother hen with them."

"All I want is to do good work and bring them home safely."

"Does your father work for the company, too?"

Something I wanted to discuss even less than my mother. "No. Just me, Mum, Emmett, and Brie."

He nodded slowly, his stunning blue eyes falling to the table. "My mother died when I was little. I can barely remember her or what my father was like before that."

"I'm sorry." I'd also read that in the background check. What was he trying to gain by telling me? Was he guessing we were in the same situation, so he could use it to find out more about my father?

Dad hadn't been in the picture since I was twelve. I visited him a couple of times each year, which left me with a swirl of emotions I wasn't prepared for in the middle of the pub. I wasn't prepared to handle the emotions of dealing with my mother, either. I had just enough to deal with Emmett. Once he was free, everything could go back to normal.

Malcolm put his hand on mine, curling his fingers between my palm and the glass. "I know what it's like to lose someone you love. We will not lose Emmett."

His hand was cool from where it had been on his glass. Firm grip, with a hint of hesitation, or discomfort for sitting together, in a pub with a woman he barely knew, holding her hand.

Unlike after the architect's office, I didn't fling it off. Instead, against what would have been my better judgment, I held on. I needed to maintain control for the team. Around every mark, target, or any person I needed information from. Malcolm was a one-job contractor. He'd be in my life for a week or two and then gone.

Let him think what he wanted about the ice princess. Every once in a while, I needed to pretend I was halfway human with someone other than my three girlfriends. "Thank you for yesterday."

He inched closer and lowered his voice. "I didn't like how she talked to you."

"And I don't enjoy sitting here in a pub when we should be planning."

"Everyone's gotta eat." He stretched his arm along the top of the booth, so it was behind my shoulders.

Why was I still holding his hand? "Since we're alone, we should review the levels of physicality for tomorrow."

He stroked my knuckles with a thumb, sending an unwelcome wave of heat through me. "We've already gone over that at least a dozen times."

I squeezed his hand. "Then what level is this?"

"One." He lifted my hand to his lips and pressed a kiss to the back. "And that skipped all the way to three."

I pulled my hand away. "We're not at the party. Keep your lips to yourself."

His intense eyes remained locked on mine. "And always ask permission."

Maybe Heather was right last Saturday night. I needed to get back into the game sometime, but this was hardly the right time. And he was hardly the right guy. If I could just convince my stubborn body to believe that. "Always."

Visions flitted through my brain. Of every *only one bed* romance novel I'd ever read. He'd be staying with me tonight, but in a suite. I'd already slept there since Monday. There were two whole bedrooms, with a sitting room between them. How was I going to sleep with him so close?

Damn Rav and his change to our plans. Hell, I'd slept in the same bed as Rav more than once, and even after a few drinks, nothing ever happened. Our relationship was special. He was my protector, and I was his savior.

But goddamn Malcolm Sharpe. Mr. Didn't Like How My Mom Treated Me.

"Except every time I touch you, you pull away." He went to take my hand again, and I dodged it. "How do I know that's not going to happen tomorrow night, even if I have your authorization? Because one little flinch could give us away."

He was right again, and I hated him for it.

"Because it's part of my job, Malcolm. You can be sure I'll handle every situation exactly the way it needs to be handled. Trust me, if it's appropriate, there will not be any flinching whatsoever."

"There won't be any on my end, either." He shifted closer. Too close. So close I could smell his bergamot and vanilla cologne. See the tiny rim of green along the edge of his right iris, despite the dim lights. His eyes flashed down to my lips and back up again. Heat poured out of them and through my entire body. "I may be the newcomer to your little team, but I'm a professional, too."

More visions. Of me grabbing his shirt and yanking his lips to mine. Of running my fingers through his hair and reveling in how soft it would be. Tasting the beer on his tongue. Inviting him to share my bed tonight.

Something slammed on the table, and I jumped away from Malcolm. Rav had taken a glass from the tray, more forcefully than need be, sloshing its contents over his hand. "I won."

Malcolm lifted his glass in congratulations, no fear at the threat in my security specialist's eyes.

Like he'd said. Not a flinch.

CHAPTER 22
SCARLETT

AFTER LAST NIGHT at the pub, Malcolm and I had walked back to the hotel together, his arm around me, chatting and laughing. His luggage had already been moved into my room, so we were a couple to the outside world.

I'd barely slept. Every quiet noise sounded like him creeping toward my room. Some insane part of my brain hoped it was true, but he stayed away. He even showered and got dressed in the morning before coming out of his room.

Dec and Jayce were at Will's place, going over the plan ten more times. Rav had spent most of the day with them but was collecting the Bentley.

Malcolm and I fell into our roles with ease. I'd put on the engagement and wedding rings I traveled with for cover, and he'd donned the one we picked up for him. We had brunch together in the hotel restaurant and wandered the hotel's small art gallery. At three o'clock, I went off to the spa for a massage and beauty treatments, while he had a professional shave and a manicure.

Had it not been for the hours meeting virtually with the

team before heading to the spa, I could have called it the perfect day. Pretending with Malcolm was easy. He took the job seriously and didn't try to irritate me or throw me off once. Instead, he told jokes, talked about the places he'd visited, and asked a million questions about growing up that I couldn't answer. Work was also off the table. As was my father. And his father.

We had a surprising amount in common, particularly the way we both had so many forbidden topics.

I stared at myself in my bathroom mirror. The ankle-length navy dress was covered in vertical pleats, with a halter which tied behind my neck in a large bow. Gold cuff bracelet, diamond drop earrings, and crystal-studded three-inch heels to match the clutch. Hair piled high at the back of my head with loose strands to frame my face, designed to highlight the plunging back of the dress.

It was almost go time. I dropped my phone, lipstick, fake ID, and a credit card into my clutch. Will had made quick work of adding a secret compartment within the lining for lockpicks, just in case.

Deep breath in. Deep breath out. We'll get the Chalcis Ring and bring Emmett home.

Head held high, I strode out of my room, rolling my suitcase behind me. We weren't coming back after the party. Where we were headed with the ring was anyone's guess, though.

What I should have seen was Malcolm, ready to go. Instead, he stood there with a buttoned tuxedo shirt, cuff links on the sitting room table, and a half-tied bow tie. He dropped the ends of the bow tie, his eyes dragging down the length of my body.

The dress wasn't tight, but it skimmed over my curves, the subtle pleats leaving little to the imagination. That was the goal, but the way he looked at me, drank it all in, I felt utterly naked.

"I'm useless with a bow tie."

"Try an internet search. Lots of sites will give you instructions." I turned away from him, and he made a noise deep inside his chest that ricocheted all the way to my toes and back up to my core. The fabric of my dress shifted with each step, gliding over my hips, the plunging back falling to a few inches above my tailbone. Each movement had me imagining his hands exactly where his eyes likely were.

"You could tie it for me?"

I retrieved a bottle of sparkling water from the fridge and twisted it open. My makeup was perfect. Drinking from a bottle would leave a cranberry-colored stain on the bottle and I'd need to touch up. I didn't actually *want* the water. I needed something to hold on to. "We should review the levels of physicality one more time."

"Of course." A video began playing behind me, with bow tie instructions.

I should have done it for him and left it at that. "Level one is holding hands. Two is a hand on my waist, back, or shoulder."

"Or your hand on my waist, back, or—"

"Level three is a kiss to exposed skin." A tingle ran up my hand from where he'd kissed it at the pub.

"Does that include everything your dress is exposing?" A smirk tinged his voice, and the heat inside me grew. His lips at the base of my spine. Up my sides. On the sensitive skin at the hollow of my shoulder.

Don't take the bait. "Level four is hands to any non-genital area of the body not yet allowed. Five is mouth to mouth."

He hummed aloud, the video still playing. "What's level six? You've never told me that one."

"Groin." I spun, just about ready to hurl my water bottle at him. "Specifically, my knee into yours."

His bow tie was a mess. "You say the most romantic things, Eloise, my love. I assume we're going in at level three?"

"Level two." I had to go over there and fix the tie for him. I didn't want to do that. *Oh yes, you do.*

He feigned a pout. "So the whole experience with the architect soured our relationship somewhat? You're upset with me for not coming to your rescue?"

"More like I'm not the PDA kind of woman."

He picked up one of his cuff links, gold with black enamel to match my cuff bracelet. "And if you need CPR? Do I need to clear us for level four before that? Or let—"

"Shut up, Malcolm!" I couldn't do it anymore. I couldn't deal with his jokes or his sexy-as-sin self standing there in the hotel room with me. We had a job to focus on. Goddamn London and their ban on plastic water bottles. Throwing a glass one would make a fucking mess. "I swear, I should have hired some shmuck off the street to help us! Someone who'd see this as something other than a joke!"

"A joke?" The teasing smirk rapidly evolved into a curled lip. "After everything with your mother on Thursday? Last night at the pub? And the day we spent together? You honestly think that's all this is to me?"

"Everything out of your mouth is designed to drive me up a fucking wall!"

His head fell backward, and he shook his fists at the ceiling. "I'm doing the best I can."

"The best at what? Pissing me off? Throwing me off my game? What are you, secretly working for those clowns who took Emmett?"

"Really?" He dropped the cuff link and yanked off his bow tie, throwing it to the ground. "How dare you."

"How dare *I*? Seriously? It's my brother whose life's at stake here!"

He began unbuttoning his shirt, stalking toward me.

"What are you doing?" I hadn't questioned for a second if I was safe alone with him. Should I have?

"You want to know the truth?" He pulled out the hem of his shirt. His eyes were on fire, an intensity taking over his being so complete I felt it in my gut. "You want to know why I wouldn't join you for a massage like the adorable married couple we are?"

I stepped back, bumping into the fridge.

"Here." He undid the last buttons and ripped the shirt off, exposing ridiculously chiseled abs and strong pecs and the faintest smattering of hair. And oh my god, how dare he look like that?

My throat ran dry, and a shiver exploded up my arms.

Malcolm Sharpe was even more gorgeous half-naked.

"Does this look like a joke to you?" He turned and I gasped, nearly dropping the bottle to the floor. Sickly black and green bruises covered his left side and back, with one large white bandage over his kidneys.

My knees went weak, and I flailed for the counter, dropping the bottle onto it, barely keeping it upright. "What's that?"

"What do you think it is?" He turned back to me, unclothed from the waist up, so close I could feel his heat.

My hand reached for him—completely against my better judgment.

He inched away, practically snarling, "I didn't clear you for level two, *Eloise*."

"They did that...?"

"Just because they didn't hit my face doesn't mean they didn't have a little fun."

I stepped closer, but he pulled the shirt on and stormed away from me. All I wanted was to wrap my arms around him and apologize. I'd been so wrong about him. "Why didn't you say anything, Malcolm?"

"I shouldn't have had to." He busied himself with the buttons and picked up his phone to restart the bow tie video. "Emmett told you to trust me, so I'd hoped you actually would."

"Let me do your tie."

He tossed the phone onto the table, abandoning his latest attempt. "One more thing the perfect Scarlett Reynolds does better than anyone else?"

I took a sip from my water bottle and returned it to the counter, crossing the distance to him so slowly it was as though I were wading through tar. Once I arrived next to him, I'd have to apologize. It was the right thing, but it lodged even more firmly in my windpipe than my rapidly escalating desire.

Get control of yourself. Do up the bow tie and step away. Don't slide your hands over his shoulders or down his chest. No inhaling his cologne, either.

He sagged onto a chair, still facing away from me. "I know I'm not your precious Rav, but I—"

"Don't." I stepped around the chair, moved his cuff links back, and sat on the low table in front of him.

He looked away from me and gave his head a little shake. "You're infuriating, you know that?"

"I've got skills. What can I say?"

He snorted and rolled his eyes back to me.

"You've done a good job here and I'm..." I picked the bow tie up from the floor and draped it around his neck.

"You're what?"

I shrugged one shoulder, crossing the two ends of his tie and tucking one side up. "You know."

"Oh my god, I've found something that Scarlett Reynolds sucks at. You can't say it, can you?"

"Of course, I can." I tightened the first loop more forcefully than was necessary.

He cocked his eyebrow at me. That son of a bitch cocked his eyebrow at me and smirked. That was another taunt.

"You're an asshole," I said, unable to contain the laugh that came with it. I folded the shorter end, pinched and looped the longer one behind it, and pulled it into shape.

His gaze fell to my hands as I finished tightening and straightening the bow tie. "Although I concede you're better at that than I am."

"My mom taught me when I was fourteen." I patted the bow tie, admiring my work.

"Did you ever get to be a kid?"

That was what my girlfriends had been for. They'd been my respite from Mum's expectations, and to this day, that's why none of them knew what I really did for a living. I could be me with them. Sometimes with the team, but only while we weren't on a job.

He put his fingers under my chin and lifted my face. We were too close again, especially when we were alone in this suite. "I don't know what level this is right here, but—"

"Level two." I swallowed hard, the heat continuing to pulse through me. "It falls under the shoulder portion of waist, back, or shoulder."

"We go in at level three." A muscle in his jaw flexed. "It's a wedding. We're pretending we've had a few drinks, and I should be able to kiss your shoulder, your hand, and your cheek. You can't tell me that's not reasonable."

"You're right. It's reasonable."

"Does a peck on the lips count? Or is that still level five?"

"Five," I breathed. *Don't lick your lips. Don't*—I sucked my lips into my mouth, moistening them where he couldn't see. Imagining that cranberry stain marring his gorgeous face. How much time did we have left before we had to leave? *Focus, Scar. This is about Emmett.*

"I'm not arm candy. We're partners tonight." He leaned closer, his cologne enveloping me. God, he smelled divine. Underneath it, the same need wafted off him as it must have been off me. His words slowed and voice dropped, so deep it joined all the other energy pooling between my thighs. "What if a peck on the lips is necessary?"

"We need clear communication at every level." Not want. Not need. Not stupid decisions. Communication. It was a job. But still, those lips. What would he taste like? Were his lips as soft as they looked? Would he be the kind of man to grab my throat if he kissed me? The back of my neck? Tangle his fingers in my hair? Caress my cheek? "Some degree of improvisation is occasionally required."

"I can improvise." His voice was so quiet. Had he said 'right now' at the end of that, or had I imagined it?

I wanted Malcolm. Was that wrong? Was it wrong to be a woman and to want to feel desired for who I actually was? Not for the act I put on?

Mum tapped my fidgeting hands. 'That's a tell, and anyone who knows this game will spot it. Scrunch your toes if you need to get control of yourself. Do it often enough and it becomes so deeply ingrained in your psyche that it can snap you out of anything. Never wear sandals or they'll see that, too.'

No matter what I wanted, the timing was all wrong. I shifted back on the table, releasing my chin from his grasp and my entire body from his spell. "When this is over—"

Someone pounded on the door, and Malcolm spun in his seat as though he could see who it was. "Mr. and Mrs. Stone?"

"That's Rav." I stood, collected the cuff links—and my willpower—and handed them to Malcolm. "We need to go."

CHAPTER 23
SCARLETT

THE BACKSEAT of the Bentley was buttery soft, camel-colored leather. The trim was actual wood and metal. Smooth ride, despite the added weight of the armored panels, it was the perfect vehicle for our bodyguard to chauffeur my bored billionaire husband and me to the wedding of our dear friends. Or our friends' children, cousins, or besties, depending on who asked.

Malcolm had reached for my hand more than once on the drive, slipping into character too early. If I hadn't been mentally reviewing every step, every mitigation, every risk of the evening, I might have accepted it as a kindness. But until my brain was fully into Eloise Stone, I couldn't afford his distraction.

"We're almost there," said Rav from the front seat.

I took a deep breath. Eloise Stone. My interests included high fashion, parties, and travel. My husband, Lucius, was a successful investment banker who'd scored big with a few deals five years ago that almost landed him in jail for insider trading. But he had an excellent lawyer.

"Avoid any discussion of how we know the couple," I muttered.

"I know," said Malcolm. "Flutter my eyelashes and let you take the lead."

There was a stifled laugh over the comms.

"I'd say we should do a mic check, but from your response, Brie, I can tell yours is working and so is Malcolm's."

"Sorry, Scar. All my systems are online, and I'm ready for any data feeds that come in. I'll go on mute now."

"Everyone else who is not going to giggle at us, please check in now."

"Will's here. My systems are all up and running. I'm also ready for any feeds that come in."

"Declan's magic fingers and magic brain are ready to go."

Jayce laughed at her partner for the evening. "Jayce's magic *everything* isn't just ready, but raring to go."

"This is Rav. I'm pulling the car into the driveway, making the circle at the end. Stopping. The man approaching the car is my friend who secured access. Let him open your door."

"Stay safe, everyone," I said.

As my door cracked open, Malcolm leaned over, kissed my cheek, and whispered, "Showtime, sugar butt."

Eloise Stone. You're Eloise Stone. And you're flattered that your husband loves you so much. I took the security man's hand and slid out of the car, my heels crunching on the pea gravel, tearing the gorgeous red soles to shreds. What a sin.

Malcolm climbed out after me and handed our invitations to the man. "Mr. and Mrs. Stone."

The man—a behemoth who reminded me of Rav, with the look in his eyes like he knew fifty-three ways to kill you and hide your body where nobody would ever find it—consulted a tablet, nodded, and returned the invitations to Malcolm. "Dinner is just wrapping up now, but the cake will be out, and dancing will begin any minute."

"Thank you," I said, pulling my wrap tighter. With the sun already down and it only being early May, the evening was cool, with a dampness in the air. The house was brilliant, every light inside turned on, plus dozens of lights around the bushes and perimeter of the house.

"Cold?" Malcolm wrapped an arm around my shoulder, and I walked closer to him, appreciating the warmth.

"Leaving now." Rav pulled the car away as the security man walked us to the front door. "I'll only be two minutes away."

We entered through the grand front doors to a very different scene than the one on Wednesday. Instead of wide-open spaces, the grand hall was dotted with lemon trees in huge urns, a balloon garland in silver and gold cascaded down the imperial staircase, and a five-tiered champagne tower sat off to the side. A server in black pants and vest chatted with a couple, carefully retrieving glasses for them.

"If the front room looks like this, I can't imagine the backyard," said Malcolm.

"Then you should go see, honey." I stopped and faced him, sweeping my hands across his chest as though smoothing the front of his tux. "I want to wander a little."

"You should start in the library at the front of the house. I imagine there's some fascinating reading material in there." He cupped my cheek, kissing the opposite one and hopefully not noticing my sharp intake of breath.

Tell me we've got this, I mouthed. How was I leaving so

much in the hands of a man I barely knew? How did my gut already tell me that—no matter how much he liked to piss me off and despite our argument at the hotel—I could trust him? It was the bruises. Clear as day, it was the memory of those bruises and the bandage and the idea of him being beaten along with my brother.

We've got this, he mouthed back. "Just don't get carried away with any of the books. I want to share a dance with you later."

"Good idea. I'll see you in a few." I retrieved his hand from my face and smiled at him. A kiss wouldn't be out of the question. *A level-three kiss. Not to the lips.* I scrunched my toes, prepared to return the cheek kiss, but he leaned in and touched his lips to my nose.

"I'll hold you to that, sugarplum." He winked and turned on his heel, heading through the snooker room.

I watched his vanishing form for too long. The broad shoulders, the tousled hair, the way he waved and nodded to people he passed as though he knew all of them. He was comfortable in this role, which settled a little of the sick feeling in my stomach.

"Are we clear?" came Jayce's voice, snapping me to the moment.

I strolled to the nearby library. A man and a woman in their finest sat at the table at the center, playing a game of chess. She was going to win in three turns, if she had any idea what she was doing. I made my way to the far wall and knelt on one of the window seats, peering outside.

The eastern side of the house faced the tennis court, which was surrounded by tall hedges and would be shaded by mature trees in daylight. Garden lights gently illuminated the stone pathway around the edge of the house, while the occasional bright red or blue flashed from what must have been the dance starting outside.

"Peaceful view," I muttered to myself, advising Jayce and Declan that the first room was clear. With a brief nod to the woman at the table, I left the room, put a hand up to decline a glass from the champagne tower, and made my way through the drawing room. A few people sat on the opulent couches, another sat at the piano by the bay windows, while another couple considered the artwork on the opposite wall.

The curved turret room-like space which held the piano provided a floor-to-ceiling view of the grounds beyond, still on the east. A quick scan showed no people on this side of the house, no guests wandering the yard. "Nice to have the wedding on such a clear night."

"There's security walking the perimeter of the roof," said Malcolm. "I only see one, but he's on the west side."

Jayce and Declan would approach in shadow and make their own determination. Were there people on the upper floors who could see down? More security personnel patrolling the roof walkway? Guests I hadn't seen?

That was our first abort point of the night. My signal, their judgment. They could call an end or postponement to the entire thing. The latter meant I'd be stuck in a loop of visiting the library and the drawing room. Fortunately, other people were milling about, so it wouldn't raise too much suspicion.

"Going up." A blur of black caught my attention, but they were out of sight as quickly as they'd come into view. Up the side of the turret, to its top, between the windows. Scale the side of the house to the walkway.

Jayce would go up first, as the experienced climber. She'd then help Declan, who'd complained every second they'd practiced pulling, hoisting, or shoving him up. When we got home, he was going to have to spend more time training with her.

I stood by the piano, smiling at the man who played a few bars.

He patted the seat next to him. "Do you play?"

"I do, but I don't think my husband would appreciate me playing." I winked at him. "With you."

Flirtation was all well and good, and it helped avoid my standing out. But I had a job to do, which required me in the backyard.

"Security's heading your way," said Malcolm.

All along the rear of the house, the tall windows showcased the stunning reception display. The sun may have been down, but it was practically daylight in the backyard. A tremendous white tent had been erected outside, and strobe lights in every color swayed in concert with the DJ's music. The song choices were modern, but with beats which encouraged couples to dance as though they were listening to old standards.

I'd expected a live band for a black-tie event, but obviously the happy couple had different ideas. Screw class. It was time for a party.

"Malcolm, how's the west side look?" I pulled my phone from my clutch and held it to my ear as I passed the people admiring the artwork, making my way to the family room.

The concentration of guests was far thicker, and there were tables set out with more drinks, sweets, and savory snacks.

"The pool's nice, but the party's getting all the attention. The security guy stopped at this end, then headed back. I'm moving closer to the north side and the party to have a look."

"Careful."

"Just one guy I can see."

I didn't need to remind him of the plan, but for some reason I did anyway. "Don't forget to watch out for signs of another team working the event."

Malcolm drew in a slow breath. "I know."

"I'm leaving the family room for the backyard."

Jayce and Declan would cross the roof in silence. Eyes out for security, avoiding the view of the dormer windows, and listening for our guidance. The original plan included Will monitoring with another drone, but he had nothing small enough to go undetected with so many guests and a security team in place.

The second plan included Brie hacking into their security system and watching through their own feed. But the system was fully contained within the house, with no access from the outside. Not enough time to tap any hard wires, either.

The third plan included Rav monitoring with binoculars, but the house had too many trees around it. It was also too far from the road for him to both stay in the car and see anything.

So old-fashioned eyeballs were what we had.

I crossed the stone terrace behind the house, decorated with a half dozen patio heaters, interspersed between more lemon tree urns and three-foot-tall pillar candles in giant hurricane vases. My phone went into my clutch as I turned to walk backward a few steps, surveying the house. "I only see one guard up there. He's on his way to the east end, so you should be clear to the west and the staircase."

Two taps came over the comms, Jayce's signal that they were still moving forward.

Malcolm said, "No guards here and no one inside the staircase. You're clear from my sight."

Please be right, Malcolm. Just please.

CHAPTER 24
MALCOLM

THE OUTDOOR POOL deck was covered in stone, like that covering the house. Pale and smooth, cut into immaculate rectangles of various sizes. It produced an organic feel—chaotic, yet predictable.

I glanced at the house, with its turret-like staircase, which Jayce and Declan were targeting. The security guard was on his way to the other side, and no one else was in the area.

Behind me, a close-cropped lawn extended beyond the stones, leading to gardens with a few early blooms. Beyond that, the boxwood hedge. We'd reviewed the last moments of the drone's life before Brie lost it in the bushes, so my unspoken goal was to find it. Maybe win a few points.

I nodded, pacing back and forth on the far side of the pool, pretending to talk on the phone. No one could excuse a businessman for needing an escape from the hubbub for a call.

The party had ramped up, the music more muted than some guests probably wanted. Rav's contact had indicated it would end at eleven thirty, a concession to their neighbors who preferred a silent evening.

"Still clear at this end, on the roof walkway and in the stairwell."

Two taps on the comms were followed by Scarlett's terse, "Homeowners are on the dance floor with the bride and groom."

The stairs were in a two-story turret off the side of the house. The top was crowned with a circular paned skylight that appeared on the drone video as though it could be opened. That was Plan A. Plan B would be to use the glass cutters and pull a section out of the top.

Plan C was all Jayce—swing down into one of the side windows. Too high risk of visibility for Scarlett and too high risk of broken limbs for Declan. There'd been some good-natured ribbing about his fear of heights, which he claimed was a lie. Then Scarlett went off on a tangent about an escapade they'd had when they were fourteen. The two had broken into fits of laughter, and only a portion of the story had been intelligible. From the reactions of the others, the story had been recounted many times.

I didn't have a single person in my life I shared stories like that with. Once upon a time, I'd been close with my father, but then—

"Lucius Stone!" I spun to see Bruce White approaching from the other side of the pool.

Shit.

I held up a finger and tucked my head as though I were finishing a call. Under my breath, I said, "The architect's here."

"Tabarnak," hissed Rav.

"Do you need me?" asked Scarlett.

"No, no, all good. I'll call if there's any news," I said in a voice loud enough for Bruce to hear. Hopefully, it was also clear to the team I wasn't ignoring my job. I slipped the phone into my pocket and smiled at Bruce. "Good to see you again."

He gestured behind himself toward the house, giving me an excuse to scan the facade again. For a half-second, a black smudge moved in the shadows cast by the turret, landing on top of the skylight. *At least one of them made it.*

"And you!" Bruce's gaze roamed down my body as he sauntered closer. "I thought you were flying to Tuscany on Monday afternoon?"

"Change of plans." I had to be careful with my words. "Not really a change of plans. Everything's fine. Eloise and I simply decided to stay in town a little longer."

"I made sure to visit everyone I knew during dinner and didn't see either of you." He stopped a few feet from me. "I wouldn't have missed *you*."

If Brie hadn't muted herself, her snorts and giggles would have filled my ears. Flirting with him had produced results on Monday, but he was an unwelcome addition to the evening.

"And you didn't tell me you knew Hugo Albrecht."

This was dangerous territory. *Change the subject.* "And where's your plus-one?"

He shrugged, waving a hand vaguely at the party. "She's over there somewhere, chatting someone's ear off, I'm sure."

How could I get rid of him without having to leave my post? "Why don't you bring her over? I'd love to meet her."

"Don't get in deeper with him," whispered Scarlett.

You think I don't know that, woman?

"To be honest," continued Bruce, moving nearer, "I don't enjoy her company very much, so the busier she is with feeling over-important, the better."

"Do you think you could arrange for a tour of the house for Eloise and me?"

He barely lifted one shoulder. "How about a private tour? Maybe I can show you where that safe room is?"

From the twinkle in his eye, it was clear I'd done an even more convincing job on Monday than I'd thought.

"Skylight opens." Jayce's voice was barely a breath, but unmistakable. The first part of the plan worked. Once they were inside, they wouldn't need me in this position until it was time to leave.

"A private tour would be wonderful." Was I really the one being reduced to the eyelash flutterer again? No matter how many successes I had with this team, it still felt like I couldn't win. "But I'm dying to know. Where did you hide the safe room?"

"Oh you just wait, Lucius." He gave me a wink and patted my chest before turning to leave. Over his shoulder, he said, "I'll talk to Hugo. Give me fifteen minutes. Maybe twenty if he's dancing."

Fuck. "The security guy on the roof is headed back in your direction. Either hide or get in fast."

One of them tapped twice—what did going forward mean at this point? Hiding? Or entering?

"You did a good job with him," said Scarlett. "Nice try on the safe room."

I stared after Bruce's form as he crossed the side patios into the backyard, head on a swivel. He'd be insistent, searching for Hugo Albrecht as quickly as possible. We couldn't take a tour that went to the safe room.

What was my play when he came back? Avoid him? Hide?

I squared my body to the tent, appearing to the world as

though my focus was on the party. But my eyes were everywhere. I watched the guard finish his walk to the corner, checked for figures in the stairwell, kept eyes out for anyone I might need to distract.

Three taps came across the comms. Now what?

"Can you talk?" asked Rav.

Three long taps. Double fuck.

Something was wrong. But the guard was too close, and they couldn't tell us.

"Talk to me, dammit," said Scarlett. "Lucius?"

"I can't see them. The guard's—hold on." I stumbled along the edge of the pool, careening into a lounge chair and helping it fall into the pool. That would get the guard's attention. I didn't have time to look though. I lurched twenty feet across the lawn, to the hedge, and threw my upper body forward into the bushes. It wasn't likely anyone could hear me beyond those listening on my earpiece, but I made the loudest possible retching noise I could.

"Are you okay?" asked Will from his cushy little seat at his mom's.

"Fine. Just trying to distract the security guy." I made the retching noise again and stumbled into the bushes—spotting my backup goal—then staggered back, wiping a dramatic arm across my face. Wobbling, I swiveled to face the party again, gaze flicking toward the roof. "And it's working. He's focused on me."

"Good job," said Scarlett again.

I shuffled back to the patio next to the light well, obviously avoiding the pool deck. I craned my head up, doing my best to look like a drunk, unable to make any subtle movement. The guard stared intently at me, lips moving. Likely talking to his team. I waved enthusiastically at him, and he just shook his head, continuing in the direction he'd come from. "He's on his way to the rear of the house. You're clear again."

If he'd dispatched someone to escort me out, surely he'd monitor me until they arrived. Hopefully, I was in the clear all around.

"I owe you a beer," whispered Declan. "We're in the stairwell."

"So does Will," I said.

"Why me?"

"Because when I wasn't actually throwing up into the bushes, I found something you misplaced."

"Then I owe you the beer!" squealed Brie, so loud I jerked.

A quiet laugh sounded in my earpiece, one I was fairly sure was Scarlett. "Focus, people."

"Sorry! Going back on mute now!"

Time to mingle and make myself look like a guest until Jayce and Declan were done. But how long could I avoid Bruce White and his lusty glares?

Time to find my wife.

CHAPTER 25
SCARLETT

Almost everything had gone according to plan so far. Malcolm and I were in. Jayce and Declan were in. Comms were up. Rav was close.

And Malcolm hadn't *only* saved my thief and safecracker from being discovered, but he'd somehow found Will's drone. Yeah, when this whole thing was over, he and I were going to have a moment. My core flip-flopped in anticipation, and I rubbed my thighs together to release a little of that energy, magnifying it instead. *Down, girl.*

I stood next to a table by the dance floor where I'd dropped my wrap. It was plenty warm under the tent, with all the bodies and the heaters. A few men still wore their jackets, but most were in vests or shirts, ties and collars undone. It looked like fun. Couples danced—some more scandalously than others—and people sang along with the loud music.

The girls and I hadn't been out to a club in five years, since we started getting too old and too responsible. Husbands, children, and busy jobs. Now I attended parties regularly, but I was always working. No alcohol. No letting my hair down. No closing my eyes and simply feeling the music inside of me.

Instead... Hugo and Camilla Albrecht were chatting with a couple at my two o'clock. Violet Albrecht-Bancroft was at my eleven o'clock, dancing with her new father-in-law. Orlando Bancroft was at my ten o'clock, off the dance floor, and enjoying some laughs with friends around the bar.

My eyes were peeled for any sign of Bruce White. Although from the sounds of his discussion with Malcolm, he'd likely avoid me and head straight back to my fake husband as quickly as he could get the go-ahead from Hugo.

I held a champagne flute full of sparkling cider in front of me, swaying to the music. They were inside. Malcolm would be right, and the bookcase was a hidden door into the safe room. The ring would be there, Jayce would grab it, and we'd rescue Emmett.

Where we'd rescue him was another matter. The kidnappers hadn't called since Saturday, so we had no instructions on where to go. Back to New York? Home? Or had they come to London for it?

No matter where it was, we had cars and a jet at the ready to go wherever we needed to.

We would get that damn ring and rescue my brother.

And then I could think about Malcolm.

My phone rang and I popped open my clutch. My stomach clenched. Unknown name. It was a few hours shy of one week from the last time I talked to the kidnappers, but they had Malcolm's regular phone number, not mine. I placed my glass on the table and pulled out the phone, hitting the answer button that would dial in the entire team on mute. "Hello?"

"Do you have the ring?" It was a different distorted voice this time. Possibly the one who'd spoken second on the call—not the one with the red hair.

I dipped my head to keep the call private, but continued monitoring the floor in case anyone got close. "Not yet. Soon."

"Your week is almost up. I'd rather not have to ship your brother to you in parts."

Malcolm and Rav both swore, while my stomach tied up into tighter knots.

"Soon means minutes. Where's the meet?"

"Venice. Tomorrow. I'll text you the address."

Venice? That strengthened our suspicions the Codex and ring had a Venetian link. Should I mention we might need an extra day? No. If we did, we'd either reply to the text or send someone to the meet in Venice while we finished the job. "See you tomorrow. He'd better be—"

The call ended abruptly.

I held my muscles steady and put the phone back in my clutch, picked up my flute of cider, and squeezed my tongue against my teeth to stop them from chattering or letting my jaw flex. "How did they get my number, Brie?"

"Ah..." Brie stumbled for a few syllables. The phones Will built and she programmed weren't hackable. That's what they'd said. "We must have worked with one of them before."

Shit. Of course. The more work we did, the more successful we were, the bigger that risk became. But would a happy customer kidnap Emmett? "We've only failed a few contracts. It's got to be one of them behind this. Or maybe a contractor we hired in the past?" Had one of them been on the other team at the Maguire mansion?

"I'll get on it as soon as you're done tonight," she said.

I took a sip from my glass and checked the family. I shouldn't have taken my attention off them, but they were all in the same spots.

Who did we know in Venice who could act as proxy if we needed an extra day? Or one of us could go? If we needed to try again tomorrow, Jayce would have to stay here, so maybe Declan could go ahead. Or maybe Rav. I couldn't leave the team.

Stop. Focus on tonight's job.

We would get the ring. We would meet them in Venice tomorrow. It *had* to work.

Inside my clutch, the phone pinged with a text. I popped it open to see the details. The meet would be at ten in the morning. We could do this.

The air grew thick behind me, and the scent of bergamot invaded my nostrils, loosening the threads deep in my stomach. The man who fried my senses was sidling up behind me, just when I needed him the most. His hand would slide up my bare back, and he'd make some quip about trailing his fingers up my spine only being level two. He'd kiss my shoulder and proclaim it was only level three.

As the newcomer neared, I didn't catch any hint of vanilla. Damn. Not Malcolm.

"Small world." If the vocal fry hadn't tipped me off, the other note in his cologne would have.

Pineapples.

Thomas Gregory Maguire.

My mark from last weekend.

All the warmth fled my body, and I scrunched my toes inside my shoes. *This* was why I never went in unprepared. If we'd had the guest list, I would have known he'd be there. I would have worn a disguise.

Worse yet, there was no way to tip off the team. I'd pretended not to know his name at his father's birthday party, so I couldn't use it now. He was too close for me to whisper or tap on my earpiece.

I released my straight posture, one hip easing in his direction, and purred, "Feels like it's about the right size to me."

"I didn't see your husband here." He took a step so he was beside me, standing precariously close. His fingers brushed the length of my arm, taking the same liberties as he had in the library of his father's mansion. Hell, the liberties I'd invited him to. "Traveling alone?"

One fake husband was being held by thugs. I hadn't prepped my other fake husband for this possibility. Fuck. *Change the subject.* "How do you know the lucky couple?"

Ignoring my question, he took my drink from me. "Do you dance, Eloise?"

Double fuck. If distracting *him* had been the job, I would have called this too easy. But to be a convincing partner *and* monitor the Albrechts *and* the Bancrofts *plus* watch for signs another team was after the ring would be a challenge.

"We're on the second floor," whispered Jayce over the comms. "Proceeding to the bookcase."

Was there any way Maguire could help us? We didn't need to generate any level of chaos to throw off a suspicious guest, and unless he knew where the ring was, there was no value in talking to him. Although if he knew the homeowners, he might introduce me, and I could kick up a conversation and prod for details if Jayce and Declan couldn't find the safe room.

I gave my toes one last curl and produced a lazy smile for Maguire. "A dance sounds like fun."

He placed the glasses on the table next to us and leered at me, a far-too-obvious scan of my breasts, waist, and hips. No doubt he was wishing I'd worn the low-necked gown from last weekend, rather than tonight's halter. Except the back was so low, there'd be no avoiding his slimy hands on my skin. "Excellent."

You got this, Scar.

He gestured to the dance floor with one hand, the other circling my waist to herd me forward. No touching. Not yet.

"I'm not a very good dancer." Was I being clear enough for the team to know what I was doing? "What was your name again?"

Thomas stopped between couples—all of whom were excellent dancers—and took my right hand, while his slid to my back.

How was I going to get out of this elegantly? One dance and say I needed to hit the powder room, probably.

He drew closer—too close—and whispered, "You can call me Daddy."

"Ew," whispered Brie over my comms.

Thanks for coming off mute for that insight, Brie. I smiled, responding with the most vapid thing I could think of. "But you're not old enough to be my dad."

The leering continued as the dance began, the waltz giving way to a game of cat and mouse. With each step he took forward, I had to take a larger one back than I should have, preventing him from getting closer. His hand crept lower, one vertebra at a time.

We glided across the dance floor with the other couples, a

dizzying array of tuxes and gowns in every shade of jewel. Rubies and sapphires and emeralds and everything in between.

At least he was a good dancer.

I closed my eyes for a moment, muscle memory taking over, inhaling his delicious cologne and pretending the pineapples were vanilla.

Get a grip, Scar.

I needed to get Malcolm out of my system. Either by freeing my brother and saying sayonara for good or finding a secluded spot with a locked door. But then I'd have to turn off my comms and that was a no-no, so I'd have to continue suffering. And everyone was listening, so I had to suffer in silence.

When this is over, Scar. Be patient.

Scrunch the toes, recite Mum's lessons, and maintain the professional exterior. And keep on dancing with Slobbery-Mouth Ma—

He stopped short, and I slammed into him, my eyes flying wide to see the man himself standing here, as though I'd conjured him out of a dream.

"Malcolm." Thomas glowered at him as if he were little more than an irritating fly.

"Mr. Maguire, fancy seeing you here." Malcolm eyed me, the same slow look Thomas had given me, but this one caused my heart to skip. "Do you mind if I cut in?"

Thomas didn't loosen his grip on me. As far as he knew, I was married to some other man who wasn't in attendance, and I was his if he wanted. "I think I'd rather keep dancing with her, if you don't mind."

"Can't say I blame you." Malcolm placed a hand on

Thomas's shoulder when he tried to restart the dance. "But I need to leave soon, and I'd be remiss if I didn't have a single dance with the most stunning creature here. After that, she's all yours."

Bimbo. Bimbo. Remember your role, Scar. I giggled and extricated my hand from Thomas's near-vice like grip. "Just one dance."

"I warn you..." Thomas leaned forward to Malcolm. "She's married."

Malcolm held out his hand, and I accepted it gratefully. "Just my type."

What did that mean? Or was that part of the role? Because *we* were supposed to be married? In all the fantasizing and attempting not to flirt with Malcolm, I hadn't thought to ask if he was single. He could have been genuinely married for all I knew.

Thomas's fingers skimmed across my back before I was out of reach. "I'll be waiting for you."

"Thank you," I breathed as Malcolm towed me between other couples.

"Note how I kept my earpiece on this time." He winked as he lifted my hand, encouraging me to spin slowly before we started.

"You should have given me a heads up you were on your way."

His smirk didn't even falter. "You're welcome."

"Sounded like you and Maguire know each other?"

"I told you." He scanned the crowd as we danced, as alert as I should have been. "I've done work for his father."

That didn't answer the question.

His blue eyes landed on mine, narrowing slightly. "Of course, you also looked awfully close to him."

"He's handsy."

"You didn't seem to mind."

Was that an accusation? "That's my job."

"He's not your job." Malcolm's jaw flexed. What was the act? The jaw telling me he was jealous? The flirtatious smirk? Or the way he'd been doing his job, watching the crowd as though he were simply guiding us around the dance floor.

"But he's going to be if we're still here when this song ends."

"You told him we were married?"

"No." I kept my gaze up at Malcolm, flicking off to the side and back again, searching for Thomas or the architect. "That was Emmett last weekend."

Malcolm's step faltered. "Do you think he suspects you were behind the Cod—"

I took an extra-long step to close the distance between us so we could almost whisper. "Don't say it out loud."

His nostrils flared and his hand eased down my back, leaving a trail of fire in its wake. It was all part of the act. Get close enough to keep our conversation private, except for the team. But when his chest met mine and his hand ceased its descent at my tailbone, I had a momentary flash of the impossible—of encouraging it lower.

Yeah, Malcolm Sharpe was a problem for me.

"I thought Bruce White and his come-ons were going to be an issue, but if he talks to Thomas, we're in bigger trouble. If they realize you've got two different husbands, what are we going to do?" He pushed me away with one hand to spin, then pulled me back so we were cheek to cheek.

There was no level of toe scrunching that could fix the feeling inside of me. I was still on the verge of panic about the call from the kidnappers, but there was something else underlying it. It was even worse than it had been with Noah at the start. He'd joined us as a contractor on a single op four years ago. But our immediate chemistry was something Mum couldn't pass up, so she hired him full-time. Before I knew it, he'd practically taken over the number-two position, we'd moved in together, and got engaged.

That wasn't about to happen with Malcolm Sharpe. He was a lone wolf. A renegade. Teams weren't his thing.

Teams. Emmett. *Focus.*

"How's it going, Dec?" I watched the crowd from over Malcolm's shoulder.

"One sec... Got it!" whispered Declan. "The bookcase had a simple hidden switch."

Malcolm's head drew back, but not enough for me to see his face. He must have been as surprised as I was.

"No security to keep it closed?" I asked.

"Yikes," said Jayce. Coming from her, that was never a good thing.

"Inside, we've got two wall safes and a standing safe." Declan could be a cocky joker in his everyday. Laid back, but always analyzing things, searching for connections and patterns. On the job, his tone was light, but it masked cool efficiency. "I'm guessing it's hidden for easy access, but from the inside, they'd be able to secure it with... holy shit, this is some serious security."

Malcolm's hand tightened on my back. "Any sign of the ring?"

"I'm starting on the small one." Jayce could crack just

about any simple wall safe without pre-planning. The 'small one' must have been something in her wheelhouse.

Declan let out a long breath. "Standing safe has biometrics. Thumb or fingerprints required. It'll take more time."

"Use the magnetic case to attach the phone next to the keypad," said Will. "Hook it up so it can start processing, then do the other wall safe."

"Copy that," said Declan. "Plus, there's a bank of displays. I think it's the security desk."

"That's probably why it's easy to get in," said Brie. "Show me video."

Hugo Albrecht strode across the dance floor with a few men in his wake, fast enough I only caught a snippet of their conversation. "...bottle of DRC 2015 that I picked up for this occasion. It's downstairs in the..."

"Hugo's headed inside," I said. "The rest of the family's still out here."

"Working as fast as I can," said Jayce. "Any chance he's headed up here, you think?"

"The men nipping at his heels are likely business prospects. They'll make a beeline for the lower floor and the wine room." Malcolm's thumb stroked my back. "Song's almost done."

As we pivoted in the dance and other couples shifted in position, I glimpsed Thomas Maguire, still watching me. "Thomas is going to pounce. We should sneak off."

Malcolm spun our dance more forcefully, navigating us farther away from Thomas. "You told him one dance and you were his."

"I was hoping he'd find someone else to slobber over."

"We'll have to sell it." His fingers flexed on my back. "Permission to move to level four?"

"Granted." *Bad choice, Scar.*

Malcolm's hand trailed down the side of my hip, barely brushing my ass. If that weren't enough to sell it, his mouth neared my ear—the one without the earpiece—and he breathed, "We should head to the light well behind the garage. There are stairs down to the bottom floor, entering close to the glass-walled lounge and the stairs to the safe room. We'll be out of Maguire's view and can help Jayce and Dec if they need it. Plus, if Albrecht is going there, we have an excuse."

"Good idea." Anything to end this dance and separate myself from his body. "We can—"

Before I could finish, Malcolm hauled me off the dance floor, between other couples, in the opposite direction from Thomas Maguire.

"You see that USB connection at the bottom right?" said Brie. "Plug the phone into that one and let me see if I can get into the security feed."

"We're on our way." I lifted the hem of my skirt to prevent it from tangling in my shoes as we crossed the stone patio toward the pool by the garage. "We'll sneak up the stairs and keep an eye out for security."

Malcolm grinned over his shoulder, eyeing me like a mischievous teen sneaking off with his girlfriend. "How does getting thrown out of a black-tie wedding fit into your master plan?"

Don't look at me that way. No one's watching. "Good point. We can stand guard by the safe room. If security winds up there on patrol or Hugo wanders too far from the wine cellar downstairs, we play it by ear. If either of us suspect they'd be heading into the control room, we need to ensure they escort us to the front door."

He slowed as we passed the final guests and wrapped his arm around my waist. Surely, in case anyone *was* watching, he leaned in, making it look like he was nipping at my ear while we walked. "Dec and Jayce, be ready to grab your equipment and run if that happens."

CHAPTER 26
MALCOLM

How Scarlett moved so fast in those shoes was a mystery. She kept up with my rapid pace across the patio, only slowing briefly when we crossed a patch of lawn she should have sunk into.

"Biometrics is proving difficult on the large safe," Will said over the comms. "Brie, I think it's wired into the security system. How's that coming?"

"Almost into the system."

"Safe one is open," said Jayce. "No ring."

"Dammit." Scarlett's hand clenched around mine on her waist. "Dec? Any progress?"

"Safe two's being a little bitch. Give me another minute."

I skirted the edge of the pool, keeping my arm around Scarlett in case she needed balance anywhere.

The devil on my shoulder told me to run that hand down her hip again, over the ass she gave me permission to touch. There was no one to sell it to at the moment, so it was doubtful she'd appreciate it.

I'd never worked with a woman like her. Gorgeous women, sure, but all grifters and gold diggers, women who wanted more than I was interested in giving. All Scarlett Reynolds wanted at that moment was help getting her brother back.

The garage loomed to our left, separated from the patio by the light well. I peered over the railing which divided it from the patio. We'd already passed the turret stairwell Dec and Jayce had entered through. At the far end of the little alley, stairs led down to an underground staff apartment and would take us directly into the indoor pool area. From there, it was through the lounge and into the turret. Then up to watch for security.

"I'm in the security system," said Brie. "I've opened up a wireless connection, so take out the USB. I don't need it anymore. Will, I'm getting you in, too."

My heart crashed, adrenaline spiking through my system. We were going to pull it off. We were going to get that ring.

Scarlett and I rounded the corner to the stairs into the light well. A rope hung across the top, the same as in the grand hall.

I let go of her waist, taking her hand while she lifted her dress and stepped gingerly over the rope.

Declan swore under his breath. "Safe two's open. No ring."

"Shit," said Jayce. "I'm running the metal detector around the room in case there's a hidden safe somewhere. Maybe the floor."

"We don't have time for this." Scarlett hurried down the stairs, dress still hitched up to her thighs. "What about the biometrics, Will?"

"Working on it."

"Say the word and I'll pull out the drill," said Declan. "Scoping the lock may help, but it makes it awful easy for them to figure out someone was here."

Scarlett let her hem fall to the ground, practically running to the pool door. Her cool was completely evaporating. When she reached the glass door at the end, she stopped, took a deep breath, and put the professional mask back in place.

A man's voice floated down from above us, and I put a finger to my lips. We were on the other side of the rope barrier and couldn't risk being caught. At least, not down here.

She nodded and put a gentle hand on the door, pulling it.

Locked.

The door was locked.

The fucking door was locked!

The voice grew more distinct. "I'm sure I saw them head this way."

There wasn't enough time to pick the lock and nowhere to hide in the light well. It was a straight path from the stairs which descended into it to the pool door. The wall to the car gallery floor was on one side and the door into the staff suite on the other.

Scarlett pointed at the suite door. If someone was inside, that would look like a break and enter. Not the right choice.

Footsteps approached on the patio stones above. If they looked over the railing into the light well, they'd see us.

I yanked Scarlett to me—her eyes flying wide in surprise—and did what my body had wanted to do since the first time I laid eyes on her. I flattened her against the wall and my lips landed on hers. One of my hands threaded into her hair, while the other gripped her waist.

She'd been caught off guard and barely reacted.

Did level five include tongue? Probably not. We didn't need tongue if we were going to spring away from each other and look embarrassed for being caught.

"I think you'll like them," said the voice above us. Closer than before, I recognized it. Bruce White again. The architect.

Fuck it. He was going to get a show that would make it clear I wasn't interested in whatever *house tour* actually meant to him. I slid my hand down Scarlett's fine ass, cupped it, and pulled her against me. Heat burned through my body, and I crushed my lips against hers, encouraging her to open for me. *Give up your self-control for a second and let me in.*

Her back bowed away from the wall and her lips parted, her tongue joining mine in the deception. She tasted like apples and wedding cake. Smelled like lilies and vanilla. Her hair was silky soft, and I wanted to comb my fingers through it, but the updo denied me.

"Lucius, there you are!"

I eased out of the kiss, keeping my eyes on Scarlett and shifting my hand to her waist. "We're a little busy here, Bruce."

God, she was gorgeous. Those deep-brown eyes and swollen lips. The way her chest rose with each rapid breath. She'd enjoyed that. It wasn't an act. Her face rolled away from them, playing coy.

I took over, turning a glower on Bruce and the woman with him. "A little privacy?"

His shoulders dipped down, but he lifted his chin. Disappointed, but too proud to admit it. "My wife also wanted a house tour, if you care to join us?"

"Maybe later." I shifted my gaze back to Scarlett, who canted her head and looked at me from the corner of her eyes.

"Of course." Bruce and his wife left, bickering quietly. I only caught snatches of conversation, but from the sounds of it, there was no plan for it to be just me and Bruce. She'd wanted in on the action.

"You made quite the impression on him." Scarlett smirked, and my brain went into a tailspin. She didn't push me away or ease out of my grip. My hands were still on her, and she was still pressed up against the wall.

"I hear someone else coming." I didn't actually hear anyone. The door was locked, the team was doing their thing upstairs, and all I could think about were those lips.

She looked up toward the railing, no doubt hearing little more than the same distant voices I did. "I don't..."

My hand glided along her jawline, around the back of her neck, and I locked my thumb under her chin. It was slow and deliberate, matching the pace of my other hand trailing down the curve of her hip and my repeated lie. "I hear someone else."

Her gaze, under a creased brow, returned to me. She gave no hint that my hands or the kiss meant anything but the job. But then she quirked her eyebrow—the quirk that prompted for the rest of my story—and I was done for.

I dipped my head down and our lips met again, one of her hands sliding up my chest, the other wrapping around my waist, pulling me closer. Either she *had* heard someone, or this kiss was real.

A tiny moan escaped her throat, too quiet for anyone above to hear. That was for me. It had to be real.

Fuck me, I was in trouble.

I deepened the kiss, and her thigh rose high enough I could grip it against my hip. Thank god for thigh-high slits.

This was the wrong priority. We were supposed to be searching for a way to get upstairs, but I couldn't stop myself. Every ounce of self-control fled my brain whenever she was near. Usually, it came out as taunts and teases. This time, it was the honest carnal need deep in my gut.

She ground her hips against me, pulling me tighter, her tongue plunging deeper into my mouth. Her leg shifted, wrapping around me, demanding more.

My cock reacted. Hardened. I pressed into her, fisting my hand in her hair.

"Here now!" came a voice from above.

I flung my hands off her, but when I tried to step back, Scarlett's leg remained latched around me.

It was one of the security team. "You're not supposed to be down there!"

"We were..." I looked from him to Scarlett.

"Mr. Albrecht said the party was moving to the wine cellar by the indoor pool." She wiped one lazy finger across her mouth, not looking the least bit shaken by being caught, and using that vacuous voice she'd used on Thomas Maguire. "The door down here's normally open."

The security thug stepped over the rope at the top of the stairs and descended. "You're friends of Mr. Albrecht?"

She shrugged one shoulder, still leaning against the wall, and let her leg slide down my side. "Friend of his older daughter."

I straightened my tux, concealing the hard-on, which would have been obvious had I not been wearing a jacket. She must have heard him coming, otherwise she would have reacted differently. The leg was her plan and I fell for it just as much as the guard had.

"It's supposed to be closed for the party." He walked past us to the door and swiped a keycard over a panel next to it. When it clicked, he held it open. "Don't cross anymore ropes tonight, alright?"

"Absolutely." Scarlett took me by the hand and patted the guard on the chest as we passed him. With a wink, she said, "I'll let them know what a great job you're doing."

Once the door shut behind us, she closed her eyes and let out a slow breath. Was that breath for almost being caught twice or for the kiss? It had to be about the kiss and her leg wrapped around me.

Three couples stood on the indoor pool deck, another woman walking toward them. From our location, I couldn't see into the lounge, which was around the corner and at least three voices carried from it.

I leaned close to keep my volume down, waving a hand toward the light well. I needed to know. "What was all that?"

"What was *that*?" Her gaze fell to the front of my pants, accusation instead of excitement all over her face.

"Don't flatter yourself." I hauled the tiny drone out of my pocket, sure to maneuver my hands so she couldn't see the truth, then tucked it away again. "Let's get to the stairs."

"One sec." She took my hand, pulling me against the wall inside the door. No kiss, no fondle, but a brief continuation of our act to cover further discussion. "How's it going up there, team?"

"There's more cameras than we knew about," said Brie. "I need to knock them out, wipe the history, and cover my tracks. I can't work on the biometrics, too."

"I'm getting there," said Will. "But I don't know how long it's going to be."

"Alright, Lucius and I are on the way in case we need to redirect any security guards." She pulled me around the corner, and we stepped into the glass-walled lounge.

The room was occupied by five women, admiring the art and sculptures in the display shelving across the room, while the lower-level garage contained as many men. Probably couples splitting off to appreciate their different obsessions.

The stairs—so close—were roped off. Crossing this barrier with so many people in the room would be obvious. There weren't any other stairs we could use. How would we get up? What was the next plan?

"I'll distract them," whispered Scarlett. "You go upstairs and if security comes, do the drunk act again. Let me know if you need help."

I nodded and pulled her close, planting a kiss on her cheek. Unlike the one outside, it was a mock-inebriated kiss. "You're the best, sugar lips."

She separated from me without a second look and wandered over to the women. "Evening, ladies. What are we..."

Four of the women faced the artwork with her. The other smiled at the rear door of the room as a man returned from admiring the cars. Could Scarlett distract all of them? All at once? And could she do it before too much of the party made their way inside with Hugo Albrecht?

Scarlett held her clutch behind her back, her free hand moving toward her opposite wrist. She moved slowly. Deliberately. What was she—

She snapped her fingers three times before gripping her wrist.

It wasn't a casual gesture. That was the danger count. "What a beautiful jewelry display. That gold ring, though? It looks…"

Oh no. It couldn't be.

This was bad.

"It looks positively medieval."

CHAPTER 27
SCARLETT

THE CHALCIS RING sat directly in front of me, alongside three other pieces of gold jewelry with the same soft, worn edges. They all looked as though they'd been buried for centuries. A golden broach with red enamel, a small box with cloisonne in blues and greens, and a belt buckle with granulated gold beads covering it.

All behind a layer of glass.

My world went silent, the chatter over my earpiece fading into the background. We'd spent all week making plans, discussing alternatives and mitigations, deciding on abort points. None of those plans had included me standing in front of the ring with a group of women.

"It wasn't there Wednesday," said Will. "I'm reviewing the feed, and Scar didn't look directly at the shelves long enough for a clear shot, but—which shelf is it on?"

I'd willed it to be in the safe room. Didn't want to negotiate a delay with the kidnappers or risk them making a show of Emmett, to prove they wouldn't be crossed.

"There's a camera in there," said Brie. "Patch into the feed with me."

A blond woman in her forties next to me said, "Camilla has the most amazing jewelry collection. She loves showing them off at her parties."

Another of the women said, "Were you here for the Christmas party? Did you see the diamonds she had on display?"

The blond shook her head. "No, that was the New Year's Eve party. The Christmas party was the Chinese Jade."

I couldn't rip my eyes off it. I was the planner. The boss. I was the one in control of everything. But all I could see was Emmett's bloody face on the video Malcolm had brought to me last Saturday night. There was a way to fix this. I just had to figure out what it was.

The women continued talking. The ones who frequented the Albrechts' parties spoke about the jewelry, the art, and the paintings. If she was a collector, maybe she didn't know it was stolen? The ring wasn't particularly remarkable to look at. If she had other medieval jewelry pieces from roughly the same time period, maybe she bought it at auction. Maybe whoever stole it sold it to someone who then sold it to her?

We always researched our jobs. We only recovered stolen items for their actual owners. Even if it had originally been stolen, if she'd purchased it under good faith, she was a legitimate owner. Then it would be up to the legal system to get it back for the museum, not us.

But what did that matter today? This wasn't about my ethics and principles. It was about my brother.

Think, Scarlett.

Think and don't talk because you're surrounded by strangers.

Malcolm. Where was Malcolm? Did he make it up the stairs like he was supposed to? Or was he waiting for me to distract everyone?

"I can't see it beyond all the women," said Will. "They're blocking the camera."

Malcolm whispered, "Where?"

The whisper and the brief response told me he was still in the room with me. If he'd gone elsewhere, he could've spoken more freely.

"From the angle of the shot," said Brie, "I'd say the camera's in the wall. Maybe in a painting or hidden by a sculpture or something? On the side opposite from where Scarlett's standing."

Malcolm said, "And you'll be able to wipe it all?"

"That's my job," said my little sister.

Cameras mattered tomorrow. Today, it was people that mattered. The layer of glass. There were no obvious hinges, so I couldn't pull it open and take the ring. The women would raise a stink, the men in the car gallery would join them, then all the people milling about the pool. Someone would grab Hugo Albrecht from the wine room, and then security would come for me. It wouldn't be a matter of getting tossed for making out or being drunk. This would be an arrest.

I didn't have time for this.

"Jayce, Declan?"

"Yeah, Malcolm?"

"You two need to get out. The ring isn't up there, so we'll abort your part of the mission. Can you get out without Scarlett and I there to watch?"

Jayce had been a cat burglar when I first met her. She knew how to sneak. Getting out was easier than getting in. Every step was another one closer to freedom. Declan was a specialist. My engineer. If nothing else, he was a runner.

"Scarlett?" said Jayce.

I couldn't get either of them down here. The plan hadn't included hiding a ball gown and tux under their clothes. There was no way to clear everyone out of the lounge, unless we called in a bomb threat or something. Although, if we did that, I'd wait for everyone else to leave, smash through the glass, and take the ring.

So long as I did it before I had to deal with security or a bomb squad.

Still too many variables.

A big hand slid up my arm, and the scent I'd been craving by the dance floor hit me. Malcolm whispered in my ear, "Just say yes, sugar lips."

I pivoted my face to look at him—handsome, charming, and intense. "You're right, honey."

Chaos erupted on the line. Jayce and Declan were busy removing fingerprints, closing the safes, and ensuring Will had a backup of his progress on the standing safe's biometrics. If we had to come back and the Albrechts moved the Chalcis Ring up to the safe room, that would speed things up. Rav was counting things down, minutes and seconds, keeping everyone on pace with Plan I-couldn't-remember-which. The plan we were to follow if the ring wasn't in the safe.

Brie and Will went back and forth about the security system, the cameras, and wiping the data.

My team was doing what they were good at. And what

was I doing? Staring at the goal of the clown's mission, completely useless.

Malcolm pulled me away from the display and the chattering women. It was probably overwhelming him, with all the voices in our comms and all of them chatting. Not to mention the echoes of voices coming from the pool area just outside the lounge.

We stopped by the rear door, the entry to the lower-floor garage. Keeping up pretenses, he wrapped his arms around me and pulled me close. His voice remained barely above a breath. He was hard to hear over everything else. "Can we get it?"

"I think…" I was not saying this. I wasn't giving up on my brother. "I think we need to abort and regroup."

There had to be options other than a bomb threat.

Malcolm ran his hand over my cheek, and I nestled my face against it.

I just needed a minute. Maybe two. I needed to think. There had to be a way out of this.

"Thomas Maguire's in the pool area, on the other side, talking to someone. He's still watching you."

"Calling in a bomb threat is not an option."

Malcolm's brows drew down. "What?"

Rav's voice rose above all the others in my earpiece. "I can do that."

"I can trigger an alarm from inside the house," said Brie. "Fire, police, whatever you need."

As though Malcolm were in my head, he said, "No, that'll just ensure the security personnel clear every room and we wouldn't have any time alone in here."

"Unless you hide?" suggested Will.

Two men strolled into the lounge from the car-ogling area.

"Can't believe Hugo pulled that off," said the taller one. "I told him there was no way he'd find someone willing to sell, but—"

"The man's a genius." His companion raised his glass full of amber liquid and the two joined the women. "What's Camilla brought out tonight?"

There were now eight people in the lounge with us, two men in the car gallery, and I didn't want to check how many around the pool. If Thomas Maguire caught my eye, he might make his way over. If he wasn't already.

I cupped the back of Malcolm's neck and pulled him close, so I could keep my mouth hidden from the pool deck. "Brie, keep an eye on Maguire. Let us know if he moves in our direction."

"Got it, but I have a lot going on here right now."

"Fuck," I breathed. "Call Ash and tell her she's got a job once she's no longer working for the US government."

"Seriously?"

"Yes, seriously." I needed more high-level analysts on the team. And if Ash's boyfriend were doing his job and accompanying us on this mission, she would have been keeping the same hours Brie was to bring us home safe. "Now I need ideas."

Malcolm pulled back to look at me. "There's only two people left with the cars. We should go in there. More privacy."

"But it'll be too quiet." I could nearly talk at full volume in the lounge, since there were so many people around us. "Talking's easier here."

"We look suspicious just standing together." His gaze moved past me, to the wall of shelves.

"I can see you on the camera," said Brie. "You look like you're having a quiet conversation and are giving off total give-us-privacy vibes."

"We can work with that." Malcolm ran a hand over my cheek, letting it drag down my neck. If the adrenaline wasn't spiking so hard through both of us, it might have been tender. "Brie or Will, can you get into anything beyond their security system? Personal computers? Network? Cloud access to files? Maybe the blueprints?"

"No," said Will. "We tried."

Malcolm's hand trailed down my arm, which kept up the privacy vibes very well. "What about the glass over the ring? Thick? How does it open? If we've got control of the security feeds and we can pop it open, we just need to keep everyone's eyes off what we're doing."

"I didn't see a—" I started.

Brie cursed under her breath. "The security program also lists every alarm contact. Front door, back door, numbered windows—"

My stomach dropped before the words were out of her mouth.

"—and one that's called Lounge Jewelry Display Case."

My head rolled forward onto Malcolm's shoulder. "You can disarm it, right?"

"I've already cut all signals to the outside world from the security system, unless I'm the one sending them. So yes, I can stop it from alerting the police. But what I can't stop—"

"Is a local alarm in the room?" Jayce finished for her.

Brie sighed. "Yeah."

Declan said, "We're packed up here. Want us to leave? Or

hide out in the stairwell and grab the ring after everyone leaves?"

That was too risky. If they stayed in the safe room, security might show up if alarms started going. Hell, they were already risking it by being in there too long. Hide in the stairwell and it was a guarantee someone would find them before the party wound down. "Maybe the pantry?"

Malcolm inched back, so I raised my head to look at him. "The evening is being run by caterers. It's likely they're staging some of their food in the second kitchen, which is attached to the pantry. They can't go down those stairs—too big a risk."

I nodded. "Where's Thomas Maguire?"

Will said, "Still on the other side of the pool, in a heated discussion with some guy."

Dammit. This evening was so far off the rails... How was I going to get control again?

Malcolm's gaze flicked to the side. "Not good. Really not good."

"I need ideas, not more problems, Malcolm."

"Meaning... you don't want me to tell you Thomas Maguire, who thinks you're married to Emmett, is speaking with Bruce White, the architect who believes you and I are married?"

"I'm coming to get you out," said Rav. "You can't stay there. We'll reformulate a plan tonight. Go back in—"

"No." My voice remained calm, the way I'd been trained. But inside, my stomach was roiling. Would the kidnappers give us more time? Where would the ring be tomorrow? Still in the lounge? In the safe room? In the safe room behind the biometric lock Declan and Will couldn't get through? At least Will had learned something about it and we knew the layout of the house. But what if they moved it to the walk-in safe in the bedroom? Or hell, what if Camilla Albrecht had a safe deposit box where she kept all of her jewelry and just took it out for displays for parties?

We didn't accept jobs where there were so many variables.

I placed my hands on Malcolm's chest, his big arm circling my waist. If I'd hired some shmuck off the street, he probably would have bolted already. For how much Malcolm complained about all the voices over our comms and how he frowned every time someone suggested an idea counter to his, he was still here. Holding out until the end with me.

I stared up into his big blue eyes. Tonight, they were deep blue, like The Heart of Eternity diamond. He'd been throwing me off my game all week, but in that moment, I found calm in those eyes. An inner calm to match my outer one. "Alright, here's what we need. All the people in this room looking at something other than the display. At least one other alarm going off somewhere in the house when we trigger the one from the display case. Breaking it will be too obvious and too many witnesses. Give me ideas, people."

Malcolm nodded and kissed my forehead. It was too intimate, but it increased my calm. It was exactly what I needed. "I have an idea that may tick all of those boxes. It's a little crazy though."

"Crazy?" All the chatter faded to the background and my world was Malcolm. "Do you see what we're dealing with? Crazy's probably our best bet."

CHAPTER 28
MALCOLM

Scarlett was a professional. To the outside world, she was nothing more than a woman holding onto her man. She'd smiled, she'd chatted, she'd mingled with the women by the display shelves. The men who'd come into the lounge from the car gallery had nodded their heads or to their glasses at us, no idea what was going on.

But she was in my arms. I could feel the way her heart rate had sped up, felt the shudder in her breaths, and saw the changes in her pupils as the information unfolded.

Yes, she was a professional.

But she was panicking.

"Well, I'm going to need your help here." I inclined my head toward the car gallery with a smile.

Scarlett shook her head. "I told you already. It's too quiet in there."

"Do you trust me?" Three hours ago, I was pretty sure she would've said no. But things changed when she saw the bruises. "Can you imagine, Velatti has a monitoring system that allows them to see the status of every one of their cars around the world?"

Scarlett's eyes narrowed a sliver. "I seem to recall somebody telling me that. I wonder how secure that connection is?"

Will blurted, "You're kidding me, right? You don't seriously want us to try and hack into that car?"

Scarlett walked with me, her hand in mine, and we left through the rear door of the lounge. By the glass wall, on the stunning white marble floor, the Aereus rotated slowly. Camilla Albrecht wasn't the only one who liked to show off. Her husband had built a room designed specifically to generate envy. It would've been one thing if the car simply sat on its round elevator platform, but turning? Pretentious bastard.

Brie groaned. "I've got too much going on already. Can you do it, Will?"

"I... um... They just use it to monitor the car. Telemetry, maintenance needs, flat tires. What do you want to do?"

The two men in the gallery were focused on the Ferrari. They'd meandered around the Velatti several times while Scarlett and I were dealing with the discovery of the ring. That left just the two of us staring into the windows, but she was right. It was quiet in this room. The two men spoke to each other, so we couldn't have an open conversation about my plan. But Scarlett's team was sharp. As soon as I'd mentioned the monitoring system, Will immediately knew that I wanted him to hack into it. Somehow, I had to subtly suggest everything else I wanted him to do. "Have you ever piloted a drone, Eloise?"

Scarlett leaned over, peeking into the open driver's window. She didn't crouch or hunch her back. No, she bent fully at her hips, resting her hands on her bent knees. Her long legs and fine ass were on full display. She shimmied side to side, ever so slightly. If we weren't in such a dire situation, I would've deeply appreciated the movement.

One of the men at the Ferrari tapped his friend and smirked at me.

Clever woman.

I looked pointedly at each of them and gestured toward the lounge with my head. In case it wasn't obvious enough or they'd had a few too many to drink, I waved them away as well. The first one made a rather crude motion, like slapping her ass, but fortunately hauled his friend out of the car gallery.

We were alone.

"Do you have us on video?" I ran my hand down Scarlett's back, over the curve of her ass. "You know the people in the lounge are watching us, right?"

She tilted her head up at me, the same look as when Bruce White had discovered us in the light well. The pretend-coy look. "Hopefully, it will keep everyone out of this area."

"I apologize for being so touchy-feely this evening."

She rested her arms on the driver's side window frame. "It's a job. Important enough that we need to pull out all the stops."

Right. Just a job. "Here's what I'm thinking. Can you get the car moving and—"

Will spluttered. "You're kidding me?"

I'd said it was crazy. No idea where the cameras in the room were, I shrugged in response and leaned next to Scarlett, looking inside. It was gorgeous, and this was probably a sin. "Think of it like your drone. Get it moving, smash the glass wall of the lounge, hopefully into the shelving, and cover our tracks."

Scarlett nestled her mouth against my ear as the car turned enough on its pedestal that everyone could see us. "It's definitely crazy. But if there's a chance it works, it would clear out the area. Brie could trigger several other alarms around the house—"

"And it might be enough chaos to get the ring."

"It does telemetry!" Will practically squealed. "It's not a drone. It's a three million dollar car with monitoring systems!"

Another couple of minutes and the car platform would be turned enough they wouldn't see us. I shifted my hand to her hip, pulling her tighter against my side. It wasn't exactly a hardship to convince anyone still watching that we were counting down the seconds until we were in bed together. "Which also has a remote starter and central computer system that controls everything."

"Will, my clutch is hanging inside the car. Is my phone close enough to any central processing system or anything for you to get a feed from the car itself?"

"You two are insane," Will said.

Rav chuckled. "Brie, before you wipe the security cameras, promise me you'll download this?"

"Download it?" Will groaned. "I don't even know if I can..."

Scarlett and I looked at each other when he trailed off. Had he figured it out?

"That was easier than I expected." Will's voice was far calmer now. "I'm in."

From what little I knew about the Reynolds proprietary

phones, they were a technology marvel. They also made an absolute mess when they self-destructed.

"It's not a self-driving car, so I can't pilot it like a drone. I can remote start it in neutral or park, but there will be safeguards in the program that prevent it from starting—"

"Wuss," said Brie.

"You are not ganging up on me with them."

"I totally am."

"Fine. If you can release the parking brake and put it into drive, I'll see what I can do."

It had rotated enough that Scarlett and I were on the far side of the car, with it blocking everyone's view of us. She pitched forward quickly, balancing on her waist, half inside the car. "Done and done."

I helped tip her back up as Will continued.

"All it's going to do is roll forward, so I don't know how much chaos you were hoping for, but this will only be a little chaotic."

"Here's what I'm thinking," I said. "Scarlett and I go back into the lounge. We admire the items on the shelves, and when the car is facing the display with the ring, you start it up. If we're lucky, it careens into the shelf, breaks the glass, and there's enough attention on the car that one of us can grab the ring."

Scarlett stood, looking up and down the length of the car. "And if we're unlucky, someone has enough of their wits about them to hop into it and put it into park."

"Brie, I want every alarm in this house going off the second either of us gets close to the glass in the lounge display case."

"Can do. I have eyes on you in the security feed and have most of the alarms at the ready."

I straightened and offered Scarlett my elbow, which she took. "Eloise, my love, let's go look at those beautiful jewelry pieces you were admiring earlier."

"Jayce and Declan," she said, "with the alarms going off, you have a fifty-fifty chance that the guy patrolling the roof goes inside or becomes more vigilant. But there's a one hundred percent chance someone will race to the security control room. You two need to get out of the house now."

Brie said, "I'll shut down the internal feeds, routing all displays to my system. Once you're clear, I'll start wiping their recordings back to Wednesday when you were in the first time."

"Back that up to Tuesday," said Scarlett, "so we avoid any chance they detect the drone and it will give them additional suspects with the event planners."

I placed a hand on the glass door and paused before opening it. "I'm surprised you're going along with this."

Scarlett squeezed her arm around mine. "It's just crazy enough it might work."

"*I* can't believe I'm doing this," muttered Will. "My first chance to operate a super car and I'm going to intentionally crash it."

We strolled into the lounge together, while another pair of men left to admire the cars. More people clogged the space around the pool, older socialites from the looks of them, more interested in a chat than in the loud music outside. Three new women stood in front of the display wall, focused on a foot-high blue-and-white Ming vase with images of warriors on horseback.

"It's coming around," said Will. "Make sure nobody gets hurt."

I slid my arm around Scarlett's waist, letting her guide me, while I kept my head down and split my attention between her and the car. It was almost pointed in our direction. So long as Will aimed it at the display, where we stood, there were only a few people I'd have to move.

Scarlett pointed at the belt buckle. "You see the little golden balls? That's called granulation. Very difficult work for the goldsmiths. They'd cut small pieces of gold and put them under fire until they balled up like that, and then fused them to the buckle. One wrong move, a little too much heat, and the whole thing—"

"Why, Eloise..." said a man in a deep, creaky voice.

Scarlett's body tensed for the barest of a moment—something I would have missed if I didn't have my arm around her.

Shit. Thomas Maguire had snuck up on us while we were plotting. "That hardly sounds like the woman who thought illuminations were lightbulbs."

"Oh, don't be silly." Scarlett adopted an airy quality to her voice, which didn't suit her brilliant brain. She also shifted her posture, to one reminding me of how she stood by the Velatti, playing up her natural curves and the scandalous dress. "I heard someone else talking about it."

"You promised you were mine after one dance." He stepped closer to her and gripped her arm. "And, Malcolm, you said you were leaving."

A growl built deep in my throat at the way he touched her. Like she was a thing to be possessed. I'd never liked that man, but we could hardly get into a pissing match right now. "She changed my mind."

"Oh, boys." Scarlett swatted his chest and thrust out one hip. "You're not going to duel over me, are you?"

"Time to change your mind again, Malcolm." Thomas didn't bother to look at me. It didn't matter that I was inches taller or that I could have picked him up and thrown his skinny little ass into the pool. It didn't matter that my arm was around her or that he'd watched us practically making out for the last half-hour. He was used to getting his way, regardless of who he had to go through.

"Don't touch her unless she asks you to," I snarled, prying his fingers off her arm.

"I just need to bypass the security on the—got it!" As the words shot out of Will's mouth, bright lights flashed at us from the car garage, and the Velatti inched forward, its engine purring as beautifully as I'd imagined, even without anyone testing the acceleration.

A chorus of gasps surrounded us. "What's going on?" layered over "Is Hugo playing a joke?" and "Is there someone in it?" A couple left the lounge, the others watching the car as though something magical or entertaining were about to happen.

"Jayce, Declan," snapped Brie. "Hugo Albrecht is heading in your direction. Get out now."

"Going radio silent, but going!"

"Eloise?" Thomas was either oblivious to the car creeping toward us or didn't care—as if his father's money put him above little physical threats like a super car rolling in his direction. "You can do better than this charlatan."

It moved faster than I'd expected. The hood of the car plowed into the glass and the wall exploded into a million shards. The gasps switched to screams.

People hurried from the room. Plastered themselves against the far wall.

It headed directly for us. Gained speed.

The loud rumble of the engine nearly drowned out the crunch of broken glass under its tires.

Scarlett shoved Thomas away just before the car reached us, and I spun her against the display shelves.

An alarm sounded in the distance. Had Brie triggered that one? Or had Jayce and Declan been caught? Someone would have said something if they had, right?

Something clipped me—a mirror?—and I careened into Scarlett. She grunted, the glass behind her shattered, and she fell.

The high-pitched local alarm screeched in my ears, the scent of exhaust filling the room.

More screams. I covered my ears.

The car tore through the glass wall on the other side of the lounge.

Where was the ring? It wasn't in its display case. None of the medieval artifacts were.

The car hit maybe ten miles an hour and dipped—oh shit, I was going to hell—it drove straight into the pool.

Scarlett lay crumpled in a heap on the floor, blood splattered across her skirt. She was hurt. Where? It had to have been the broken glass scattered around us. Or the shattered Ming vase. A painting, another sculpture, and golden jewelry littered the floor in front of the display case.

Narrowly avoiding the glass, I dropped to the floor next to her. "Are you okay?"

Without moving, she whispered, "Got it. We need to go. Play up the injuries."

"Eloise!" I bellowed. "Oh my god, Eloise!"

"Less than that," said Rav over the comms.

"You need a doctor. Can you walk?"

"I..." She sat up with my help and put a hand to her head. "I'm not sure. Maybe?"

"I'll take her." Thomas stood next to me, looking even more dramatically down his nose than usual from his vantage point. He sucked at taking hints. "I have a car waiting outside."

I shot to my feet and swung at him. My knuckles connecting with his cheek was one of the most satisfying things I'd experienced in my entire life. For every time he'd talked to me like I was less than him. For the way he'd touched Scarlett. Fuck, just for the way he'd looked at her and thought she was his plaything. "Get your own woman, asshole."

He stumbled into one of the men coming to check on Scarlett. From the way Thomas clutched his cheek and blinked repeatedly, mouth gaping open, it was obvious no one had ever hit him before. Good. I was glad to have been the first.

And even better, his caving shoulders made it clear he wasn't coming after either me or my woman.

My woman.

I knelt beside her, surveying the damage. Blood had soaked into her skirt and stained her hands.

"I'm a nurse." A woman joined me and put a gentle hand on Scarlett's shoulder. How she maintained that calm with the drowned car, the alarms going off everywhere, and the screams, I didn't know. Maybe she was a combat medic? "Can I check your legs?"

Scarlett nodded and took my hand. She gave one quick

squeeze to get my attention and flicked her eyes to the stairwell, then the pool. We needed to get out, not spend the evening being treated.

"Can I take her to the hospital?"

The nurse lifted Scarlett's dress to her knees, nodding as she did. "It's mostly scratches, but it looks like a few pieces are lodged in her shin."

"Everyone out!" yelled a man from the direction of the pool. It was one of the security guards. "The house is being evacuated. Medical attention is on its way!"

Scarlett grimaced as the woman prodded at her injuries. "I can walk. See if anyone else needs help."

The nurse leaned forward to look Scarlett straight in the eyes. One pupil, then the other, and she turned to me. "Help her get outside and be sure she doesn't leave until a paramedic looks at her."

"I will. Thank you." I took one of Scarlett's arms and draped it around my shoulders, then slid my arms under her.

"What are you doing?"

"You're hurt." I stood slowly, attempting not to jostle her as I picked her up. "I'm getting you outside."

She pulled closer and spoke directly into my ear, as though anyone could hear her talk over the continuing alarms. "You're getting me to the Plan F rendezvous point."

Plan F? She was bleeding and all she was thinking about was Plan F? That was the one where she and I got caught and needed to run from the backyard. Hug the eastern wall, where Jayce and Declan would be descending, slip between the tennis court and the trees. Pickup by Rav at the neighbor's house instead of at the Albrechts' front door.

"Fine." I walked carefully over the uneven glass covering

the floor, said a silent good-bye to the beautiful car, and followed the chaotic foot traffic to the central staircase.

CHAPTER 29
SCARLETT

Pain screamed up and down my leg.

Smashing my clutch into the glass covering the display case was a smart plan. I'd be flung back from the car, my hands would fly up in the air out of control, and I'd break the glass. Simple. Grab the ring. Also simple.

But Malcolm had collided with me and my simple grab had turned into a mad flail. I'd knocked everything out before I'd fallen. By some miracle, when I opened my eyes, the ring was right in front of me. Malcolm decking Thomas Maguire gave me the perfect opportunity to palm the ring while everyone was even more distracted.

No matter how many plans we'd made for the wedding, none of them had panned out. The only thing which had worked was Malcolm's quick thinking about the car. He was good. Clever.

And he'd punched out the guy who'd touched me. Obviously not the first few times he'd wanted to, but at the exact right moment, he found an opening and took it.

I wasn't as fast on my feet as he was. Rav and Emmett were better at that—Noah had been the best though.

Malcolm had done everything right tonight, and I'd pretty much failed at everything.

No, not everything. I had the ring tucked away in a special hidden compartment in the neckline of my dress.

But I wasn't leaving under my own power. I hadn't heard anything from Jayce or Declan since Brie gave them the warning to get out of the safe room. And I was being carried out of the house by the most infuriatingly sexy man I'd ever met. "Status update, everyone?"

The alarms surrounded us, blaring from the basement, the main floor, and upstairs.

"I tripped all the alarms I could find," Brie said. "I haven't seen Hugo Albrecht on any of the feeds yet, so he's probably in the safe room. I saw Camilla heading there a few minutes later, so they're probably locked away in safety."

Malcolm crested the landing of the central staircase. Instead of heading for the back door, per our plan, he followed the crowds being herded out the front doors by the security personnel. "Any updates?"

"I can't hear Jayce or Dec over the alarms," I said.

"I'm sure they're fine." He kept his eyes forward. "Is the car ready?"

"Pulling into the neighbor's driveway now," said Rav. "Are you sure you don't need me to come for you?"

"Malcolm's got me."

"I'm on my way." Rav had never trusted my security to anyone else, no matter what he said.

"No. Stay in the car." I looked up at Malcolm, who

twisted his body as someone got too close to me. Why wasn't he arguing with Rav? He'd been following the team's lead more and more the longer we worked together, but this was almost like— "You lost your earpiece, didn't you?"

Malcolm nodded, and my breath hitched.

"Where? When?"

"When the car hit me."

I pulled closer to him. "Hit you? Put me down!"

"No." His pace slowed as we funneled through the front doors. Over a hundred people stood in the driveway, more joining with every passing second. Irritated guests who didn't know what was going on, frantic guests who must have been downstairs, and more than one person limping. Either the car had hit more people than just Malcolm and me, or the panic had resulted in twisted ankles and banged up elbows as people fled.

Over Malcolm's shoulder, I glimpsed a soaking wet man and woman who must have wound up in the pool. Thomas Maguire was nowhere to be seen.

Will had certainly underestimated the level of chaos.

"Brie, Malcolm lost his earpiece. I need you to destroy it." Our command center had remote access to every piece of our tech, including the ability to release a chemical agent that would eat every molecule of DNA and render it not just unusable, but untraceable.

"I'm busy with the security system. Will, you do it."

Will huffed out a breath. "I just drove a Velatti Aereus into a pool. I can do anything."

"I have one camera on the roof," she added. "When the alarms started, the security guy ran the length of the roof and once he was clear, he went inside. Jayce and Declan are moving slower, likely keeping quiet, but the path looks clear."

Flashing lights lit up the evening and sirens competed with the continuing alarms.

One of the security guards approached us—a burly man with a scar across his right cheek and a dark suit—and held up a hand. "Paramedics are almost here. Come with me and I'll get you to the front of the queue."

"Get out of there," said Rav. "You can't wait around while there's a risk they discover the ring's been stolen."

The guard put his hand behind Malcolm's back, steering him toward the driveway and the flashing lights. Not good. Really not good.

"Put me down?" I patted Malcolm's chest and he frowned at me. "My head's swimming and I need to stay still for a sec."

"Then you definitely need to come with me." The guard was too insistent. We were surrounded by people. Sure, I had a little blood on my dress and hands, but why the focus on us?

"Give the lady a minute." Malcolm carried me toward the eastern end of the house, out of the way of the throng of guests waiting for rides, paramedics, or for the party to resume. "Can you walk? Those gashes look nasty."

"You carrying me is gaining too much attention." I scanned the crowd as he eased me to the ground, and sure enough, not only was the security guard still watching us, but several of the guests were.

"It's too cold out here for you." He shrugged off his tuxedo jacket and draped it around my shoulders. "Where's your wrap?"

"I'm not a porcelain doll. I'm a woman on a mission and we need to get this ring out of here. Help me walk."

He did as I asked, supporting me with one arm. Louder than necessary, he said, "Are you sure you should be walking?"

"It feels better already." My dress was dark enough no one would see the blood unless they were next to me. And hopefully, moving around would prevent the guard from forcing me into the ambulance.

We made our way to the end of the house, turned around and walked back to throw off any suspicion, and headed for the end of the house again. The eastern end. The egress point. Rendezvous.

"Earpiece destroyed," said Will.

"The historic records of the security cameras are also done," said Brie. "I'm downloading tonight and once everybody's free, I'll delete these too."

"Good." I leaned more heavily on Malcolm's arm. Every time I put any weight on my right leg, searing pain flooded my system, like knives flaying skin. I needed to get off my feet and have Rav take care of this. "Is Brian ready with the jet?"

Rav said, "He is."

Malcolm hunched over enough to pull my right arm around his shoulders and gripped me by the waist. "We're far enough away from the crowd. You don't need to pretend you're alright. If you won't let me carry you, at least let me do this."

I tried to smile at him, but the best I could do was a grimace. "For a single operator, you treat your team members pretty well."

He chuckled as we rounded the corner. Not a person in sight. "When I'm not pissing them off?"

"Something like that."

"How are Jayce and Declan?"

I'd almost forgotten he lost his earpiece and couldn't hear any of our conversations. Whether it was perfect timing, or they heard him from my earpiece, two taps came across the comms. "One of them wants you to know that everything's alright."

"Only one of them?"

"Probably your drinking buddy."

"I didn't think you were supposed to know about that." He gripped me tighter, practically lifting me off my feet. If I wasn't going to listen to him, he was going to force me.

"It's my team, Malcolm." We passed the library windows, heading to the turret where the piano was inside. I did my best not to groan with each step, but it was useless. The farther we walked, the quieter we became. Gradually fading away until we could sneak into the woods without anyone noticing. The house was empty, and the eastern end of the house was bare of people. "They're my family."

"We can move faster if I carry you."

"Not a chance." Nothing that would draw attention to us, in case somebody was watching. We'd fallen into a rhythm, with me hopping on my good foot while he supported me. His strong arms and the delicious scent wafting off him and his oversized jacket helped contain some of my nerves.

"Always in control, right?"

"Always." I inclined my head toward the tall hedge around the tennis court and he nodded. A hundred and fifty feet in the shadow of the bushes, across the secondary driveway which was only used for deliveries, and we'd be in the neighbor's yard. Another hundred feet beyond that, and we'd be at the driveway and Rav's car. I whispered, "At the corner of the tennis court."

The pain was growing worse. The hem of my dress clung to my right leg, blood soaking it. I stopped and braced my hand against a nearby tree, nudging Malcolm away from me. The issue wasn't that I had a big ego. It was that my mother had taught me not to show weakness. I was the team lead and had to remain in control. Being carried around like a damsel in distress ruined that image.

But sometimes I had to accept help. Even if that was as humiliating as being carried to the car. Everyone needed help sometimes.

"Are you going to let me carry—" Malcolm stumbled backward suddenly.

A dark-suited arm latched around his throat and a gun appeared at his neck. The man holding him growled in the darkness, "Give me the ring or he's dead."

The air rushed out of me and my knees buckled. There *was* another team here for this job, after all.

"Scarlett!" hissed Rav. "What's going on? I couldn't hear."

Malcolm's hands rose to the sides, his gaze not leaving mine. "Eloise, honey, take off your rings and give them to the nice man."

"Not the ones she's wearing, you idiot." The man pulled Malcolm farther away from me, tightening the arm around his throat. The house lights were all behind him, but a glint of moonlight cut through the trees enough that I saw his face. The security guard with the cheek scar. He *had* been after us. "We both know your little stunt inside was to recover the Chalcis Ring. Give it to me."

What was I going to do? Hand it over and lose my brother? Or keep it and lose Malcolm? I had to choose Emmett. Had to. That was the right decision.

How could I save both of them?

How was I losing someone else on a mission?

"I... I don't know..." I couldn't do it. I couldn't risk my team. Malcolm was part of my team. For two years, every time we were on a job, I barely breathed for fear of it ending the way the diamond recovery had ended with Noah. And here I was, on the job I knew we shouldn't do, about to lose someone else.

I took in a shaky breath, goose bumps prickling my arms and legs. My shins throbbed with pain.

I couldn't do it. I could give the ring to the thug, but what would I do with the kidnappers? They wouldn't give me a third job. They'd kill my brother.

"Say the word, Eloise." Rav appeared next to me, suppressed pistol pointed directly at Malcolm's assailant's head. He was supposed to be in the car, but he was never very good at listening when we were in danger. He stepped in front of me. "And I'll take him out."

Malcolm's eyes widened. "Let's not get too crazy here."

"Stay back, Frenchman, or I'll put a bullet through his head."

"He's a contractor." Rav's words were cold, and I knew he wouldn't hesitate. He was trained, too, but by a military who'd deployed him into far more dangerous situations than we went into.

I wasn't ready for bloodshed.

"Give me the ring and your brother lives."

I launched from the tree, prepared to pull Rav's gun away from the man, but my right leg gave out underneath me and I landed on the ground at Rav's feet. Through a strangled sob—

part pain, part desperation, part fear—I said, "You're lying. This isn't the pickup point. Who are you?"

A tiny spark flickered by the man's head, and he collapsed, entire body convulsing. The spark followed him to the ground.

Everyone moved so fast, while my head spun. Malcolm dodged away from the man, Rav disarmed him, and Declan slid his stun gun back into his belt holster.

Thank all the powers that be. I blew out a shuddering breath and let my head fall into my hands. *Reynolds women don't cry. Reynolds women don't cry.* But still, the stinging hit the back of my eyes, and I saw Noah's car fly over the edge of the bridge one more time. Communications failure. Dead. Malcolm had lost his earpiece. And could have died.

This was why you didn't get involved with people in the business, let alone on your team.

People died.

Someone was putting zip ties on him and unrolling duct tape, probably for his mouth. I couldn't look up. I couldn't move. My leg was on fire, and my stomach wanted to throw up everything I'd eaten all day.

Calm down, Scarlett. People died, but nobody had died tonight. *Reynolds women don't cry.*

Strong arms tucked under me, and I opened my eyes to see Malcolm's beautiful blues.

"I've got you. Let's get you to the—"

Rav was in front of us. "Give her to me."

Malcolm didn't puff his chest or argue. Didn't eye him with the same disdain he'd given Thomas Maguire. He simply shook his head. "I've got her. You make sure everyone else is safe and that we all get to the car."

"Let me get a photo," said Declan.

Rav said, "That doesn't matter. We need to hurry."

Malcolm was already carrying me toward the car.

There was a flash of light behind us, and Declan said, "What if he really was the pickup guy? Or what if someone was double-crossing the clowns? Or he's from another crew? This face could be leverage."

CHAPTER 30
MALCOLM

By two in the morning London time, we were all on the jet, on our way to Venice. Everyone had their turn in the heads to clean up and change. Declan, Jayce, and I sat in the forward cabin's oversized leather chairs, happy to be alive.

I tried not to stare at the door at the back and failed miserably. Rav had sequestered Scarlett in the VIP cabin, tending to her injuries. What was taking so long? Was he coming out at all?

Declan sank in his seat facing me, reaching his long leg across to nudge mine. That man had saved my life tonight. "How you holding up?"

"You *did* check to see if the guy's finger was on the trigger first, right?"

Declan grinned. "Of course, I did."

Why didn't that inspire me with any confidence?

Jayce chuckled from the seat across the aisle, one leg curled up in front of herself. "I think his words were, 'I'm pretty sure his finger isn't on the trigger.'"

"Do you always treat the new guy this way?"

"New guy?" Declan snorted and glanced at Jayce. "Thought you weren't interested?"

Any team I'd worked with in the past would have abandoned me to the gunman, unless they worried I'd slip up and reveal their identities. Not this team. They were a family. It was irritatingly inspiring. "Temporary guy, then?"

The door to the VIP cabin slid open, and I jumped out of my seat. Rav closed the door behind himself and pulled open the storage compartment above the table to store the large first-aid kit.

I made my way to the aft cabin to join him. "How is she?"

Scarlett had swatted me away when I tried to take some of the glass from her leg. Declan and Rav, acting like more protective big brothers than I suspected Emmett ever had, both yelled at me to leave everything in place. No matter how much pain she was in, the order was clear—wait until they were on the plane and Rav would clean it up.

Had he been a medic? Or just familiar with combat injuries?

He latched the cabinet closed and turned slowly to look at me. "She's fine. She's a tough cookie."

Tough, but there had been such vulnerability, such fear in her eyes when the man's gun was on me.

When did Scarlett Reynolds get to be a woman?

Probably not until we had her brother back safe and sound, if nothing else.

The stoicism may not have been pummeled into her quite the same way it had been with me, but the result was the same. A parent with expectations that were so high, we spent our entire lives under that shadow. She nearly crumbled underneath it, isolating herself; while I'd fought so hard against it, I was a stranger to my own father.

"I'm going to—"

Rav's hand was on my chest before I made it a half step. "She needs rest. We all do." He jutted his chin toward Declan and Jayce, raising his voice. "That means you two as well. We only have two and a half hours on the flight to Venice, and we've been up all day. We don't know what's going to happen when we get to the meet, so we need everyone prepared."

Declan nodded. "How do we prepare when we don't know who we're meeting or what's going to happen? All we have is one phone call with an address in Venice and a time."

"Exactly." Rav pointed at their seats. Without argument, they stood and began the process to convert them into beds. "And that's why everyone needs to be at their sharpest. Fast reaction times. Quick decisions."

While Will had been following our schedule for the past week, Brie had been at their office twenty-four hours a day. She napped when her programs were running queries and searches, woke to adjust, then took more naps. For a computer geek, she had amazing stamina.

I placed my hand on Rav's wrist and slowly removed it from my chest. It was obvious he only needed one of the two to kill me if he so chose, so there was no reason to move too quickly around him. "I just want to check on her. It was an intense evening and I—"

Rav looked pointedly at the seat next to me and slid into the one opposite it. In the area next to the VIP cabin, that meant chairs facing each other on either side of a worktable.

Great. Another heart-to-heart with a Reynolds man. Another reminder to leave Scarlett alone.

All the same, I sat. We had two and a half hours. I had time to talk to her, but I had to get past her guard dog if I was going to before she dozed off. "She was upset about the gunman, and I wanted to be sure she was alright."

"He was threatening one of her team. Of course, she was upset."

"She's normally so controlled, but she froze. It was..." I glanced at the door beside him. "It was like she panicked. An absolute level of terror I wouldn't have expected from her."

Rav folded his arms, as he did so often, showcasing the ridiculously broad chest and bulging biceps. Protective mode was amping up even higher. "How much have you heard about Noah?"

Was this an ex? "I don't know who that is."

"He was our 2-IC on every job—"

Definitely military, otherwise he would have at least said 'second-in-command.'

"—until we had an incident two years ago and he died."

"She's mentioned that. Losing a team member after some communications problems?"

His gaze grew darker, reminding me of my screw-up at the architect's office. "He wasn't just a team member. He was her fiancé."

How did that relate to her reaction during our escape from the party?

"We'd recovered some diamonds which were stolen from a museum, but the thieves heard him on the way out." His gaze unfocused, no doubt going back to the moment. "We had two cars for the getaway. I was driving one. Zac—our regular driver—had the other. The thieves came out firing and..."

"They shot him?"

"Our comms were down, so I acted based on what I could see, and that was men with guns coming after Scarlett. I jumped out of my car, lay down covering fire, and got her into Zac's car." He shook his head. "Noah was only a few minutes behind her, so he took the second car and caught up with us."

It came as no surprise he would have jumped in front of a bullet for her. They obviously had history that went beyond normal friendship.

"They shot out his tires while we were crossing a bridge and he went over the side."

"And she saw it?"

He unwound one arm from across his chest to point at me, refolded it, and gave a slow blink. "I held that woman down in the back of Zac's car while she screamed at us to go back for him. Not only have I seen her grief, but I've caused it to keep her safe. I've seen true terror in her eyes, and been there when she's dealt with all of it. So, you listen to me—when I tell you she's fine, I mean she's not the kind of woman who needs a white knight to save her."

She probably hadn't been fine in a long time.

Rav leaned forward on the small table between the two chairs. "And in case this is about your dick, she's kissed me on an op too, so don't think that meant anything but saving her brother."

I leaned forward to match him, so he'd understand my honest reply. "That's not why I was going to see her."

Maybe not so honest.

"And Declan." He pointed over my shoulder. "And Zac and several of her marks."

I didn't clench my jaw. At least, not too tightly.

"And sometimes our contractors." His serious expression didn't falter. "They always have the worst time with it, because they think Scarlett on the job is a real person. But she's an act."

I nodded, as though none of this was a surprise to me. My biggest question was, where did Scarlett *on the job* end? Was Scarlett in the car after the architect's office *on the job*? Was Scarlett in the pub *on the job*? And was her bowed back and hungry moan all part of the job?

No matter what, I needed to know. I needed to hear it from her, not from one of her guard dogs, for once.

"I understand." All too well. Despite our vastly different upbringings, Scarlett and I ended up too similar. Put on the mask, shut people out, and get your job done. "But I still want to talk to her."

Rav sucked his tongue against his teeth, driving his intense gaze into me.

I wasn't backing down.

He stood and rapped on the door before sliding it open. "Malcolm wants to talk to you."

Scarlett's voice was quiet from the other cabin. "So, why are you standing there instead of him?"

"Because you need your rest more than he needs to talk to you."

"I'm a grown woman."

"Who sometimes needs a reminder she's not invincible."

She chuckled. That was a good sign. "Make sure you never say that around my mother. She'd fire your ass so fast."

Rav stepped back from the door and waved me in. "She's all yours."

Fifteen minutes ago, I thought that was true. In the hotel, she'd started to say something about when this was over, and I'd assumed, or maybe hoped, it was personal. Now? I was pretty sure I was about to fall flat on my face.

CHAPTER 31
SCARLETT

Rest? How was I supposed to rest after all of that?

Malcolm had braced my leg on his lap the entire drive to the private airfield. He'd ensured that even the few bumps we felt in the Bentley didn't jar anything. His new tuxedo pants were stained with my blood, and he waved it off like it was nothing.

Our husband-and-wife pilot team, along with their daughter, our flight attendant, had us in the air a half hour after we arrived.

Rav had forced me into the rearmost cabin on the plane, where he'd injected lidocaine into my leg and removed every shard of glass. He muttered the entire time, mostly in French, which told me how pissed off he was about everything. He'd never been good at sitting in the car.

But now my leg was bandaged and propped up on the divan, we were in the air, and Malcolm was standing in front of me. I turned off the tablet I'd been reviewing mission notes on and slid it into a side compartment.

I gestured to the single large seat in the cabin. "What's up?"

He slid the door closed and latched it. "I wanted to make sure you were okay."

"I'm okay. That's hardly a question you need to lock the door for."

Instead of taking the seat, he knelt next to me, his gaze resting on my leg. "You really gave me a scare."

"Me? You're the one who had a gun to his head."

He swallowed hard and shook his head. "You froze."

I pulled myself closer to the end of the divan and the wall, sitting up straighter. "I don't freeze."

"And you were crying."

"I don't cry."

He eased himself up, only far enough to sit on what little space there was available next to me. "You're in some serious denial."

So what if I was? I lived a fake life with fake people. I lied for a living. Wasn't the next logical step to lie about all of my feelings, including to myself? "You barely know me."

"True." His hand flexed over my thigh. "Permission for whatever level it might be to pat your thigh in support?"

My heart rate picked up at his silly request. "Permission granted."

He rested the hand on my mid-thigh, his touch feather soft. "In the hotel this afternoon—before Rav arrived—you were about to say something to me."

This was the conversation that required a locked door. "Was I?"

"You were." He inched closer. "You said, 'When this is all over…' and stopped. What were you going to say?"

I was supposed to be reading Brie's report. Mum would already have gone through the entire thing and picked out fifteen mistakes I'd made. I needed to spot them before she called me on them, so I had a retort.

More importantly, I needed to look at what she'd sent me about the man who pulled the gun on Malcolm. Declan's photographs had included a shot of his bound hands and a tattoo on the web between his thumb and forefinger. She suspected it was related to some organized crime family or gang but hadn't figured out which one yet.

But all I could see was the gun at Malcolm's neck. Other images bled into the periphery of my memory—him carrying me, the mischievous look in his eye when he brought up the idea about the Velatti, and the kiss. The all-consuming kiss in the light well that made me want to throw everything away.

I didn't know Malcolm Sharpe, not really. My brother trusted him. Some of my team even liked him. Was any of that enough for me? Did it really matter? "I was going to say, when this is all over..."

His hand crept up the outside of my thigh, toward my hip. "Yes?"

A pulse exploded from my core, and the same pathways lit up as when he'd kissed me. "I know you're going to go back to your old life, that you don't want to be part of a team, but I want you."

His hand skimmed up over my hip to my waist as he leaned in. "Reynolds Recoveries wants me? Or Scarlett Reynolds wants me?"

I sat up from the pillow Rav had forced behind me. I talked my way around people and situations for a living. Why was it so hard to tell him how I felt? "We have an opening."

We'd brought Malcolm on board for this mission because we were two down—Emmett and Zac. The truth was, we'd been one down before that. One down for the last two years, in a position we filled with a string of faceless contractors who didn't fit with the team. Malcolm barely fit, but somehow he did.

His big hand circled my waist, and he pulled me so close I felt his breath on my lips. "That wasn't the answer I was looking for."

Kissing him in the light well had been easy. It was the job. Until suddenly, it wasn't. The two of us sitting on my team's plane, no one watching us, no recording devices, no sneaking around—could it be as easy?

I still had two shirts left.

Noah would have wanted me to be happy and move on with my life. Not sit around for two years using him as an excuse.

There was no sign of hesitation or doubt in those beautiful blue eyes. All I saw was the same desire burning within him that was inside me. My heart raced at the thought of finally giving in to the attraction that had been simmering between us for too long.

I brushed my fingers over the side of his head, cupped the back of his neck, and pulled him to me. Our lips met and his grip around my waist grew tighter as his tongue plunged into my mouth. His other hand gripped the side of my neck as he ravaged my mouth.

It was real. It wasn't a job. He didn't need anything from me except—I shuddered. Except me. I threw my other arm around his back, and he jolted. Fuck. His bruises. "Sorry."

He shook his head and pulled closer. He kissed me again, deeper, hungrier.

I pressed my body against him, lifting my leg until the pain screamed up it again and I stiffened. "Shit. My leg."

He sprang up from the divan, brow creased with concern. "I'll get Rav."

"No." I grabbed his arm and pulled him down next to me. "We're both hurt. And I'm still not made of porcelain."

"What do you need?"

What was holding me back? I knew what I wanted. I wanted Malcolm. For one night, two nights, maybe a week. Get him out of my system and maybe go back to the real world. Throw those two shirts out, take down the last photo of me and Noah, and find a nice man who didn't mind how much I traveled.

I swallowed hard. "Scarlett."

He twisted his head, as though he hadn't heard what I'd said. "You need yourself?"

My body sank against the pillows and I stared up at the ceiling, laughing at how my command of the English language was failing me. "The one that wants you. That's me."

"That was a better answer." He braced a hand on the back of the divan and loomed over me. "Now tell me, what do you like?"

"What do you think I like?"

"I know you liked that kiss in the light well, no matter what you said after."

What level of physicality was latching my leg around his ass? Or the hard-on he'd pressed against me? "I wasn't the only one."

"You weren't."

"You were hard for me, Malcolm. I liked that, too."

He lowered himself, running a trail of kisses down my neck. "You seem like a woman who wants to be in control all the time. Wants a man who'll focus on what you already know gives you pleasure."

My breasts heaved as his lips continued to the hollow of my throat and along the V-neck of my sweater.

"I think you paint a pretty picture for the world and part of you is begging to let it all go. To surrender."

Surrender? More like escape. Let someone else take the risks and be in charge. Skip on getting the kudos and taking the blame. It was exactly what I wanted. But I couldn't say it—I'd dropped too many barriers around him already. "Or you're so cocky you assume the behavior you crave in a woman is exactly what they all want."

"And yet, here you are..." His fingers ghosted over the curve of my breast, and I arched into his touch. "Letting go so I can take over."

"Doesn't that mean I'm still technically in control?"

He lifted his head to smirk at me. "Permission to skip level six and the knee to my groin, boss?"

"Good answer." I tore my sweater off, revealing my favorite black silk bra with ivory frastaglio embroidery. "And permission granted."

"Fuck me," he breathed, his eyes consuming every inch of my exposed skin. "And I'd thought your dress last weekend was the sexiest thing I'd ever seen."

"It gets better." I slid a hand down the front of his pants, stroking the outline of the growing bulge. "The thong matches."

He tucked one arm behind my waist and edged me along

the divan, so I was lying down and he was between my legs. "There. You're supposed to be resting."

"I'm not interested in rest right now." I popped the button on his jeans, my fingers deftly navigating through the fly of his boxer briefs to wrap around his hardening cock. "This is what I want."

"No." He removed my hand from his pants, pinning it above my head with one hand, while he redid his zipper.

I tried to lift my hand, but he held it firmly in place. "What are you doing?"

"Taking control. Now stay put." He loosened his grip, but I didn't move. "With your permission?"

"Kiss me," I whispered. "Like you did the second time in the light well."

"With pleasure." His fingers threaded into my loose hair, and he lowered onto an elbow, settling some of his weight on me. The kiss was slow, his tongue sweeping across mine as he ground his hard cock between my legs.

I moaned into his mouth, keeping it as quiet as possible, too aware of the team being on the other side of the door. Unable to keep my hands above my head, I wrapped an arm around the uninjured part of his back, the other driving into his hair. A bed would have been better. Hell, a floor space wider than the aisle between the divan and the chair would have been better than the tiny couch.

He broke from the kiss and licked his lips. "This doesn't fold out into a double bed, does it?"

"No." Sadly.

"We'll have to make do, then." He kissed and licked his way down my chest, folding the waistband of my tights down so he could see the top of the thong. "That *is* nice."

I ran my hands over my breasts, into my hair, closing my eyes to live in the sensations. It had been far too long since someone else had pleasured me, and I was going to take every second he'd give. "Keep going."

Malcolm left the tights in place, his lips warm and gentle as he kissed the sensitive spot at the inside of my hip, grazing down the front of my thigh. The man was a tease, which shouldn't have surprised me. "Patience."

"You want me to beg, don't you?"

He chuckled, warm breath spreading through the fabric, heating the juncture of my thighs. "I don't think you ever would."

I bit down on my lip, trying to contain my smile. "Please?"

"That's not begging." He winked at me, locking his eyes with mine as he trailed kisses back up to where he'd started at my hipbone, avoiding what I wanted.

"Pretty please?"

He ran one lazy hand between my thighs, applying too little pressure, and paused. "You suck at begging."

I shivered, grinding myself against his hand. When he tried moving it, I clamped a hand over his and applied the pressure myself.

"Told you so." His nostrils flared, the hunger in his eyes palpable as he withdrew his hand from my grip and curled his fingers around my waistband. He eased my tights down, inch by infuriating inch. "A woman who knows what she wants. I like that."

"Good." I took a handful of his hair, lifting my hips so he could undress me. "Because I want your mouth—"

A fist pounded on the door. "Scarlett!"

"Go away!" I shouted, louder than need be.

"The tattoo! It's Fenix!" said Rav, his voice growing more insistent. "The one from the Barton Safe company."

I shot up to sitting, nearly knocking Malcolm to the floor. "What?"

"Brie just sent the details." Rav—or someone—attempted to open the door. "We need to talk. Now."

CHAPTER 32
MALCOLM

I KNEW three things about phoenixes. One, they were mythological birds that rose from their own ashes. Two, the rest of the flight to Venice had been dominated by discussions of phoenixes, the Fenix Group, and the identity of the mysterious man who pulled the gun on me. And three, the phoenix was the most successful cockblocker I'd ever experienced in my life.

Two weeks ago, I'd stolen the Reynolds getaway driver's phone, after receiving a tip from my only team member I'd met face-to-face for the Codex heist: Reynolds had the schematics for the Codex's case, and we needed it. We'd thought that gave us the upper hand, since we'd taken that information away from them. Despite it all, Reynolds had still beaten us to the prize.

While my balls attempted to recover from the not-close-enough call in Scarlett's cabin, I discovered Reynolds had broken into the company that designed the case—Barton Safes just outside of Boston—and secured a second set of specs.

There, they'd stumbled on a duplicate set written up for something called The Fenix Group.

None of it mattered to me. The Codex job was a grand failure, but it was in my past. Their second sighting of Fenix wasn't important to me, either, since that was a longer-term concern for Scarlett and her team.

Perhaps Scarlett and I had made too much noise, so Rav used it to stop us. Because after the flurry of discussion, he barred me from entering the back cabin with her.

After touching down in Venice, we took a water taxi to St. Mark's Square and our hotel. Everyone collapsed for a few hours of sleep. I'd hoped Scarlett and I could have picked up where we'd stopped on the plane, but I was as exhausted as the rest of them. Now, we were on our way to the meet point.

Everything was finally going to plan. It had been a screwed-up path to get here, but the five of us were walking across a small bridge to a large dark-wood doorway. On the other side of that doorway would be Emmett Reynolds and the end of this ordeal.

I could barely keep my eyes off Scarlett, our bodies practically vibrating when we got too close to each other. The temperature was far warmer in Venice than in London, and she had her hair up in a messy bun. She wore dark-gray pants and a silk blouse in ivory, which reminded me of the lace on her bra. What was she wearing under this one? Once we had Emmett, we'd go back to the hotel, and I'd find out. And with nothing else to bother us, I'd find out a hell of a lot more.

The narrow bridge led to an even narrower road between the two buildings ahead of us and to the double-doors of the house where we were to meet the clowns. The bridge crossed a narrow canal, with a water door built into the side of the home—arched with a portcullis-style gate which could be raised to allow a boat inside.

Rav walked at the front of the group. "I'm going in first."

"You'll do no such thing," snapped Scarlett. "We're playing this exactly the same way as we play every other situation where I'm negotiating. I go in first and you're behind me."

"Where will Malcolm be?"

"Beside me."

The big man looked like he was about to snap my neck. How much would it take to earn his respect or trust? Or until he stopped glowering at me like the man who was risking Scarlett's life? Probably a lot. Probably a lifetime.

Her lips tightened. "He was the one with Emmett when they took him. He was the one who was supposed to deliver the Codex to them. He is going to be up front with me."

Rav gave her a curt nod. "Then I open the door, I go in first, but I hold it open for the two of you." He inclined his head toward Jayce and Declan behind me. "You two, stay by the door."

Declan put up his hands as if in surrender. "Don't need to tell me twice."

From what I'd learned, Jayce did all of her work in secret, and Declan was a very sheltered member of the team. If it was going to be an issue, they should've stayed at the hotel. However, this was a family affair. They all wanted to be sure Emmett was safe and had refused to stay back.

"Brie," said Scarlett, "you got eyes?"

We hadn't had time to see Will before flying out of London, so we'd brought the drone I'd recovered with us. The damage from landing in the hedge had been slight, and Will walked Declan through minor repairs while we were on the jet. The plan was for it to hover fifty feet above the open courtyard in the center of the palazzo we were to meet them at.

"I do. There are two men with clown masks inside."

Rav said, "Inside the courtyard?"

"Yes, but no sign of Emmett."

"There were three of them at the poker game." My every instinct told me to take Scarlett's hand or put my hand on her back. Something to show my support. What was coming over me? I didn't show people support. I worked. I did jobs. This whole team thing was screwing with my brain. "The one with the green hair was the only one who talked. He was also the biggest. Red hair was the smallest, and blue hair—even though he never said anything—felt like he was in charge."

Will chimed in, "I'm going to maneuver the drone around a little. The opening in the roof isn't giving us a full picture straight down. There's an overhang, so maybe he's hidden from sight."

Rav paused before opening the door.

Brie said, "The third clown was hidden underneath an overhang. He's standing in front of a door in the courtyard that's closed."

Emmett had to be safe. As stressed as Scarlett was, I was feeling an equal weight of guilt. He'd saved me from a beating all those years ago, and then he'd received one... Why? Because he was the one with the family and I wasn't. If I'd had anyone I could count on to save me, maybe I would've been left behind as the leverage.

Just don't be a trap.

Against my better instincts, Scarlett's warnings, and Rav's

threats, I slipped my hand around hers. I gave it a quick squeeze. "He's in there. This'll be over soon."

"One way or another." She squeezed back and withdrew her hand. That wasn't how professionals behaved. Showing her feelings was a weakness. How many stupid rules had her mother ingrained in her head through her life? Rules that isolated her as much as I'd isolated myself.

Rav pounded on the door twice, right hand at his waist, where he carried his concealed gun. He eased the door open, moving as though he were breaching a stronghold. Slow, observant. I could have imagined him with an M4 or something even more lethal in his hands.

"Come in," came a distorted voice from inside.

Rav pushed the door open wide, and as planned, he stood in the doorway as Scarlett and I, then Jayce and Declan walked in.

The palazzo courtyard was small. Maybe four hundred square feet, covered in a pale stone that looked like aged marble, with a wide stone staircase heading up the right wall to another door. Windows overlooked the courtyard from the second floor, and the terra-cotta roof was visible above. No sign of the drone, but it would be up there.

Exactly as Brie and Will reported, only the clowns were in the courtyard. Red hair stood behind a three-foot high stone well, blue hair stood next to the stairs, and Greenie—the mouthpiece—stood by the single door on this level. Each had a gun at their waist, but they were all holstered.

Blue hair nodded toward the door, and Rav closed it behind himself. The courtyard was a couple of steps lower than the entryway. The water entrance took up part of the floor space, nothing more than a small pool behind the portcullis. Jayce and Declan remained on the high ground, while Rav loomed just behind Scarlett and me.

Greenie didn't budge from his spot by the door. "Where's the ring?"

Scarlett said, "Where is my—"

Greenie put up a hand. "You're not the courier, Malcolm is. I don't want to hear any of your pretty little words."

Whether Scarlett was fuming underneath her polished exterior, I couldn't tell. I'd have to know her far better than I did to have any clue about that.

I said, "The trade was the Chalcis Ring for Emmett Reynolds. We have the ring, so where is Emmett?"

Greenie knocked three times on the door, which opened. Relief flooded my body when I saw a bruised, but not broken or dead, Emmett.

Scarlett's shuddering breath was so well-masked that I only noticed it because I was next to her. She reached into the front of her waistband, into the hidden compartment where she'd secured the ring, and pulled it out. "One ring. One man."

The clown with the red hair gripped the well in front of himself and looked at the one with blue hair. Blue hair nodded, and Greenie approached Scarlett, gloved hand out. "We need to verify it's the real thing."

She gave him the ring, and Greenie disappeared into the room, shoving Emmett out as he went.

Emmett's face was various shades of yellow, green, and blue, but both eyes were open, and he only walked with a slight limp. "Sorry, Scar."

"Well, I only told you not to get arrested. I guess you did that." She cracked the faintest hint of a smile, but the long blink told me her *Reynolds women don't cry* mantra was flitting through her head. She wrapped her arms loosely around him and whispered, "Thank god you're okay."

"Don't you go getting emotional on me now, sis."

She let go of him to cock her eyebrow.

Greenie burst out of the room and over to Blue's side. "He confirmed it's the real thing. We've got it."

Red-haired clown said in a distorted voice, "We need to get it to the island."

Emmett held his left hand out to me, keeping the right one close to his body. It must've been injured, as well. "Sorry for getting you tangled up in all this."

"It's been an adventure." I looked down at Scarlett, at her strong, impassive features, and felt a swell of desire. I'd never met anyone like her before, and now that we had Emmett, I'd have my chance to explore her further. "And your team is... impressive."

The door cracked open behind us, and Rav said, "Emmett first."

Emmett smiled at me in a way that reminded me of his sisters and mother. It was the eyes—they all had the same eyes, despite the different colors. He patted my arm and walked past me, as Rav gave instructions to Declan and Jayce next.

Scarlett and I took slow steps backward, not taking our eyes off the clowns. It felt too easy. Were these gun-toting maniacs really men of their word? Maybe easy wasn't quite right, considering everything we'd had to go through to get the ring. But if that was all they wanted, we were home free.

The clowns with green hair and red hair toyed with the ring, but blue hair watched us from behind his mask.

I took the first half-step up to the entryway level, but Scarlett's ridiculous heel caught on it, and she stumbled. I grabbed her elbow and steadied her.

Blue hair lurched forward at the same time, reaching for her. "Scarlett!"

Her body went rigid. And her mouth slowly fell open, along with her eyes.

His voice hadn't been distorted. I recognized it.

Rav spat, "Get your ass out here! Now!"

"No." Scarlett gripped my hand so tight her fingernails could have drawn blood. "No, it can't be."

CHAPTER 33

SCARLETT

Someone was holding my hand, keeping me upright. If I wanted to know who, I'd have to look away from the clown with the blue hair. The clown with the voice I knew. That had been my constant companion for years.

My stomach twisted and flopped, and I was sure I was going to either vomit, faint, or scream. I took a step toward him. It couldn't be.

"Those damn shoes," said Blue Hair. It was him.

I didn't have to see his face to know. I let go of the hand which had held me up and took the few steps which separated me from the greatest lie of my life.

His scent was still the same. Some strange combination that reminded me of baby powder and musk. Not cologne, just him. I still had that scent on two shirts, so I knew it too well.

Greenie grabbed him by the shoulder and spun him around. "What are you doing? We're almost there. We need to go."

The blue-haired clown pulled off the mask and faced me.

"Noah," I breathed. The tears clogged my throat, spreading up my sinuses until the pressure built so high in my eyes they leaked out. A thousand memories flashed through my brain. The jobs we'd done together, dinners with my friends, our engagement at Niagara Falls. Watching him go over the side of the bridge, to the river below. The funeral with the fake ashes.

I had nothing to say. No words formed in my brain.

Someone was talking behind me, maybe several someones, but I couldn't make anything out. My head was swimming. Which one of my mother's lessons was supposed to prepare me for this?

Someone grabbed my hand and tugged me backward. Rav? It was probably Rav. He was the one who always took care of me. He was the one who held me down while I watched Noah's car go over the bridge.

A single word escaped my reeling brain. "How?"

The tugging on my arm switched to an arm around my waist that lifted me up, forcing me backward.

Noah sprang for me and grabbed both of my shoulders, but my protector pushed him away. "If you want to know the truth, meet me on San Michele at eleven o'clock tonight."

CHAPTER 34
SCARLETT

By seven o'clock, I was still wired. Brie and Will had used the drone to follow the clowns, but with so many close buildings, overhangs, and covered walkways, they lost them. Not that it mattered, because if I wanted the details, I knew exactly where to be.

Scream, Scarlett. Break something. But whatever you do— Reynolds women don't cry. No matter how many times I told myself that, the tears streamed down my face, as much an insult to my pride as discovering Noah was alive.

I picked up one of the sleek dining room chairs with its blue leather upholstery and carved wooden frame, heaving it into the air. Before I could carry through with smashing it, I let it drop to the floor and sank down next to it.

Alive. He was alive. The words were a dagger in my heart. Two years he'd been alive and never came for me. Never sent me a message. Didn't come home. Left me to fucking mourn him.

If it had been amnesia, I could've forgiven him. He could have at least fucking lied and said it was amnesia. But no, he just spit out my name, plain as day, with no hesitation. What the hell had he been doing for the last two years?

Why kidnap my brother? Why not come directly to us? Why did he want the Codex? Why meet in Venice? Why San Michele?

I crumpled, resting my forehead against the warm parquet floor, and just let it flow out of me. This wasn't supposed to be how today turned out.

Why reveal himself?

Noah was experienced in this game. He worked with Reynolds for two years, and we didn't hire anyone but the best. He was a planner and a manipulator. Everything he did had a reason.

That included showing his face and telling me to meet him. What else did I have that he wanted?

I had to put him out of my mind. Focus on the good things. I was in a beautiful city with my team. My brother was safe. We'd taken him to the hospital where they checked him over, ran a few tests, and they were holding him overnight for monitoring. Once our flight crew had time to rest and Emmett was out, we'd fly home, and life would go back to normal. We would take on some low-risk jobs for a few months and breathe.

And the first thing I'd do when I got home would be to burn that photograph of Noah. Maybe stab it a few times. Run it through a shredder. Then I'd burn it.

Someone knocked on my door.

"Go away!"

The knock came again, followed by a gentle voice. "Scarlett? It's Malcolm."

I sprang off the floor, rubbed my hands over my cheeks as I

dashed toward the door, and ripped it open. I snapped, "What do you want?"

He looked me up and down, not the way he had every other time. Not the way that said he wanted in my pants, and not even in a way that said he was judging me for my disheveled appearance. Bare feet, half-tucked blouse, and all the hair I'd ripped out of my bun. No doubt smeared makeup to complete the picture.

"Rav said he came to talk to you and you tried to hit him." Malcolm grimaced. "I suspect he would have let you if it would help."

I blinked at him a few times, and an almost laugh burst out of me. "I also threw a chair at him, but he caught it."

Malcolm stifled a laugh. If he really wanted to hide it, he could have. He was likely testing my mood. "I'm not so sure I could catch a chair if you throw one at me."

Good thing he hadn't arrived ten minutes ago.

"That was quite the... ah... moment after we got Emmett?"

I dragged the back of my hand across my eyes, drying the slowing tears. "Do you want to come in?"

He nodded and walked in past me. "The tears were a surprise, I've got to say."

"Reynolds women don't cry." I locked the door and pressed my forehead to it. "Tears are a tool."

"If we're speaking plainly..." His arms slid around my waist from behind and he rested his head against my shoulder. "They're a pretty effective tool."

I sank into him, running my hands over his arms and holding tight. That was so much better than the floor. "They weren't for you."

"Still..." He pressed a gentle kiss to my neck. "I know Emmett was our focus, but all I wanted to do was hold you. Make sure you were okay."

"You were the one holding my hand, weren't you?" Everything that happened after I saw Noah was a blur.

"I was."

"All the way up the stairs and you shoved..." I shuddered, gripping Malcolm tighter. "You shoved him off me."

"Apparently, I don't like men trying to manhandle you."

I turned in his embrace so I could look up into his eyes. Run my fingers through his dark-blond hair. Marvel at his serious expression. This crazy moment between us was almost over. Back to reality. "They should release Emmett from the hospital tomorrow. Once the jet's ready, we'll fly home. I can have them file a flight plan that takes you back to New York after that, if you want?"

"What's your plan tonight?"

"That didn't answer my question." It avoided my real question: Was there a chance there was something else going on between us? Something other than a need to get him out of my system?

"Because I need to know the answer to my question first." His arms remained firm around my waist. They didn't move, didn't lower to my ass, he didn't even draw little circles with his thumbs. "And in case there's any doubt what that means—I want to know if you're planning to run off after him tonight."

"Does it matter?"

He raked his teeth over his bottom lip, gaze roaming the wall next to us before returning to me. "Before we got Emmett back,

I had every intention of finishing what we started on the plane. Maybe even inviting you to spend a few days in Venice with me so we could fully scratch the itch we both obviously have."

My stomach clenched. I'd hadn't been sure if I wanted more than one tumble in the sheets with him, but the second those words were out of his mouth, everything was clear. I did want more. "Just an itch?"

He shrugged. "We've only known each other a week. It takes time to figure out if there's more than that."

I removed his arms from my waist and led him through the sitting room. My former fiancé—was he even former now that he was alive?—had vanished, letting everyone believe he was dead. I couldn't pass up the one chance I had to find out the truth. Otherwise, I'd spend the rest of my life wondering. "I'm going to San Michele tonight."

His grip tightened and he halted, bringing me to a stop. "I'm coming with you."

"I can handle my—"

"I'm not arguing with you over this." He yanked me to him, so my free hand landed on his broad, muscular chest.

"What are you?" I tilted my head back, licking my lips in invitation. "Jealous?"

His eyes narrowed as he pinned my held hand behind my back. "Yes."

I blinked. That was supposed to be a tease. We hadn't known each other long enough for him to be possessive, let alone protective. But there it was. The fierce gleam in his eyes and the way he held on when I mentioned going without him. It wasn't something I expected. How was I supposed to react to that?

Malcolm had stood up to my mother and was trying to stand up for me now. How had we gotten so far, so fast?

"I'm only going for information." My chest swelled, and the need I'd felt on the plane threatened to take over my ability to speak. "You're the one I want. In my bed."

One breath passed between us, and his lips crashed into mine, stealing my breath and echoing my words in one swift movement. His tongue was in my mouth and his hands on my blouse.

This was what I needed. An explosion of emotions and release. Shutting off my brain. I popped the button on his jeans, while he did the same with my pants. His shirt flew, I undid my own, and we only made it as far as the table with the chairs I'd wanted to smash.

He tossed a foil packet onto the table and ran a hand over my breast. "Pink bra tonight. I like it."

"I want it fast and hard, Malcolm." I twisted my fingers in his belt loops and pulled him closer. "Right here."

"You want to be in control this time?"

"No." I held him firm, his hardening cock pressed against my abdomen. I lifted on my toes to kiss him, but he avoided my mouth.

"Then take off your pants and underwear."

I did as I was told, easing them to the floor. Before I could step out of them, he picked me up and I wrapped my legs around him. "Table's too low. That wouldn't have worked."

Effortlessly, he swiped the condom and carried me to the bed, tossing me onto the plush covers. "How's your leg feel?"

"How's your back feel?"

"Lay down. Spread yourself open for me." He stood at the

foot of the bed and undid his pants, stroking his hard cock once it was free. "I want to taste you, Scarlett."

I tossed my shirt and bra aside, then shifted backward.

He dropped the pants and crawled over the bed, the mattress dipping with each movement. He retraced his path from the plane, kissing up the inside of my thigh, skipping the part of me that burned for him, climbing up my abdomen.

"Please."

His long fingers circled my breasts and he squeezed, sucking one nipple into his mouth, then the other. "That's still not good enough."

"I said fast and hard, dammit," I gasped.

"Screw that."

Heat pulsed through my core, spreading out to every cell of my body. I grabbed his head and pulled it up so he had to look at me. "Screw *me*."

"The lady's demanding, isn't she?" One of his hands left my chest and landed on my clit, just like on the plane. Not moving. Not doing anything. Trying to kill me. He whispered, "Say it."

"Please, Malcolm. Oh my fucking god, please." My fingers dug into his scalp, the intensity inside me escalating. "I need you inside of me. Now."

He chuckled, so low and rich it jostled in my stomach. Inch-by-inch, he moved down my body, his tongue continuing to taunt and tease until his face arrived between my thighs.

I let my head fall back onto the pillow, waves of pleasure washing over me the second his mouth touched me. He was good. His tongue was as magical on my clit as I'd imagined.

That was it. One good orgasm and I'd have him out of my system, then I could get back to the real world.

Or maybe a half-dozen.

"A half-dozen what?"

Shit. So much for my inside voice. One more ounce of self-control he'd ruined. "Orgasms."

He lifted his head and quirked an eyebrow, those infuriatingly sexy blue eyes sparkling with mischief. "I knew you were demanding, but—"

"Shut up and get back to work."

"Taskmaster." Without taking his eyes off mine, he sucked hard on my clit. He caressed the hollow where my abdomen met my hip with one hand, the fingers of his other skimming my cleft. "Did you see where the condom landed?"

"No idea."

He grunted, not moving, not looking for it. He'd make me wait for that part.

That was okay. I just needed one. One fast, one hard, one whatever he was going to give me. I just needed one. I groaned, "Malcolm. Please."

Two fingers delved inside me, bringing what he was doing with his tongue to a crescendo. He worked them in and out, keeping rhythm with his tongue. Up and up and up, my pleasure rose. He sucked again, hard, maintaining the pressure until my body clenched around his fingers. Pain streaking up my leg from the cuts and stitches, and I didn't care.

Every muscle drew tight, and I cried out his name, "Malcolm!" as the orgasm crashed over me. It drove through my entire being, drowning out every voice, every worry, every moment of stress. Perfection. Bliss. Wonder.

His fingers slowed, remaining deep inside, and I blew out one very long, arduous breath.

"Oh my fucking fuck, Malcolm."

"So... good?"

"You're an ass," I said with a laugh, my eyelids unable to reopen.

The bed moved and dipped as he made his way up to my face. "Look at me."

I did as he asked and was rewarded with a broad smile. "Yes, good."

"Excellent." He took one of my hands, limp as it was, and wrapped it around his shaft. "Because we've apparently got five more to go."

CHAPTER 35

MALCOLM

Scarlett stroked my cock, sucking her bottom lip into her mouth, as though she were fantasizing what I'd taste like.

I bucked my hips, and her grip tightened. My head rolled back as she gained speed, sitting up as she worked me. Watching her release had been such a turn-on, I was already breaking. Too soon.

Her lips found my neck and she nipped at the skin under my ear as she continued pumping me. "Come for me, Malcolm."

"Not yet." I groaned and snapped upright, every ounce of my being protesting. I shoved her onto the mattress so hard she bounced. "Where's that condom? I need to be inside of you."

She didn't search for it, just ran her fingers between her legs, rubbing them against her clit, dipping in and out of herself. "Yeah, that's what I want. I want that big cock fucking me."

Shit. I froze, watching her pleasure herself, watching her

writhe under her own touch. Scarlett Reynolds was the sexiest thing I'd ever seen. And she was mine. Right now, in this moment, that woman was all mine.

This was a mistake. Our relationship was built on lies and mistrust. From the moment I'd first seen her, it was all lies.

Except the way my heart swelled whenever I saw her. The way it sank when I'd seen the blood on her leg. The walls I'd built up to protect my heart from getting hurt were crumbling one brick at a time, and I was useless to do anything about it.

Yeah, this was a mistake. But it was one I was going to make, no matter the fallout.

My hand wandered over the sheets to find the condom, while I leaned forward to press my lips against hers. It was slow and deep, our tongues exploring every inch of each other's in a way that magnified the throbbing in my cock. I needed to sink myself into her wet heat.

She ground herself against me, bracing my shaft against her clit to give us both friction until I found what I needed.

The tightness at the base of my spine intensified, and I could feel my release coming. Still too early, so I pulled away from her to search in earnest.

"You'll need to be better prepared next time."

"I get a next time?" I snagged the foil wrapper from where it had landed by the pillow, and she took it from me.

"So far, so good." She ripped the packet open and guided it over me with an inspiring speed and eagerness. "Check in again later."

Before I had time to think of a witty response, she was on her back and had latched a leg around my hips, pulling me to her. I paused when my tip pressed against her folds, fighting against her insistence. From the moment we'd met, she was strength and control. A few tiny slips here and there, but she never handed herself over. "Now beg."

Her leg tightened. She was stronger than I'd expected.

I slipped inside her, no more than an inch. Sharing the tiniest fraction of her heat. All I wanted was to see her vulnerable. That should have been what I saw, with her naked and sprawled on the bed, but she still thought she was running things.

"Let go," I growled, rocking my hips from side to side. "Show me you want me. Don't just tell me."

She closed her eyes and clenched her jaw, obviously fighting with herself. What was going through her head? Angry she'd given in to the first orgasm so easily? Turned off because of my play?

I sank in another inch, her walls stretching around me. "Show me this isn't just an itch, Scarlett."

Her eyes flashed open and she blinked slowly, as though trying to absorb my words. "Why didn't you tell me about the bruises earlier?"

The clowns—her former fiancé and whoever else was with him—had claimed they didn't know which one of us had taken the Codex. But Noah knew. The second he spoke to her in the palazzo, I recognized his voice as my anonymous employer from the Codex job. The manuscript and the ring were definitely linked. By him. "I think we have other priorities right now."

She lifted her hips, and I pulled away as she did. "You didn't want me to think you were weak."

"And you hide your feelings from everyone because you don't want them to think the same."

"Please, Malcolm?" She covered her face with her hands

and let out a shaky breath. "You've seen me more exposed and weak than anyone outside of my team. At first, I couldn't help it, but now..."

I pushed into her, sinking deep inside. My body screamed at me for going so slowly, but it would pay off in the end. I didn't want just sex. I wanted the connection she'd tried denying me.

A full-body shudder wracked her.

"But now *what*, Scarlett?"

"He hurt me, Malcolm." Her voice quavered, and when she pulled away her hands, there were tears again. "I want to remember there's good things and good people in the world. That I'm worth sticking—"

She didn't finish, but she didn't have to.

Fuck me, but that wasn't begging. That was miles beyond what I'd hoped for. It was vulnerability. Honesty. "You're worth so much more than that."

She swallowed hard, the honesty obviously sticking in her throat as tightly as it did in mine. "Show me."

I pulled out and slammed into her, and she cried out. I did it again and again. Harder and harder, until I was pounding into her like she'd wanted me to. I couldn't go slow. Couldn't stop the need. I wanted her too much. Needed her too much.

She wanted me too. The only words that escaped her lips were moans of *yes* and *more* and *please*. The tears vanished, evaporating in the furious heat between us.

I gritted my teeth to hold back the tidal wave building inside me. Being with her was too easy, and I was already too close. I reached down, stroking her clit as I pounded into her. "I want to see you come on my cock."

"I can't." Her eyes squeezed shut, her head thrashing back and forth on the pillow. "Not yet."

"You're so fucking tight. You fit me so perfectly." I slammed into her, and she arched up beneath me. "You can do anything."

Her breath caught, every muscle in her body going rigid.

I kept going. Kept touching her. Kept shoving her to the edge of another release.

She tossed her head back, pleasure and pain warring on her face. The orgasm consumed her, and she opened her mouth, but little sound left her lips. She just moaned and moaned, and I rode the waves of her climax as her pussy pulsed around me.

I tried pulling out to flip her over and finish her from behind, but her leg tightened around my waist.

"Let me watch you." She was still breathing hard, eyes barely fluttering open. "Please?"

I let go of her clit and dragged my hand up her chest, to her neck, and I wove my fingers into her hair. My voice was raw as I continued driving into her, burying myself as deep as I could. "Scarlett."

The orgasm ripped through me, a shockwave of pleasure so intense I could barely function. The pleasure went on and on, and I couldn't do anything but ride it out. Couldn't think of anything but the woman beneath me.

She opened her eyes as I collapsed on top of her. Her lips parted, but she said nothing.

I pressed my forehead to hers, unable to do anything but breathe.

The stress over my failed heist, the guilt over leaving Emmett behind, the stupid need to prove myself to this amazing woman. It all faded as her arms wrapped around me.

It was me, Scarlett. I was working with the gunman in Boston. I stole Zac's phone. When I saw Emmett at the poker game, my first thought was to get the Codex from him. The truth was all right there, and I wanted to give it to her. I wanted to be as vulnerable as she'd been—to show her she wasn't alone. There was something real between us.

But if I told her, she'd leave.

She'd see the real me and toss me aside like everyone else did.

I rolled off her and lay on my back. She followed, draping her hand over my chest. My heart slammed against that hand, begging to escape. I had to leave her before I gave any more of myself to a woman I didn't deserve. But I didn't want to leave.

After a quick glance to find the trashcan, I removed the condom and tossed it in the general direction.

"So..." Scarlett propped her head up on my chest. "Was that a half dozen total or each?"

I chuckled and combed my fingers through her hair.

Her lazy smile appeared, and another truth came over me.

I'm falling in love with you, Scarlett.

A fresh wave of panic crashed into my brain. This was definitely a mistake.

CHAPTER 36
SCARLETT

THE THICK PLUM comforter had landed on the floor at least an hour ago, pillows strewn across the room, and the thin white sheet lay in a crumpled heap. Twilight settled through the room from the ceiling height terrace doors which overlooked St. Mark's Square.

"Three more to go for you." Malcolm's fingers trailed up and down my forearm, draped across his bare chest.

I chuckled and closed my eyes, nestling my head in the crook of his shoulder. "I can't believe I said that out loud."

"*I* can't believe you said that out loud." His breathing was soft and rhythmic, a dramatic departure from the heated grunts and pants which had occupied my ears for the last two hours. "It means you'll need to agree to a few more days here with me though. Not sure I can take care of all that by tomorrow."

"It's a little late to ask now, but..." I curled my leg higher on his thigh, pressing my body to his side. "You're single, right?"

"As single as someone can be."

"Good." Me, too, except for the suddenly alive fiancé. *Stop thinking about him, Scar. You're naked and wrapped around another man. Noah's your past.*

"I, ah..." He shifted, so the arm I was lying on ran down my hip. His words came out quiet and hesitant. "My father moved us around a lot when I was younger, and I had a hard time making friends."

"Hard to believe."

He shrugged. "It took me a while and several boarding schools, but I eventually figured out that people expect specific behaviors from you. After you reach a certain age, everyone wants the new kids to be the same as them. Adapting was the best way to make friends."

"Like flirting with the architect?"

"I may be a private investigator and spend a lot of time sitting in cars, watching people for the information I need, but I've..." His heart rate sped up underneath me. "I've used that skill when it's needed."

So long as he didn't tell me that's all this was, it didn't matter. It meant he was like me.

"That's why I didn't tell you about the bruises when I showed up on your doorstep. Your friend's reaction indicated flirting with you was my best bet, and that wouldn't have meshed with sympathy for the bruises."

I fought against rolling my eyes at the memory. Heather had just finished pointing out that Noah wasn't as perfect as I'd convinced myself he'd been. Was there any way I could tell them the truth about him without revealing the extralegal portion of my job?

"When flirting didn't get me the results I wanted, I figured you'd use whatever excuse you could to leave me behind, so I kept it quiet."

"I like hearing about the real you, Malcolm."

He pulled me tight against himself, and his heart continued skipping. "Sometimes, it's hard to remember who that is."

"I know the feeling." That was why, no matter how busy life got, I held on to my girlfriends. I covered up the true reason for most of my trips abroad, but there was more than enough legitimate work for them to hear snippets of my boring tech security or data recovery jobs. It was also why I clung to the core of the Reynolds team—most of them had been my friends or family since I was young. Since *we* stopped moving.

"Your mother trained you, didn't she?"

My childhood had been more like a ridiculous story from a movie than a real childhood. She didn't launch Reynolds Recoveries—at least not officially—until I graduated from university, but she'd had me help her on jobs long before that. We'd always done good work. It took its toll on our relationship, but that was my job as the oldest—bear the brunt of everything and protect Emmett and Brie.

"She's a thief? Or..."

My mother had never told me the entire truth. All I knew was that she had contacts around the world, knew how to do things normal mothers didn't, and that she refused to talk about what she did before I came around. "My dad was the thief. Is? I don't know what the right word is there."

"What does that mean?"

"He's in prison. Has been since I was twelve."

Malcolm shifted underneath me, and I craned my neck up at him. "Twelve? Your father's a lifer?"

"Twenty-five years. Espionage." It was a matter of public record, so there was no point in hiding it. All my friends knew the basics. Most of our clients may have even known. In some circles, it gave us credence.

"And here I thought it was like mother, like daughter." He eased back down and pulled me tighter.

He was right.

The unspoken truth Emmett, Brie, and I had agreed long ago to never dig into was that we all suspected Dad had taken the fall for Mum. Why else would she have given me a lock-picking set for Christmas when I was twelve? One I'd shared with Declan, my buddy who loved puzzles and breaking down things to figure out how they worked? How else could she have gotten my friend Zac out of his first ten speeding tickets? Or found Rav when he'd gone off the grid. "Oh, there's a lot of that, too."

Malcolm rolled and pulled me on top of him, pushing my hair back from my face. "Funny how our parents were so different, and yet we ended up the same."

"Scarred?"

"Searching for connection, while still being scared to death of it?"

Right again. I had lots of connections, but only the ones I'd had since before I knew better. I leaned forward and our lips met, tongues swirling slowly around each other. Even if this was only short-lived, it was a new connection.

The alarm on my phone went off and I startled. "Damn."

"No time for another connection?"

I crawled over to the bedside table and turned off the alarm. "I need to get ready."

He grabbed me, throwing my flailing body to the bed and pinning me. "We. We need to get ready."

Those words had sat at the back of my mind since he'd said them. Would he keep me safe? Or put me in danger? Put himself in danger? Was it a romantic gesture or—

"Stop thinking and say yes." Malcolm tapped my forehead. "If it were Rav saying that to you, I bet you wouldn't be debating."

"I am not talking about Rav while I'm naked." I shoved him off me and rolled from the bed. "I want to grab a quick shower."

"Perfect!" He shot out of the bed and threw his arms around me. "We can continue this discussion in the shower."

I quirked an eyebrow at him. He wouldn't take no for an answer. And maybe I was alright with that.

Someone knocked on the door.

Malcolm held tighter. "Ignore it."

"It's probably turndown service or something." I glanced around the room, at the complete disarray. "Why don't you get the water started, and I'll grab an extra towel for you?"

He nipped at my bottom lip, sending a pulse straight to my core. "When you say a quick shower..."

I twisted out of his grip and grabbed a robe from my open suitcase. "Just go."

With a swat to my ass, he finally did as he was told and headed into the bathroom adjoining the bedroom. The view of his backside was just as phenomenal as his front. And from the tightness between my thighs, it was clear I hadn't had my fill of him yet.

The knock came again.

"Un momento!" I threw on the robe and tied the belt as I made my way through the sitting room. This tiny space had seen such a swirl of emotions since we arrived this morning. Panic and worry about how the meeting would go with Emmett's kidnappers. Anger and tears over finding out about Noah. Passion, lust, and tenderness with Malcolm.

Before opening the door, I checked the peephole.

And my stomach dropped.

Noah. With a bouquet of flowers. The lilies I loved so much.

I shot a look over my shoulder.

If Noah was here, instead of waiting for eleven on San Michele, what would he do if he saw another man? He had flowers, dammit. "I just want to talk."

The water was already running in the shower, but how long would Malcolm wait before coming to get me? Five minutes? Ten?

I undid the safety latch and creaked the door open to whisper, "You said eleven."

He held the flowers up, their perfume washing over me. "These still your favorite?"

"What do you want?"

"To talk."

"So do I, but this isn't a good time."

He put a hand on the door and pushed. "You're coming to the island tonight?"

"I am." I pushed back, but he was too strong and too insistent.

Noah stepped in, acting like I'd invited him. He nodded slowly, looking around the sitting room. "Shower time, of course. Can't keep you away from the hot water."

"Exactly." I slipped in front of him before he got too far and could see the mess in the bedroom. Why did I care? It's not as if he'd told me two years ago he wasn't dead. But he'd also kidnapped my brother at gunpoint and had either beaten him or watched while someone else did. This wasn't the same Noah I'd intended to share my life with. "So I'll—"

"Scarlett?" called Malcolm.

Noah cocked his head. "Not a good time, eh?"

"I told you, I'll see you on the island." I pointed to the door. "Now please leave."

"Who was that?" Noah tossed the flowers onto the low table between the chairs I'd considered smashing earlier. A lifetime of emotions ago.

"None of your business."

"Scarlett, were you planning on—" Malcolm's voice cut off as he appeared from the bedroom, covered in nothing but a towel.

"Malcolm Sharpe." Noah's gaze slid past me and a smirk tickled at his lips. "Making yourself comfortable, I see."

"Scarlett, do you need me to—"

I put up a hand before Malcolm could say anything else. For all I knew, Noah had thrown down the flowers so he had more freedom to grab a gun hidden on his person somewhere. "We're fine. He came to talk."

Malcolm sounded as calm as Noah did, but underneath it all, he was likely ready for a fight. "I thought that was why you were going to meet him on the island tonight?"

My eyes remained on Noah, and I kept my body between

them. I could practically feel the testosterone surging between the two of them. "Noah, I'll see you at eleven. We can talk then."

Noah raised a finger and pointed it over my shoulder. He growled, "I paid you to bring her here, not to fuck her."

What?

Malcolm was working for Noah? I *was* just a job?

CHAPTER 37
MALCOLM

"You son of a bitch!" I strode toward Noah, rounding Scarlett.

Noah's finger remained raised as he matched my pace, moving backward toward the door. "You and I will have words, Malcolm Sharpe."

"Screw you, Noah."

"Don't forget," he said over my shoulder to Scarlett, "eleven o'clock. Center of the island."

I slammed the door behind him and did the safety latch. A thousand plans on what to say to Scarlett flew through my brain, too fast to grab. Would she believe him? What would happen next?

"He... he paid you?" The pain in her few words ate at me. We'd come so far in such a short time, and Noah was trying to undo that.

I spun to face her and saw tears again. "Are they a tool right now?"

She wiped the back of her hand across her face. "How dare you. How dare you accuse me of something like that after... After I find out I was nothing more than your mark."

Oh shit. I hurried to her, intending to grab her arms and hold her close, but she backed away. "You don't seriously believe him, do you?"

"Why shouldn't I? We had questions about you right from the beginning. Why take my brother and spare you? Why send you to convince us and take the Codex back to them? The obvious answer is that you were working with them. You were the inside man."

I took a step closer and grabbed her hands. How was I going to make this better? Tell her the truth? Keep hiding? "I did work for him, to get the Codex."

She yanked her hands away.

"I didn't know it was him. I just knew it was some voice on the other end of an earpiece that I recognized when we grabbed Emmett."

"So I'm supposed to believe you had nothing to do with the kidnapping?"

I grabbed her hand and held firm when she tried to pull it away. I bowed my head and forced her to feel the crown of my skull. "You feel that? That's where Jayce hit me on the head with a statuette."

She sucked in a slow breath. "You were the one who came into the library after her?"

"Yes, and then they were done with me. It was a onetime job, with a group of people I never met, for one item. I failed the job and they cut me loose." I let her hand fall away from my head.

"Just the way you like it." Scarlett stepped back again, so she was against the wall. "It's all about winning, isn't it?"

"Yes, but..." I gestured from her to me and back again. "This—us—this is a win."

"I con Thomas Maguire at his dad's party and leave him without what he wants, so he comes after me at the Albrecht party. Noah..." She flung her hand toward the door. "Noah finds me with another man, so he throws the biggest grenade he can find."

"Exactly." I closed the distance between us and ran my fingers through her hair, settling my hand to cup the nape of her neck. "It was nothing but a grenade. A lie."

She squeezed her eyes shut, her entire face tightening. "And my team gets the Codex before you can, so you sign on with those clowns to get it back."

"No." I wrapped my arm around her waist, searching for the woman who'd opened up to me about her family. Who I'd opened up to. I didn't open up. "He failed to tell you for two years he was even alive. How could you believe him over me?"

Scarlett opened her eyes, swimming with tears. "I'm just a tool, like my tears. To all of you. No one wants me, they just want the image of me. They want me as a prize. And not even me. I just happened to be the one in everyone's path."

I pulled her closer, so her head rested against my neck. "You're not a tool. Neither are your tears. You need to feel. Like we did when we were together in that bed, sharing things."

"Sex is a tool," she choked out.

"Don't say that. Don't tell me that you lying next to me, telling me about your father was a tool."

"It was a lapse in judgment. I need to be stronger than that." She wedged her hands in between us and pushed me away. "You should go."

I reached for her again, but she spun along the wall away from me.

"Malcolm, just go."

This wasn't happening. I hadn't let down my defenses, laid in bed chatting with her, hadn't let myself become friendly with her team. And I would not let Noah's lie ruin my opportunity to build on what was growing between us. "Scarlett, he was lying. You were not my job."

She picked my shirt up from the floor and threw it at me in a wadded heap. "No, I'm just the little cherry on top of your actual job—get the Codex. And when that failed, get the ring."

I remained still, clutching the shirt against my chest. She believed that lying piece of shit? Of course, she did. Why would she believe me? "You're just like all the rest of them."

"Screw you."

"You want people to be the same or they're not allowed inside, right? I'm not perfect, and I didn't tell you about my first job for Noah, because I didn't even know it was him. But that job has nothing to do with this. With me helping Emmett. With me wanting to be here with you right now. I'm sorry I'm not in that tiny group of people you've been friends with since you were a kid, but that doesn't mean you can't trust me. That doesn't mean you can't let the new guy in."

She threw my pants at me next. "If you're not gone in the next two minutes, I'm calling Rav. And you do *not* want him to be the one throwing you out."

"You're as bad as my father. He shut down when my mother died and left me out in the cold. Now you get one piece of news that doesn't fit in with your perfectly planned idea of the world and you shut down, too."

She turned away from me. Yeah. It was exactly the same.

I dug through sheets and pillows on the floor until I found the rest of my clothes. This was why I liked my solitary life—no one ever told you to leave. I stalked into the bathroom, shut off the water for the stupid shower, and got dressed in private. I should've known better.

Once I finished changing, I marched back out into the living room, prepared to see a defiant woman. Maybe make my case one more time when she saw me. Instead, the terrace door was open and she was leaning on the railing, watching the evening traffic in St. Mark's Square. The dull murmur of hundreds of voices mingled with the sounds of music playing at the cafés dotting the square.

I approached the door, my throat growing thicker with each step. She was still in the pale-pink silk bathrobe, with her head down. What the hell was wrong with me? Why did I care? I didn't do teams. I didn't do people.

But all I wanted to do was wrap my arms around her one more time and tell her we'd felt something real together. The sort of thing neither of us got to enjoy in life.

"Just wear sensible shoes, Scarlett." The island visit could be dangerous, especially considering she was meeting her brother's kidnapper.

She didn't budge.

It was all I could do not to shake her. "And take Rav with you."

"Go away, Malcolm," she whispered.

Letting people into your heart just produced the feelings which were surging through me, the nervous jitters, the aching gut, the indecision. *You're a lone wolf, Malcolm. You look out for yourself.*

I turned away from her and walked through the sitting room. The bouquet from her former fiancé added insult to everything I was feeling at the moment. My instinct told me to pick them up and throw them across the room. Smash their tender little petals into the garbage.

My dad's voice echoed in my head. *It's just for the semester, Mal. Maybe two. I'm sure you'll make lots of friends there.* No 'I love you' or 'I'm sorry she's gone' or even an 'I'll miss you.' Just enroll me in a new school and go to work. Maybe think about me every once in a while, or just treat me like the adult I was supposed to be the moment my mother died.

I tore open the door to the hotel room, fully intending to slam it shut behind me. I didn't want to slam it. I wanted her to come running to the door and tell me she trusted me. That had been our entire problem since day one. I thought we'd gotten over it.

Who are you kidding, Mal? You lie and sneak around for a living. Why would anyone ever trust you?

Why did I even think she might be different? She was the queen of lies and deceptions. Just not with her team. With her team, she was stubborn, loyal, and protective. That was the real her. But only with her fucking team.

Not me.

No one ever picked me in the end.

I clicked the door closed behind me and slunk down the hallway to the central staircase. I was a lone wolf. I didn't need people. I hated working with teams, because someone always let you down or they were looking out for themselves. I was happy for the clean break from the stupid Reynolds people. I'd gotten my rocks off, and I wouldn't be saddled with anyone else.

Perfect.

I needed a drink.

The front door of the lobby was open to the square, all the same sounds greeting me as I'd heard from Scarlett's, three stories up.

"Malcolm!" Declan raised a hand in greeting as he came in through the front door. "Rav and I were sitting down at the café across the square. Care to join us? I owe you a drink, after all."

Lone wolf. No teams.

I didn't even slow down as I passed him. "I don't feel like it."

"Have you seen Scarlett? You think she'd like to join us? I should probably grab Jayce, too."

Goddamn teams.

CHAPTER 38
SCARLETT

One foot in front of the other. Don't look back. Just keep moving. The words repeated in my brain over and over, urging me to continue, despite the weight sitting on my heart. I wrapped my arms tighter around myself, trying to ward off the chill of the evening.

For the blink of an eye, I'd thought there might be a future with Malcolm. Something intense had happened between us, giving me the first glimpse of a life post-Noah.

Then the truth came out about Noah.

And the truth about Malcolm.

Followed by the truth I was nothing more than the crew mastermind. The planner. The manipulator. The tool. And there I was, alone again, walking the cobblestone streets of Venice, running straight toward the ghosts of my past.

It was late and dark, but the city lights persisted. Laughter and voices came from all around me, from restaurants and outdoor cafes, and from tourists not wanting to lose the magic of the city by turning in. The ancient stone buildings held no interest, and I nearly collided with several people in the narrow alleyways.

One foot in front of the other, through the labyrinth of canals and bridges. The answers would be on San Michele. I'd get the truth, I'd close that chapter of my life, and I'd go home.

My phone buzzed and I ripped it out of my pocket, half-hoping it was Malcolm. But it was Emmett, also alone, but surrounded by hospital staff. I picked up. "Hey, Em."

"Sorry if I woke you, sis."

"It's barely dinnertime at home. And you're supposed to be sleeping."

"Always looking out for me, eh?" He sighed, barely audible over the laughter from a couple walking behind me.

"What's going on?" I turned onto Fondamente Nove, a wide street leading to the water bus station.

"I don't like this place," Emmett said, his voice low and tight. "I don't like them telling me I can't do what I want."

My stomach clenched. The hospital was far more comfortable than where he'd been for the last week and a bit, but he was practically a prisoner, all the same. "You'll be out tomorrow. Promise. Then we can take you home."

"Stopping in New York on the way or..." The twinkle in his eye was practically audible. "Any chance Mal's coming home with us?"

"He can find his own way home."

"Too bad. I usually want to hit men who look at you the way he did."

"Sorry to burst your bubble, but you probably want to do a lot more than hit him."

"Why would I want to hit him?" Emmett groaned and my

steps stuttered. He hadn't let me see the extent of the damage they'd done, but when the doctors refused to release him, a fresh wave of rage pulsed through me.

"The asshole was working for Noah this whole time."

"Bullshit," he practically coughed.

"He admitted it, straight to my face." My throat tightened as I remembered the bump on his head. His admission of guilt.

"Not a chance, Scar. He got in front of them when they started beating me. Did you know that? I bet he hid his bruises from you, didn't he?"

"It was an act." But the things he'd said to me. The panic in his eyes when he saw I was hurt. No, Malcolm was nothing more than a con man. "Noah hired him for the Codex heist at the Maguire mansion. He's the one Jayce hit with the statue."

"So he didn't hire him for the kidnapping or the ring heist?"

"Noah said—"

"A load of shit, if it came out of his mouth. Don't tell me for a second you trust that asshole."

I was not trusting Noah. Despite the fact I was heading out to a tiny island in the middle of the lagoon to meet with him in the dead of night. And I wasn't believing it just to get away from Malcolm and the look in his eyes when he first came into my room today. Or after we'd had sex—a look that made me think it could be more than that. "Malcolm's a lone wolf. He said it himself. He doesn't do teams."

"You know what a lone wolf is, right?" Something creaked on his end, likely his hospital bed. He was no doubt sitting up, pointing a finger at me.

"That's a stupid question." One that was probably going to be followed with an even stupider answer.

"Wolves are pack animals, Scar. They don't choose to live an entirely solitary life. When one's out on his own, it's because he's looking for a mate or a new pack to join."

"He doesn't fit in with us." I stopped short of the bus station, surrounded by outdoor restaurant seating, music, and too many voices. Lights strung from the building, over the walkway, around the patrons, reflecting in the lagoon next to me.

Emmett groaned, this time sounding more like frustration. "He practically hauled you out of the palazzo after you grabbed me. He was joking around with Declan and Jayce. Hell, even Rav likes him."

"Rav does not like him."

"Pfft. He likes him in the same way Rav likes people other than you. Controlled disdain."

A boat piloted to the bus landing and several people stood from their restaurant seats. Two of them, hand in hand, smiled at each other. He looked like a shorter version of Malcolm, and my heart took another tumble. I hadn't known the man long enough for any of these feelings.

It was loneliness. That's all. I had to get back on the horse, go on some meaningless dates, so I wouldn't fall for the first set of gorgeous blue eyes that drove me wild.

Emmett yawned. "Do you remember that painting I recovered in Miami last fall?"

What did that have to do with the conversation? Maybe his meds were making him loopy? "Yeah."

He'd gone to Miami for reconnaissance, so we could plan which team members to take. Through a set of circumstances and luck that only my brother could pull off, he wound up at a Heat-Celtics game, with courtside seats. The man who'd bought the stolen painting was sitting next to him, with no clue it was stolen. They had a restitution plan in place before halftime.

Mum had been so impressed with the job that she had our forger make a copy to hang as a memento in our boardroom.

"I didn't do that job alone."

"I remember. You had some source get you the tickets." My shoulders fell. His report had said he worked with a private investigator whose name he hadn't divulged. I assumed he was being all Emmett about it, calling the private eye his confidential informant, as though he were some spy or FBI agent.

"Your silence tells me you've already figured it out."

"He commented on Kiera's copy in the boardroom." And I'd been so upset I kept talking over him, instead of asking how he'd known the original had been stolen five years ago.

"I know emotions aren't really your jam and all—" He cut off to yawn again, his words slowing. "He didn't ask for payment or anything, just did it because he's a good guy and said the tickets were worth it. Same with the beating. He jumped in and tried pulling them off me, with no regard for what might happen to him."

The passengers had disembarked from the water bus, and the next group was boarding. "I need to go."

"He's a good guy, Scar. He does shady work sometimes, but what the hell do we do?"

In our line of work, trust was a luxury, not a requirement. Malcolm had earned enough of my trust that I'd taken him to my bed. But I couldn't ignore the fact that he'd hidden something so important. I needed time to think. After I saw Noah. "Thanks for the intel. Now get some sleep."

"Yes, ma'am," he slurred.

Good. He needed his rest—I hurried to the water bus line—and I needed answers.

CHAPTER 39
SCARLETT

IT WAS JUST after ten thirty. The vaporetto water bus took only six minutes to get from the mainland to San Michele. The square island was bordered by red and white brick walls with porticos dotting its length. The cemetery itself had closed hours ago, so I'd been careful about staying in the shadows until I escaped the view from the church at the northern corner. With the near full moon and clear sky, I made my way without the flashlight from my phone.

As much as it pained me, I'd listened to Malcolm and had chosen the sensible shoes I'd worn when pretending to be one of the Blur Luxe cleaning staff. There was no telling what I'd be up against tonight or what Noah's actual plan was, so it had been smart.

I was only so smart though. I'd come alone. There was no way Rav would have come with me. He would've played every dirty trick up his sleeve to stop me from going. But I needed answers.

And only one man on the planet had them.

Tall, narrow Cypress Pines, benches, and green bins lined

the path of concrete with small stones and bricks embedded in it. Signs dotted the island, directing me to different burial sections and the tombs of the most famous inhabitants, like Igor Stravinsky. It was eerily quiet, making me question my decision to come alone for the hundredth time.

"Scarlett." Noah appeared from the shadow of one of the tall crypts at a crossroads. "I wasn't sure you'd be joining me."

"I wasn't sure myself." I scrunched my toes inside my shoes. "But I want answers."

He gestured along the path I'd been following, and we fell into step together. "Do you know anything about the Codex of San Marco or the Chalcis Ring?"

"I know my brother was kidnapped and beaten because of them."

He waved the snarky attitude away, apparently unaffected. "No, about the legends about the Tesoro di San Marco."

"The Treasure of St. Mark?"

The sounds of digging battled with his words. Was someone preparing a fresh grave? My stomach tightened. Not my grave?

"When St. Mark's bones were smuggled out of Alexandria in the ninth century, his saviors brought back an immense treasure. They kept the bones in the Venetian doge's palace until St. Mark's Basilica was built, but kept the treasure somewhere else." His speech grew more rapid the longer he talked. "The Codex included a map, and the ring is the key to the chest with the treasure in it."

This wasn't the same Noah I'd lived with. He'd always been calm and collected before, but now there was a frenzy in his voice. He'd been more like me and less like a zealot, which was what he sounded like. "These aren't the answers I'm looking for. I want to know what happened. How did you survive? Why didn't you contact me?"

He paused in his steps and took me by the hand, drawing me closer. "I thought about calling you so many times."

"So why didn't you?"

He pulled my hand to his heart, the frantic energy falling away as quickly as it'd come over him. "Your mother."

"My mother?"

"She was constantly criticizing me. I couldn't live up to her high expectations. After years of that, and I couldn't stand the sight of her."

"What about me?" What made me so easy to cast aside?

"I missed you every second we were apart." He gave a rueful smile, full of regret. "Until I realized how much better I felt without your mother around."

"You knew how hard her criticisms were on me, too. Why didn't you ever tell me?" That was what people who were in love did. Who were planning on spending a life together did. They leaned on each other and talked about those things.

"Oh, Scarlett." He pulled my hand to his lips, and every ounce of me wanted to shove it in his face. "That made it even worse. I knew if I told you the truth, it would crush you. You wouldn't be able to handle how much it bothered me, on top of how much it bothered you. You would've left the company, which was too important to you. I didn't want to do that to you. I loved you too much."

We were supposed to grow old together. I'd thought I could trust him to be the beacon of honesty in the sea of deceit I lived in. But he was just like everyone else we brought in from the outside. Liars. Like Malcolm. "When did you decide to do it? The diamond job. Did the communications really fail or did you plan the whole thing from the beginning? Was going over the bridge part of your plan, too?"

"We can talk about those details later. Right now, I need you to see what we're doing."

"We who?" I didn't care about what he was doing. I cared about my questions.

He hauled me by the hand, toward the digging sounds. "This island was originally two separate ones. The southern island, the one closer to the main islands, was called San Cristoforo. It included a monastery built in the fifteenth century, which was demolished when Napoleon declared the island would be used as the city's cemetery."

I pulled my hand out of his. The thought of him touching me made me sick to my stomach.

"But we have to go even farther back than that. In the tenth century, a church was built on the northern island dedicated to the Archangel St. Michael. But on the southern island? The one between the original San Michele and Venice, they buried the great treasure. Most people believe that St. Mark's bones were the most important thing that came back from Alexandria. But they weren't."

"So kidnapping my brother..." Why was I even having this conversation? If he wasn't providing me with the details about his faked death, why wasn't I going back to the water bus pickup? "It was all about a treasure hunt? Like you think you're Indiana Jones or something?"

"Yes." He lifted his arms out to the sky, as if he were conversing with God directly. "But no. What we'll uncover here does not belong in any museum."

"You're not making any sense. Why am I here for some treasure I know nothing about?"

"I have a new benefactor with more money than your mother and all of her backers. And fewer rules. And he has such a vision." Noah ran a hand down the length of my arm. "He is going to change the world, and I'm going to be by his side. The first part is in the chest we're digging up."

"What's that have to do with me?" There was no way I'd go back to him after what he put me through over the last two years. He wasn't so delusional to think I actually would?

He stopped short again. "We were a great team, Scarlett. Once I had some distance and perspective, I realized the personal thing was a distraction. What I need is your brain. Your ability to see the angles and plan out a mission with exacting precision. I haven't been able to find anyone who can match you in that."

"So tonight's a job interview?"

His eyes twinkled in the moonlight. "I want you to see what we're about."

We felt grander than him and his benefactor.

"Where have you been?" called a man's voice.

A voice with a familiar, grating vocal fry.

It couldn't be.

Noah placed a hand on my back and encouraged me to keep moving. "Have they found anything yet?"

Most of the graves in this area of the cemetery were stone slabs with crosses or headstones. Now and then a crypt loomed or a taller statue watched over the dead. At the next cross path, there were three crypts at the corners, and a statue at the fourth. The statue stood at least fifteen feet high, a maiden gazing at the heavens. Her base was made of a large stone, probably several, with stairs leading up to it like a dais.

Lanterns sat at each of its corners, illuminating the shattered stone at the center and a pile of dirt. Two sprays of dirt flew out of the hole, along with the glint of shovels.

Standing next to the hole, another man I never expected to see again. Thomas Maguire, greasy, slobbery, over-pomaded Thomas Maguire. A predatory smile snaked its way up his face.

"Eloise..." he drawled. "Such a pleasure to see you again. But wait, is it Eloise Stone? Eloise Reynolds?"

My brain whirred. I'd conned him into opening the Codex drawer so I could get the password. I'd been afraid at the Albrecht mansion that he might have known. But if he was working with Noah to get the ring... He would have been behind the original request from the clowns to get the Codex. Had he been the one who paid Noah to get the Codex in the first place?

And why had he been at the Albrecht party? Unless it was nothing more than a game to him, and he'd been watching me?

It *was* all about winning, just like I'd said. Either winning or anger that he'd lost to me.

Thomas descended the raised platform and sidled over to me. Like every time I'd seen him, he ran a hand along my arm.

Noah shoved him. "Take your hands off of her."

Thomas's lip curled and he looked me up and down one more time like I was nothing but a prize. Something to be won. "Why does everyone insist on protecting this little piece of ass?"

"I'm not a—"

"Because she's worth a hell of a lot more than that."

"Don't forget who's paying for your little expedition here." Thomas stepped closer to Noah, looking up at him, and yet somehow looking down his nose at him. "It would do you well to remember I'm in charge."

There was no way Noah's new benefactor was this toad. He had no vision, other than a vision of his own superiority.

I said, "If Noah was the blue-haired clown, were you the red-haired clown?"

Thomas's upper lip quivered. "Illuminations are light bulbs, are they?"

"Alright, now that we've had our proper introductions..." I folded my arms and tightened my toes again. I still had so many questions about Noah and the last two years. But they were being drowned out by wanting to know what was going on between these two men. And the hole in the ground. I turned to Noah. "If you want me on your team, tell me what's going on."

Noah smirked. He thought he had me. "Thomas hired me to get the Codex. I assembled a team who weren't up to the job."

"Including Malcolm?"

"So your boyfriend confessed?"

"Not my boyfriend. Keep going."

"He failed," Thomas practically snarled. "It's as simple as that."

"Except it wasn't a complete failure," said Noah. "I heard him talking to Emmett, so I knew when the Codex was already gone once he got up to the library, that you had it."

I'd told Emmett he'd screwed up when he responded to Malcolm that night. I just hadn't realized how much. "You knew you needed Emmett to get the Codex. And—what? If Malcolm failed the first job, why pay him for the second job?"

Thomas's eyes snapped to Noah. "You didn't tell me that

loser was being paid. He failed to get the Codex from my father. You don't get paid for that."

Noah shrugged at me. "You caught me. I didn't actually pay him. I let him live after failing. Giving him an opportunity to redeem himself is payment, of a sort. But then what does he do?"

He takes what you wanted—me.

Noah was a liar and a master manipulator. He'd made the entire story up right on the spot. Nothing more than to drive a wedge between me and Malcolm.

You son of a bitch.

"What about the Codex?" I said to Thomas. "Why steal it when you already owned it?"

Thomas frowned and walked back up the steps to look into the hole. "All this talk is boring me."

Noah smiled. "You know the answer, Scar."

Of course, I did. "Junior over there believes the treasure's real. His father was going to sell the Codex, so he wanted to take it first."

"You told us the Codex was on its way back to its rightful owner. Fortunately, Reynolds is still using the same transporter for items heading to London. I intercepted him and got the manuscript back." Noah gestured to the side of the platform opposite the dirt pile. "Come and see. We're going to make history here."

I walked up with him, not wanting to get too close to the edge of the hole, in case there was some idea I'd wind up at the bottom of it, instead of working with Noah. It would be best if he thought I was on the same team as him, if I was going to get out of this alive. Otherwise, I'd learned too much and would be a liability.

Noah brought a lamp closer, shining it into the hole for me to see. Two men worked inside the hole, which seemed to be lined with brick or stone. Not dirt. How far down would the water line have been? "When they turned the island into a cemetery, they added six feet of dirt to the surface, to give them space to bury people. As soon as we found the walls, we knew this was the right spot. They would have been put in place to protect the treasure."

On the platform's deck, next to a pile of dirt, I spotted the ancient Codex of San Marco, out of its case, and the glint of gold from the Chalcis Ring. "What is it? The treasure? Gold and gems, like in a cheesy pirate movie?"

One of the men paused with his shovel over his shoulder and took a breath. He had a tattoo on his hand, between his thumb and index finger. The phoenix. And a large scar across his right cheek.

Oh, shit.

He was the one who'd pulled the gun on Malcolm.

Noah's gaze rose to mine, madness glittering in the lamplight. "Destiny. Resurrection. Immortality."

CHAPTER 40
MALCOLM

I STOOD at the Fondamente Nove water bus station, staring across the lagoon at the island of San Michele. The night was dark, but the moon was bright. The island was so close I could have swum if I had to.

It was almost eleven o'clock. The time Scarlett was supposed to meet Noah at the center of the graveyard. I'd marched out of the hotel after she took his word over mine, swearing not to look back. But I had. I looked up to her terrace, where she still stood. Instead of bowing her head like when I left, she was in Declan's arms. They were mostly in silhouette from the lights inside her room, but it was clear enough that she was crying.

Fuck me, but I liked the Reynolds crew. Declan, with his easy-going ways. Jayce, with her constant need to eat and move. Rav, who glowered at me at every opportunity, but who was just protecting the leader of his pack. The camaraderie, the support, the amazing level of trust they had with each other.

I only saw Emmett every few months when our paths

crossed, but he was the closest thing I had to an actual friend. Someone I had a history with and I knew had my back.

It wasn't just an itch.

And it wasn't just about winning.

So instead of walking away, finding my own hotel, and flying back in the morning, I'd followed her to the water bus station. I'd watched her get on without Rav. At least the fool woman had chosen better shoes.

Just before eleven o'clock, I got on the water bus. On the short ride across the dark lagoon, I hauled out the Reynolds phone no one had confiscated, took a deep breath, and called Rav.

"How do you still have one of our phones, traitor?"

Obviously, Declan wasn't the only one who talked to her after Noah's bombshell.

"I don't have time for this right now. I'm on my way to San Michele."

"And I'm going to sleep. I don't care where you are."

"Scarlett's over there. She's going to meet Noah."

"What is this? Another little trap or a double-cross? Trying to lure me over to the island? To what end?"

I gritted my teeth and shook a fist at the phone, as if it would accomplish something. "I'm not asking you to trust me or take my word for it. Check her phone. Brie should be able to track it for you, if you can't track it yourself. She's on the island. And I'm afraid she's in trouble."

There was a clicking noise on Rav's end of the call, like he was using a laptop. Thank god. He was checking.

My heart beat high in my chest, anxiety flooding me. I wanted to convince him I was innocent of what Noah had said, but that wasn't my priority. The closer I got to the island, the louder the alarm bells in my head grew.

Noah may have been her fiancé once upon a time, but he'd also been her brother's kidnapper. He'd taken part in the beatings.

The asshole had brought her flowers.

"Tabarnak," Rav grumbled. "Stupid woman. I'm sending her GPS coordinates to your phone. I'll... Depending on how long it takes, I'll either have a boat to pick you up, or I'm coming in."

The water bus slowed at its stop on the side of the island. "I'll let you know what I see when I get there. Hopefully, I'm overreacting."

Rav huffed out a breath. "Be careful. But be extra careful with her. I'll kill you myself and bury you on that island if anything happens to her."

"I wouldn't expect any less." I hopped off at the stop and ducked through the gate, keeping to the shadows. The island was small, and I had her location on my phone. Finding her would be easy—with the steadily growing worry pounding through me, going slow enough to not get caught would be more difficult.

I wove my way along the grass at the edge of the paths, staying in the shadows of the tall pines. Raised voices carried on the light wind, in the same direction I'd been traveling.

Please let that be you carrying your phone, Scarlett. Please be alright.

Lights came into view, and I slowed. I had to judge the threat before leaping in. At a cross between two of the main paths through the southern cemetery, two figures stood atop a raised grave with a tall statue. Noah and Scarlett. A third voice joined their conversation, but I could only see the two people. A spray of dirt flew out of a hole by their feet.

I neared them, slowly, heading for the ten-foot-high crypt directly in front of me. The moon provided light for me to see them, but also provided shadows at the side of the crypt. Their lamps would ruin their night vision, so I'd be nearly impossible to see.

As I crept closer, Scarlett said, "What would have happened to Emmett if I'd given your thug the ring?"

"What's she talking about, Noah?" asked another man. His voice was familiar. Like a man whose cheek I'd smashed my fist into for trying to steal Scarlett from me. How was Thomas Maguire here? And what were they doing?

I settled into my hiding spot, barely twenty feet away from them.

Noah held one of the lanterns at his side. "We would have released Emmett, exactly as he'd said."

"Explain, Noah. Were you trying to sneak the ring out of London without telling me?" Thomas's voice dropped an octave, the grating quality of it magnified. "I think the more important question is, what would have happened to my treasure if the bitch had handed over the ring?"

They were working together. Thomas was the inside source. That made so much sense. He'd given us the location of every security camera in the Maguire mansion, plus the code for the Codex's drawer.

I hauled out the phone and texted Rav. *Noah and Thomas Maguire are with her, along with at least one other guy I can't see. It doesn't look good.*

He replied almost immediately. *I'm calling the police. Get her out of there.*

The man in the hole straightened, so I could see the top of his head. "I hit metal."

Another man stood up in the hole, roughly the same height as the first. How was I going to rescue her? How fast could the diggers get out of the hole? Could I just show up and claim I wanted a cut? If Noah was the blue-haired clown, was Thomas one of them?

Were they armed?

What I would have given to have a Reynolds earpiece in my ear right now, so I could let Scarlett know the cavalry were on their way.

"Answer me!" shouted Thomas, who pulled a gun from his waist and pointed it at Noah. Fuck. That answered that question.

CHAPTER 41
SCARLETT

Thomas thrust the gun in Noah's direction, locking his elbows in the most unnatural position I'd ever seen.

Noah's eyes refocused, and he shook his head. "Put that thing away before you hurt yourself. Have you ever even fired a gun? You are quite literally pointing over my shoulder."

Thomas sneered. "You backstabbing—"

"Calm down. Our working relationship is almost at an end. You fire that gun and it's going to echo around the entire lagoon and bring the cops down on us. Use your brain."

That was exactly what I was trying to do—use my brain. I'd played right into Noah's hands. All the men around me wanted to win. But I'd done the same thing. I wanted answers, wanted to believe that I knew best, that I was strongest. Now I was in a cemetery on an island in the middle of the Venetian lagoon, with a couple of madmen and two thugs who could snap my neck without a thought.

If you don't make plans, people die, right, Scar? Right.

Noah's supposed death two years ago had planted that fear in my brain. And now here he was, standing next to me. And because I was good at planning, the lunatic wanted me to work with him.

Coming to the island had been a stupid choice. I already knew enough about what happened to Noah the moment I saw him. If he hadn't gotten in touch with me, and he still knew who I was, it had been his choice. It didn't matter if it was because of my mother—if that was even true. He made a choice. He picked himself over me and didn't have the balls to break up with me like a normal person.

At least I learned one important thing by coming here—Noah hadn't paid Malcolm. I hadn't just been a job to him. He wanted me for me. And I was likely going to get myself killed before I'd have the chance to apologize for being a scared little girl with her uncomfortable little feelings.

Thomas skirted the edge of the hole to jab the gun into the center of Noah's chest. "How's this for aim?"

This was going downhill fast. I was close to the edge of the platform and took a tentative step back. No one noticed.

"I don't trust you," snarled Thomas.

Noah moved fast. Forced the gun to the side, twisted it out of Thomas's grip, and had it pointed against Thomas's temple, before Slobbery-Mouth could react. "I don't trust you either, but this is a working arrangement. It's not a romance. It's not a friendship. You hired me to get you that treasure, and my only payment is one item from the chest. One item of my choosing. And once I have that in my hand, our business dealings are over."

Thomas trembled visibly.

I took another step back. There were crypts nearby I could hide behind, but would Noah turn the gun on me? Would the thugs in the hole come after me with a shovel and bury me?

Note to self: implement an emergency call sequence on the phone. One that could be triggered without turning the damn thing on. Maybe inside a watch.

Thomas lifted his chin and gave a quick nod. Even with a gun to his head, Thomas had to pretend he was in control.

Noah removed the magazine and emptied the chamber, then threw the gun to the ground. He took a step toward me and grabbed me by the upper arm. "Do you see what I'm dealing with? This is why I need you. I need someone to vet my clients."

"Sure." I pulled my phone out. "Let me call Brie. She's the best at that."

Noah plucked the phone from my hand. "I can't believe I forgot to take that from you." He tossed it onto the platform, next to the Codex and the ring.

Thomas peered into the hole, doing what was probably his best to sound like he was still in control. "Are you done yet?"

"Sure thing, boss," said the thug without the phoenix tattoo. He'd called Thomas *boss*, probably not a term he threw around lightly. And when Thomas had heard that Mr. Phoenix Tattoo had tried to take the ring at the Albrecht mansion, he'd accused Noah of a double-cross. Two men in charge, with one thug each. The loyalties were obviously divided.

The two men in the pit hefted the small chest out of the hole. It was only two feet long by one and a half high and deep, but from the sounds they made when they lifted it, it was heavy. Simple, dark wood, with iron bands at the back of the lid, handles at either end, and a massive lock embedded in the front.

Carved into the top was the winged lion of St. Mark.

Thomas sucked in a quick breath. "This is it. The Tesoro di San Marco."

Noah leveled Thomas with a glare. "Can I trust you to behave yourself? Remember, I only want one item of my choosing."

Thomas waved his hands frantically. "Yes, yes, whatever. Just open it."

Why was Noah so insistent on one item? And of his choosing? Did he know what was inside? A holy relic? A gem larger than my fist?

"Patience." Noah knelt in front of the chest, running his hands over the top. He grabbed the ring from the platform along with a set of lock picks from one of his pockets. Instead of using the picks on the chest, he used one of them to pop the plaques off the ring. He attached all four plaques to a short metal cylinder, securing them with an epoxy, creating a unique key. "The legend says if you don't open with the key, there's something inside that will melt the contents."

"I know what the legend says," snapped Thomas. "But fifty pounds of gold coins are worth exactly the same as a fifty-pound block of solid gold."

I leaned in for a better look as he inserted it into the lock, my curiosity too strong.

Or exactly as strong as it should have been.

One of the thugs held a lantern over the chest, and I saw the tattoo. On Noah's hand. The same phoenix. It was like a brotherhood marking and hadn't been there before he'd faked his death.

Thomas fell to his knees next to Noah, all anger apparently forgotten in the hopes of what they'd find inside the chest. "Open it."

Noah turned the key and it clicked. The two thugs huddled around their bosses, focused on the chest. Noah lifted the lid, the ancient hinges protesting the entire way. It was a miracle they didn't snap off.

The lantern light glinted off gold and gems and jewelry. It really was like a pirate's chest. A small one, but all the same.

Thomas dug both his hands in, lifting mounds of treasure, which he let pour through his fingers. "I knew it was real. I knew it. My father was a fool. But I don't need him anymore."

Noah seized Thomas's wrists before he could dig in again. "I told you—I choose first. Keep your hands out of there."

While the men focused on their little baubles, I took another step and another and another. What was my escape route? The water bus only had one stop, so if Noah wanted to grab me, he'd know where to go. There were plenty of areas I could hide out, behind the crypts, in the church, and in the cloister. If I got a solid lead, would he try to find me?

If Noah hadn't come after me for the last two years, how much could he really care? Thomas was the one I was more worried about. It seemed to be his mission to make me suffer after the escapade at his father's birthday party. It was doubtful Phillip Maguire would put any resources into tracking me down after this, but considering the wealth Thomas had just discovered, he might hire his own teams to come for me.

Noah lifted on his knees, giving himself leverage to sift through the box for whatever it was he was looking for.

I took two silent steps backward, toward the edge of the platform. Even in the rubber-soled shoes, stepping on the stone might make a noise. But if I could get down onto the grass, I'd be harder to hear. I just had to stay away from the gravel paths.

"Oh my god, this is it." Noah stood slowly, as did his tattooed thug.

I couldn't see either of their faces from the angle I stood at, but the awe in his voice was clear. He'd found what he'd been looking for.

"That's it?" said Thomas. "A feather? There's a stone in here the size of my thumb that looks like a diamond, and all you care about is a feather?"

I eased down onto the grass, one silent foot after another. The nearest tree was ten feet away on the grass. The nearest crypt was twenty, across the gravel path. The lower risk track was the higher risk hiding spot.

In the distance, police sirens sounded. What were the chances they were headed our way? Had some late-night resident or caretaker of the island spotted us? If so, the main entrance for the water bus was not an option. Even if they couldn't connect me to what was going on here, they'd take me in for trespassing. That wasn't something I could risk. We had strings we could pull in pretty much any country, but favors were best kept for emergencies rather than stupid decisions.

The men around the ruined grave didn't seem to notice. It was far enough away, but it could be on the main islands, off on Murano, or any of the other islands in the lagoon.

Thomas shot up to standing. "What is it? Why is that what you care about?"

Noah held the feather aloft, and I could see it. Made of solid gold, with barbs that glinted in the moon and lantern light. No jewels on it, no ornamentation, just a simple feather of gold. "The phoenix will rise!"

"Why do you keep talking about that? I want in on whatever it is."

They were too absorbed in what would become another argument. I took a few more slow steps back.

A hand clamped around my waist and another landed on my mouth. As the thought of screaming flooded through my brain, I caught his scent. Bergamot. And vanilla.

Relief flooded through my entire existence, and my muscles softened. I kept quiet and turned my head to see Malcolm. I gave him one slow nod, and he released my mouth. We faded away into the shadows of the trees together.

"You're not worthy." Noah stuffed the feather into a pocket in his jacket and shoved Thomas so hard he stumbled into the hole, screaming.

The tattooed thug did the same to the other guy and pulled a gun. Aimed it into the hole.

"Leg only. Leave them here for the police." Noah leaned over to talk to the men who'd been his partners. "If you tell them about us, we will come for you. You won't know when, and you won't be safe anywhere you go. Maybe Daddy can rescue you from an Italian prison, but he won't be able to save you from me. Or from the phoenix."

Malcolm pulled me tighter behind the tree as Noah spun around.

"Scarlett?" Noah grew silent, and the only sounds I could make out were Malcolm's shallow breaths next to me and Thomas's indignant protests.

The tattooed thug said, "You want me to go after her?"

The sirens grew louder. They must've been coming to San Michele. If Malcolm was here, maybe he'd called them?

"I know you're out there, Scarlett!" yelled Noah. "And my offer stands. If you want to leave here, I'll take you."

Job security wasn't something I ever worried about. No matter how my mother treated me, she was right. I was good at this job and any amount of false praise wouldn't help me get better.

"We need to go, Noah. They'll be here soon."

"I know." There was almost a sound of regret in his voice. "And we have important things to do."

Two suppressed gunshots broke the silence, followed by screams and moans. Noah and his thug ran in the opposite direction from where Malcolm and I were hiding.

Malcolm spun me in his grip so I faced him. "We can talk later or not, but Rav is meeting us at the southwest gate. We need to hurry."

I took his face in my hands and just stared at his gorgeous self for a heartbeat. We did have to hurry. The police would be there soon, and the sounds coming from the pit would bring them down on us swiftly. "I told you to leave me alone."

"I tried." Malcolm gave a half-hearted shrug. "I honestly did."

He came for me, despite everything I'd said to him. He could have left or told Rav where I was, but instead, he chose to come for me himself.

A little voice in the back of my head repeated his words, *You're worth so much more.* "Noah told me the truth, that he didn't pay you for this job."

Malcolm gripped my wrists and brought my hands down to his chest. "We really need to get going."

"I know." I gave him a quick peck on the lips, despite wanting to throw my arms around him and never let go again. "I just have one thing I need to do first."

CHAPTER 42
MALCOLM

"You're going to hell for that," said Emmett after the third time he watched the video of the Velatti driving into the swimming pool.

Declan hadn't even been there, but he narrated the entire experience as though he had. He laughed so hard every time, I thought he was about to fall off his chair.

The group of us sat around a café table at the edge of St. Mark's Square, like Declan had invited me to the night before. Round tables with chairs spilled out into the piazza. Lights ringed the entire square, every window on the first three floors of each building glowing bright. It was ten o'clock Monday night and the crowds were still thick.

An outdoor band played at our café, complete with piano, clarinet, and a string quartet. The music varied between classical background music, show tunes, and a rousing version of 'New York, New York.' Across the square, another band joined ours, playing the same tune.

Emmett had been released from the hospital that afternoon. Jayce had just finished her second gelato, Scarlett was on her second glass of wine, and even Rav had cracked a smile at the ridiculous video Brie had sent.

Thomas Maguire and his bodyguard were arrested last night, and the Carabinieri TPC had taken the Tesoro di San Marco. The only negative was that Noah and his man had gotten away. He'd be out there somewhere, but from his final words, he'd be waiting for Scarlett to join him instead of pursuing her. Hopefully, she was safe. Brie was already on the trail, tasking her support staff with finding him.

Scarlett raised her glass. "Here's to three successful recoveries."

Everyone at the table held up their glasses and clinked. After watching Noah and his thug run off, she'd grabbed the Codex and the Chalcis Ring. Before Emmett was out of the hospital, she had them safely heading back to London to their respective museums.

Declan raised his beer. "And here's to a quiet stay in Venice for a few days until poor little Em is allowed to go home."

Emmett nudged him, but winced as he did. "The doctors are being ridiculous."

Rav frowned at him. "The correct word is cautious. And I agree with them."

"Such a stick in the mud." Emmett took a sip of his water. Rav had forbidden him from consuming alcohol for a few days. No dehydration.

Jayce dropped her gelato cup onto the table. "Did Brie ever figure anything out about those Fenix people? Do you think Noah was working for them? Or did he and his tattooed buddy go through all of this for that golden feather?"

Scarlett leaned back in her chair, crossed leg swaying to the band's rhythm. "I don't want to think about that right now. Let's just have a little time to relax."

"Alright." Jayce shot up from her chair. "I need to try the vanilla. Anyone want anything?"

"Watching you eat is making me hungry," said Rav. "I'm coming with you."

The two of them wandered off, and Scarlett smiled. Her long hair was down, the lights from the square reflecting off the auburn strands. After a week and half full of stress, emergencies, and fear, she was finally at ease. Not facing the prospect of having to flee anywhere, and despite the uneven ground of the square, she was happily back in her four-inch heels. Skinny Capri pants, and light-pink silk blouse.

"Speaking of spending time together..." Declan nudged my leg under the table. "I thought you didn't do teams. What are you still doing here?"

Scarlett picked up her wineglass and narrowed her eyes at him over it. "Watch it, Ramsey."

"What?" His mock innocence was made more obvious by the smirk he couldn't keep down. "I have no idea what you mean."

The band shifted tempo, playing something better suited for dancing.

I took Scarlett's glass from her and placed it on the table. "May I have the honor of this dance?"

"I thought you'd never ask."

A few couples followed our lead, along with a mother and her young son. Nothing fancy, as I worried Scarlett would catch a heel on the stones. Just enough to hold her against me and enjoy the evening. "When's Emmett cleared to fly home?"

"Wednesday, I think. The ribs and bruises aren't really a

problem, but based on the head injuries, Rav wants him to stay put in case there's a concussion."

I nodded, unsure of what to say. After a late-night escape from San Michele and the hours spent trying to track down where Noah had gone, we'd had precious little time in the wee hours this morning before we passed out from exhaustion. Then it was vetting the new couriers, specific instructions to ensure the Codex and ring made it back safely, and time at the hospital.

Evelyn had requested they hold a Lessons Learned meeting once they got home, so Scarlett had a couple days' respite, at least.

I urged her away from me, to spin slowly under my arm, and then tucked her back where she belonged against my chest. "Any chance you can stay on here longer than that?"

"More itch scratching?"

I lowered my hand to the small of her back and pulled her closer. "More of... I don't know, everything?"

"A tall order and yet particularly vague."

"I don't know what magic you weaved, woman, but I couldn't do it. I couldn't just walk away."

Her face was serious, betraying little emotion. Not giving me much to work with. "So much for the lone wolf?"

I dipped my head to kiss her, soft lips and gentle tongue. A tiny sigh escaped her chest and her hand slid up from my shoulder to cup the nape of my neck. When we stopped, I said, "I'm not so sure that's what I want anymore."

"You want to join my pack?" Still no hint of emotion in the words. Plenty in the kiss, just not the words. Was it just a job offer? Or was she steeling herself against the possibility that a job was all I wanted?

"I've never worked with a group like this before. Never spent time with people like your team. The way you all care for and look out for each other, it's amazing." I curled our hands against my chest, the pressure bringing my attention to how fast my heart was beating. "You're amazing. And I'm hoping we can spend a lot more time together."

CHAPTER 43

SCARLETT

I stopped dancing and wrapped my arms around his neck, leaving Malcolm to do the same around my waist. "For the last two years, I've shut my feelings off, even more than normal. I've been living in the past with a man who wasn't worth a second of my time. I want to taste life again."

"I'm hoping you mean with me?"

"I do." Warmth pooled in my stomach, and I lifted on my toes to kiss his cheek. "I decided that before we even found out about Noah."

His head jerked back. "Seriously?"

"Even when you irritate me, I feel more alive with you than I have in years. I don't want to give that up."

"Shall I go back to irritating you then?"

I grabbed a handful of his hair and yanked playfully. "Don't make me sic Rav on you."

"Anything but that." He kissed my temple, and I sighed. "I'll even volunteer to tell your mother you hired me."

After talking to Noah, that meant even more than it

would have a day ago. He'd hidden away for two years to avoid her—if that was even true. Anyone who actually loved me wouldn't have been chased off by an overbearing mother-in-law. "She doesn't scare you?"

He snorted, the overconfident gesture obviously masking something deeper I wanted to learn about. "She's hardly the first tyrannical parent I've dealt with."

"Noah..." I scrunched my toes inside my shoes. How was I in the middle of St. Mark's Square, in this man's arms, with my team nearby, and still I couldn't shut off the memories of Noah? The memories of all the little things no one ever pointed out to me. He *hadn't* been worth two years of celibacy, let alone every moment I spent on him before that. "He used to say I was frigid. Unemotional. Just like Mum."

"You're careful with your heart. There's nothing wrong with that." He held me tighter, one of his hands winding its way up my spine. "I'm just happy you want to share a little of it with me."

Let it go, Scar. Show him your emotions. Be real. I let out a long, slow breath, and eased the pressure inside my shoes, instead letting the corners of my lips rise. I looked back up at Malcolm, who smiled at me. The lights from the surrounding buildings reflected in the depths of those stunning blue eyes, and for a moment, I let myself be lost in them.

He didn't just want me for me. For my brain, my skills, and my sharp mouth. He wanted my team and my family around me. Could I be so lucky he'd keep wanting that for longer than this trip?

"As much as I'm getting used to this team concept..." His hands trailed down the curve of my ass and squeezed, then leaned in to blow across my earlobe, igniting a fire deep in my core. "How long do we have to stay down here? I want to spend more time making you feel alive."

I swayed against him, encouraging him to follow the gentle rhythm playing through the square. "One more song. I like this one."

He pulled back and took me into a more classic dancing pose so I could admire the length of him. He was now mine and I was his. Maybe it would only last our time in Venice together, but the feeling inside of me said it was going to be a lot longer than that. We understood each other. From our messed up childhoods to our dramatically different adulthoods, we'd come out so similar.

I hadn't been looking for anyone to replace Noah, but what I found was someone far better suited for me. Someone who'd have my back, and who risked his life when my brother was in trouble.

Malcolm's brows drew together and his smile softened. What was he thinking about?

I tilted my head. "What?"

He pulled me close again, shaking his head slowly. "You'd be awfully easy to fall in love with, you know?"

That was unexpected. But from the way my heart did a little somersault, not at all unwelcome.

His gaze flew around the square. He hadn't meant to say that out loud. "Theoretically speaking, of course."

"Of course." There *was* more between us than this little adventure, and I couldn't wait to explore every moment with him. "I think you'd be pretty easy to fall in love with, too."

I was halfway there already.

He leaned in and kissed me again, wrapping me in his arms, abandoning any pretense of dancing. The crowds around us, the music from the dueling bands lining the square, and the hectic pace of the last week and a half faded away.

My pack had grown by one. And I couldn't have been happier.

CHAPTER 44

DECLAN

"How the hell did that happen?" Emmett snatched my second beer—the one I'd secretly ordered for him—frowning at Scar and Mal. "I told her to trust him, but figured she was more likely to take his head off."

I glanced at the happy new couple, dancing slowly to the live band. "As I hear it, she pulled a gun the first time he showed up at her place."

Emmett spluttered, covering his mouth to hold his beer in. "That sounds more like my sister."

"I just hope it lasts. She deserves some happiness, especially knowing what that asshole did to her."

"If he comes anywhere near her ever again, I swear, I'll—" Emmett winced and shifted in his chair. He should have still been in the hospital, as far as I was concerned, but that wasn't up to me.

"We all will, Em."

After the beating he'd had taken at the hands of Noah and his merry men, Emmett might make it to third in line—right behind Scar and Rav. Although, from the looks of her and ole Blue Eyes, Em might have to wait for fourth place.

I stretched my legs out and leaned back. A warm evening, good music, a crisp and citrusy Nastro Azzurro, and my best friends. Life would only be better if I had a puzzle to fiddle with and a beautiful woman by my side.

There *were* several of the latter around, but most were tourists with other men or children.

"He was going to be my brother-in-law." Emmett pressed the beer bottle to a bruise on his cheek.

"I know." My phone buzzed from the table, and I flipped it over to check who was calling. I picked it up and sat forward. "Edoardo! Long time!"

"Declan, good to hear your voice again. How have things been?"

I hadn't heard his thick Italian accent in at least six months. Suspicious timing. "Don't bother trying to play friendly with me. You never call unless you need something."

My friend chuckled. "Guilty. I heard a rumor you were on the continent."

"Up in Venice. Only here a couple more days."

"Any chance I could convince you to come to Roma for a visit?"

Emmett cocked the infernal Reynolds eyebrow. I bet if I ever pointed out that he did exactly the same thing as his mother and sisters, he'd lose it on me.

I shook my head and stood as Rav and Jayce returned to the table with far too much food. Clamping a hand over my opposite ear so I could hear him better, I said, "Why?"

"Allora..." Edoardo cleared his throat, as though he were busy swallowing his pride. "I need you to open your safe."

I'd designed a custom safe for him, hidden behind a bookcase in his immense library. But it was his safe now. "Why do you need me?"

He lowered his voice, making it hard to hear him over all the tourists and the music playing around the piazza. "Someone broke in and tried to open it. They triggered the glass re-locker. Now I'm stuck and can't get it open."

A group of pretty young things—probably too young for me—sauntered by, and one of them gave me a wink.

I returned no more than a salute. "Edoardo, you own a safe deposit box company. You must have at least five locksmiths you use on a regular basis. Send me the contact info for one of them and I'll send the details over."

"You misunderstand. Perhaps I'm using the wrong words. I have a..."

"A need for discretion?"

What he kept in there was his own business. I cracked safes to recover items, to help people who lost their combinations, or to help people after a loved one passed without providing security instructions in their will. But given the size of Edoardo's house, and the complexity of the safe he had me design, he probably kept enough in there that he wouldn't trust most people to see it—especially if he didn't even trust his own company to keep those things safe.

"Sì, exactly. Discretion."

"Hold a minute." I made my way back to the disgustingly adorable couple, put the phone on mute, and interrupted them mid-kiss. "Scar?"

She and Malcolm startled. They'd forgotten they were out in public. Good for her.

"Do you remember Edoardo Caetani?"

"Of course. Don't tell me he's had another painting stolen?" She flicked her gaze to Malcolm. "Old friend of the company. We recovered a Caravaggio for him, what, a year and a half ago?"

"Sounds about right."

Malcolm circled her waist with his overly possessive hands and held her close. "A new job already?"

I put my hands up in front of myself. "No, no. I designed a new safe for him after that, and apparently he had someone break in. Now he needs my help to reopen it."

Scarlett nodded. "Brian is flying everyone back in a couple of days. If you can wait for that, we can get the flight routed through Rome and he could drop you off? How much time do you need?"

Malcolm chuckled. "Wish I had a jet."

"Not sure how long it'll be. I need to get in and survey the damage. Re-review the specs. I've got a way in that should work, but I won't know until I see it."

"Malcolm and I are going to stay here for a..." She tilted her head at him. "Week? Two weeks?"

He leaned in and pressed a kiss to her temple. "I'll take whatever you'll give me."

I pointed my phone—still on mute—at him. "And you got Rav's warning about—"

"Killing me? Yeah, I got that back at your office. And a few times after that."

"Smart man. He'll never take it back." I grinned at him and saluted her, then left to finish my phone call. "Edoardo, I can be there in two, maybe three days. That work for you?"

"Sì, that works for me. I have another specialist arriving from the States around the same time. This should be good."

"Another specialist? You doubt me?"

"Declan, I have more than one safe in my house. I need them both opened after the break in."

"The other safe's not as good as mine, right?"

"Of course not." He laughed. "I'll see you later in the week."

I tucked my phone into my pocket and strolled back to the table. Something wasn't right. Whether it was the tone of his voice, the hesitations, or... just something niggling at the back of my brain.

"I think the pistachio's the best." Jayce had four cups lined up in front of herself, with different colored gelato in each one. She dropped a plastic spoon in front of me and nudged the cups to the middle of the table. "I need an opinion."

"You're sharing food with me now?" I hesitated before accepting the offer. "Does that mean we're engaged, or is it one of the signs of the apocalypse?"

The little ball of energy shrugged. "I might actually be full."

Emmett laughed and abruptly cut it off. The cut on his cheekbone had opened, but at least no blood was pouring out of it.

"I just got a call from a guy who needs me to re-open his safe in Rome. If I can get Evelyn to agree to it, think you can come with me, Jayce? The safe is one thing, but I'd like your thoughts on the break-in when it happened."

Her eyes nearly popped out of her head. "I haven't been to Rome in ages!"

"Scarlett said it was a year and a half."

She pointed a spoon at me before taking more of the green gelato. "Either way, I'm in."

A few days in Rome in early May would be a treat. A simple job, some good food, and maybe I'd tinker with his other safe. Mine was definitely better.

EPILOGUE
SCARLETT

TWO WEEKS LATER...

A large, warm, very naked body pressed against my back. One of Malcolm's muscular arms lay under my head as a pillow, the other draped across my waist. He breathed slowly, his heartbeat strong and steady.

I'd never been the napping type, but he was bringing out all sorts of things in me I wouldn't have believed a few weeks ago.

Venice had been a whirlwind, and then Rome had been an adventure.

He shifted in his sleep and his arm around my waist traveled lower, gliding across my abdomen. It snuck between my thighs and encouraged them apart.

"You're not asleep," I whispered.

"Nope." He lifted my top leg, pulling it backward to straddle his hip. Then those magic fingers found my clit, stroking lazily.

"What time is it?" I'd drifted off and the sun was still streaming through the tall window of our suite. I had an alarm set to be sure we weren't late for the jet's departure, but that wasn't the only priority this afternoon.

"No idea." He rolled his hips, his cock hardening against my ass.

"We have to make the call before we leave."

"You need to relax first."

I latched onto his wrist, battling between the desire to grind against his hand and with the need to get out of bed. "I can't relax until it's over."

"She'll be happy."

"I'm not talking about—" I came to a shuddering halt as his fingers delved inside me.

"Anything?"

"My mother. Not while your fingers are—" I let out a low moan.

Mum wouldn't be happy. She'd raise her elegant eyebrow and tell me 'No.' End of argument. No debate.

"I don't suppose you can reach a condom from where you are?" His fingers dipped in and out, not picking up any speed, but stringing me tight. Teeth raked my neck. Hot breath blew across my earlobe. "You're so fucking wet for me."

I was clean and had an IUD. He was clean. But we were waiting until we got home before making any big leaps. Our time together had been amazing, despite the danger and all the ups and downs, but the reality of my day-to-day world was very different. We'd been together every day for almost a month, but what if we didn't—

"Stop scrunching your toes." He nipped my shoulder. "Let the emotions out."

Let them out? Like it was that easy. I'd spent most of my life learning to mask them. They became tools in my war chest, ready to be used against an opponent as needed. But this afternoon wasn't a job, it wasn't my girlfriends, and it wasn't the team off-hours.

It was Malcolm.

It was different.

My laptop pinged from the desk, notifying me of an incoming call. "That's my mother."

"Shit." His fingers were out of me in a flash, and he bounced off the bed like a guilty teenager. "Are you sure you want to do this?"

"Yes." I joined him, throwing on clothes while the pinging continued. "I need to tell her eventually, right?"

"Easier to do it from Rome than face-to-face?"

I grabbed a fistful of his shirt and yanked him to me, feigned anger all over me. "Are you calling me a coward?"

He planted a kiss on my nose. "I'm calling you smart."

Dressed and hair finger-combed, Malcolm and I sat at the desk and answered the call.

"Darling." Mum's professional facade dropped into place before she finished the second syllable. "I was about to give up on the call. You took so long to answer."

Translation: Your top button is not done up properly, your hair is disheveled, and you are calling from your hotel bedroom.

"Sorry about that, Evelyn." My gaze flicked to the note Malcolm had written next to the laptop, with reminders. *Don't over-explain* was at the top. Don't give her ridiculous excuses like you were in the other room discussing couriers or logistics or anything else. Just leave it be. "We'll be home tonight, and I wanted to give you a heads up on some staffing changes."

"Oh?"

I scrunched my toes and Malcolm squeezed my leg. I *was* a coward. But he'd reassured me everything would turn out alright. What could she do? Fire me? "I've hired Malcolm."

"No." It was the simply monosyllabic command I was expecting, followed by her eyebrow lift.

Translation: Say more. I dare you.

Only I didn't. Without looking at the list of reminders, I cocked my eyebrow right back at her.

Malcolm Sharpe was flying home with us, to be part of my team and my life. Emmett insisted Malcolm move in with him, so he had time to find his own place. I was pretty sure that was Emmett's way of making sure Malcolm could escape if things didn't work out or move in with me if they did. My brother was still looking out for me.

"Scarlett, he's still an unknown commodity. We can take him on as a contractor, but we're not hiring until he's proven himself on more than a couple of jobs. He may be easy on the eyes, but you know there's more to this job than a pretty face."

"I do." Here we go. "But like you said, I'm the leader of this team and I'll take over the company someday. If I'm supposed to review the logistics activities, I can also step in and make an HR decision. He's everything that made Noah an excellent second-in-command, except he's also loyal."

There was a long pause, and my heart rate steadily climbed. It was ultimately her decision, and I didn't want to fight over it. I wanted her to agree.

Time slowed.

She wasn't going to cave. She'd insist. We'd argue and I'd compromise.

I didn't want to compromise.

I wanted something new.

The tiniest crack appeared in her veneer. The corner of her lips turned up, and the hint of her genuine smile appeared. "Good for you, darling. Consider it done."

Done? Really?

I kept my shoulders square instead of collapsing in a relieved heap.

That was far from the battle I'd been bracing for. Had that been her plan all along? Was she simply waiting for me to make a stand instead of nodding like an obedient little girl?

My fingers wrapped around Malcolm's.

"The paperwork will take a few weeks, of course. We're already elbows deep in Ashley's work permit, but I'll see what we can do." She looked at her desk, likely making a note. "He should be in the States to start that. Talk to Brian about refiling his flight plan if you want to drop Malcolm off in New York, but I suspect if you do that, you'll be staying there with him?"

Busted. I still couldn't pull anything over on her. "We just won't mention it at the airport."

"In that case, I'll see you both at eight tomorrow morning. We have a project board that's been neglected while the lot of you have been gallivanting around Europe." She gave a curt nod. "Good to have you on-board, Blue Eyes."

"Thank you, ma'am." Malcolm tipped his head and she cut out. He swiveled on his chair to face me, his soft smile curling deep inside my gut. "Thank you."

"For the job?"

"No one..." He ran a gentle hand down my cheek, the smile deepening. "No one's ever gone to bat for me, except your brother."

The nerve endings in my feet lit up, telling me there were emotions to suppress. Distractions to be made. Instead, I turned my face into his hand and kissed his palm.

The truth was, I was falling so hard and fast for him, that words like love and forever had started swirling around my brain. Maybe it was too soon for that, or maybe it was just right.

"Losing out to your team at the Maguire party was the best thing that ever happened to me."

"Kidnappings and beatings aside?"

He slid me to the edge of my seat and took my face in his hands. "I'd do it all again in a heartbeat if it meant I'd end up here with you."

I swallowed hard, pushing down the chaos bubbling inside of me. Joy, panic, anticipation, fear. They were just words. Words I wanted to gobble up and live off of. "Do you really mean that? You told me you had a hard time remembering who the real you is sometimes."

He pulled me to him and kissed me slowly. Deeply. A kiss like a promise of the future, not only of the next hour. When we separated, he took my hands and held them to his heart. "When we were in the car after the architect's office, that was me. And every moment after that."

"You tried to comfort me, and I pushed you away."

"True, but..." His gaze roamed my face, searching for something in the silence that stretched between us. "You let me see your emotions. Upset, frustrated, angry. Scared."

I nodded, putting myself back into my own shoes that day. I'd been so exhausted, I hadn't been able to keep everything bottled up the way I should have. "Not my best day."

"Oh, sweetheart." He pressed his forehead to mine and

just breathed, his cologne and his natural musky scent enveloping me. "You showed me the real you—not the woman with the earpiece, running an op, but the woman desperate to save someone who mattered. Your whole heart was on display and for once, I saw the fallout of my fuck-up and I gave a shit."

"I thought you were pretending, in case they were watching us."

"Of course, you would have thought that." He gave a wry laugh. "But this is the real me, Scarlett. Telling the real you that I... that I love you, flaws, emotions, and all."

I dug my toes into the rug underneath us, stopping myself from saying the same ridiculous words back to him, no matter how much the little voice in the back of my head wanted to. "Malcolm, you barely know me."

"I've seen you happy and sad, angry and stressed, relieved, anxious. I've seen you plan. I've seen you relax with your friends. We've eaten, we've danced, we've toured three of the world's great cities. I've spent every day and almost every night with you for a month. How many hours does it take before you can know a person's heart?" He dipped his head to look me straight in the eyes. "I'd bet I know yours better than almost anyone in the world."

Could this also be so simple?

The only thing we were missing was a past. The drudgery of every day. But he was right—I knew his heart. If I was in danger, he'd come for me. He'd carry me out of an evacuating building. He'd even stand up to my mother and give me the support to do the same. For better or worse, he'd encourage all the messy emotions I'd spent a lifetime suppressing to come out.

"Malcolm, I..."

"Shh." He placed a finger against my lips. "I don't want you to feel like you—"

Screw it. "Don't move in with Emmett."

"What?"

"Because it might be even crazier than your Velatti scheme, but I feel the same." I curled my fingers around his and held tight. "I love you, too, Malcolm. Move in with me, instead."

His smile grew and he stood slowly, encouraging me up into his embrace. He held so tight around my waist that he lifted me up and spun me slowly, knocking into the chairs. "Absolutely, yes."

Lightness surged through me. Lightness and freedom. I squeezed my eyes shut when he put me down, years of muscle memory reciting those ridiculous words in my head. With a deep breath, I reopened my eyes, so he could see the tears welling in them. Happy tears.

Because Reynolds women *could* cry. And there was nothing wrong with it.

THE END OF BOOK 1

BOOK 2: Declan heads to Rome with Jayce, where he meets his match: a safe designer who's as talented as he is sure of himself. When they're contracted to test Edoardo's safe deposit box company, the crew joins them in Rome, where things quickly start going wrong.

Discover Declan and Leigh's story at
https://janetoppedisano.com/TheEaglesVault

FREE NOVELLA: What was all that about the events in

Boston in the lead-up to the Maguire mansion heist? Check out the free novella *The Phoenix Heist,* the prequel to this series, starring Zac and Ashley's story—and with cameos from the main characters in the Caine & Ferraro series.

>Get *The Phoenix Heist* for FREE only at
>https://janetoppedisano.com/ThePhoenixHeist

EXCERPT FROM THE EAGLE'S VAULT
LEIGH

My heart pounded as I walked along the narrow cobblestone street early Monday afternoon. Directly ahead, the café where the Reynolds team had set up base for the initial Cassaforte Caetani reconnaissance. My heels caught in every second stone, threatening to pitch me over. Beyond the restaurant, there was a paved sidewalk, my salvation.

"You're going to break an ankle." My brother snaked an arm under my elbow, helping me balance. "I should be the one going in with Declan."

I tugged at the hem of my suit, a pale-blue Italian wool dress and jacket Scarlett loaned me, which molded to every curve of my body. It screamed money, professional, and I know my business. It also screamed look at me in a way that would have made my ex throw a tarp over me. A thousand bucks, easy. And the tiny handbag? Five times that, at least.

"You will. I'm just doing this one thing." I rolled my shoulders, trying to find some level of comfort in the rich fabric. When I'd first put it on, I'd sank into the luxury, but now it was hard to forget how tight the pencil skirt was across my butt, or how the push-up bra Scarlett had bought for me —bought for me!—made my breasts at least two cup sizes larger.

Yeah, I definitely needed a tarp.

As we got closer, I spotted the woman herself, deep in conversation with Jayce and Declan. Tall, lean Declan, with the impossible-to-read hazel eyes and sexy scruff.

I withdrew my death-grip from Isaac, tucked the handbag under my arm, and rubbed my hands together. Would sweat stain the jacket? Or the clutch's leather?

Declan leaned back from where Jayce's head blocked his view and nodded at us. He leaned farther back, blatantly scanning the length of me, a wave of heat following those eyes. He sat forward and whispered something to Scarlett.

"I brought the distraction," said Isaac as we reached their table.

At the table next to them, Rav, Emmett, and Malcolm looked up from their tablets.

"I'm not a distraction, Isaac." I lowered slowly into the chair beside Jayce and pulled off one of the borrowed Louboutins, rubbing my toes.

"Too small?" asked Scarlett.

We were practically the same size and measurements, other than the required bra. "I'm not used to wearing narrow-toed shoes."

Jayce chuckled. "She tried to get me into a pair of those torture devices once. Never again."

Declan stood and switched to the men's table. He wore a sleek charcoal suit that highlighted his broad shoulders and tapered form. *God, he's hot.* There was something unsettling about how attractive this entire team was. How much confidence of different flavors dominated the space between these two tables.

I didn't belong here. I ran a hand through my hair, shaking off the thought. This was about my talent as a vault engineer and knowledge that could help with the vault. This wasn't a heist, it was a penetration test. A safety check. Nothing more.

Read the full story, available at
https://janetoppedisano.com/TheEaglesVault

AUTHOR'S NOTE

I've always been a huge fan of action movies and love a clever heist—from the meticulous planning, to the unique characters making up a varied yet cohesive team, and to all the twists and turns on the way to success. Best of all, the danger and intensity provide a perfect backdrop for romance! It was an utter blast writing this book, with all the ups and downs the whole team went through on their way to getting Emmett back and (sadly?) losing out on the feather at the end.

As always, my first thanks go out to my husband and son. For acting as my sounding boards, for tolerating my rants about characters not listening to my instructions, and for giving me the time and space to get this book done.

To my eternal beta readers, Paula and Pat, who devour everything I send them and always provide amazing feedback: thank you for supporting me through this entire journey and being my earliest cheerleaders.

Many thanks to my editors: To Miranda Darrow for helping me develop Scarlett's difficult (to write!) personality; and to Brandi Aquino for ensuring the words were polished.

And finally, I'd like to thank you, my dear reader, for your willingness to accompany me on this journey, it means more than I can express. You are the heartbeat of every story I write.

– Janet

ABOUT JANET

Janet Oppedisano delivers award-winning romantic suspense with smart, driven women and sexy, protective men that will keep you on the edge of your seat. Her heroines excel in their fields and aren't looking for love—until they meet the charismatic heroes who fall hard and fast for them. Throw in gripping mysteries, heart-pounding danger, and a touch of history or legend, and you've got stories that keep you hooked.

With a Mountie father and a Navy diver husband, Janet's life has been steeped in adventure, inspiring her high-stakes stories. She's lived all over Canada, from the Maritimes to the Prairies, and her books reflect the authenticity and depth of her journey.

When she's not plotting her next twist, Janet is baking, hiking, traveling, or cheering for her hockey goalie son.

And if you're wondering about her last name, it's pronounced oh-ped-ih-SAH-no—just like it looks. Honest!

You can find Janet and all her social media links at:
https://janetoppedisano.com

Made in the USA
Columbia, SC
11 April 2025